The G MANN II:
Pay-2-Play

Gregory L. Heitmann

ISBN-10: 0615749267
ISBN-13: 9780615749266 (Gregory L. Heitmann)

Dedicated to the great people of the Southwest.

Gregory L. Heitmann

Many thanks to my family, gracias!

Special thanks to Dorene.

Gregory L. Heitmann

Author's Note

This is a work of fiction and usual rules apply. The characters, the conversations, and the incidents portrayed in this novel are products of the author's imagination. Nothing in this book is to be construed as real. Any resemblance to actual events, or persons, whether living or dead, is purely coincidental. Again, none of the characters are real; none of these events ever happened.

Gregory L. Heitmann

Other novels by Gregory L. Heitmann:

Fort Sisseton – Dakota Territory

Gregory L. Heitmann

Prologue:

Rio Caballo Gorge Bridge

August 27th

 In the early morning light when the sun is rising, but the rays are blocked by the Sangre de Sustantivo Mountains near Verde, a halo effect occurs. In the Southwest part of the United States, towns and geographic landmarks carry Spanish monikers. Here, locals know that Verde means "green;" same for the mountains where Sangre de Sustantivo translates to "Blood of the Savior." The highest peaks in the state, including Mount Walter, bearing a strictly English name and rising to a height of 13,761 feet, shield and diffract the morning light, producing an almost eerie glow. The town of Verde rests at the bottom of these famously high peaks on the west side of the mountain chain. The famous Verde Ski Valley and the Verde Enclave are well known tourist attractions.

 West of the community of Verde about ten miles on U.S. Highway 164, is a lesser known attraction, the Rio Caballo Gorge Bridge. This bridge spans a distance of about 1300 feet across the Rio Caballo, in English, horse river. The bridge flies above the river at just over 650 feet. It is shocking to come across this canyon in the middle of the desert whether approaching from the east or west. As you head west on U.S. 164, departing Verde, a person suddenly sees the opening in the earth, and you are crossing the bridge, noting the steep walls descending to the floor of a ravine that resembles the Grand Canyon in miniature. As you approach from the west heading east, you cross a desolate twenty-mile expanse of desert dotted with sage. Ahead of you, Walter Peak looms. The desert is dotted with self sustaining "Earth Ship" homes, mostly occupied by wealthy hippies trying to stay off the grid. The Rio Caballo Gorge sneaks up on you as you approach; the rest area provides another distraction, and suddenly you are on top of the bridge crossing a gaping crack in the earth, the result of the amazing erosive forces of the water of the Rio Caballo. Often it is the vehicle and pedestrian traffic in the area as you near the bridge that alert you to the notable crossing. Vendors line the parking area on the east side, selling their wares ranging from native foods to hand carved fetishes and jewelry. Pedestrians stream across either side of the bridge enjoying breathtaking views. They preserve the memories with an infinite number of photographs, as vehicle traffic continues to stream across the U.S. 164 Bridge. No other crossing of the Rio Caballo Gorge is available north or south for about fifty miles in either direction, increasing the amount of traffic one might expect for this remote area.

This stretch of the Rio Caballo is designated by the Federal Government as a "Wild and Scenic River." It flows unimpeded for a nice stretch and provides quality white water rafting at particular times during years of good runoff from the snowpack. Rafters can often be spotted by tourists from the bridge, passing on the river below during the spring and summer months.

The Rio Caballo Gorge Bridge is a unique spot in the United States and well worth the trip for those that purposefully venture to the area or are just passing through. It is a hidden gem tucked in the Southwestern state.

On this morning with only the slightest hint of gray in the east, a lone woman walks on the sidewalk of the bridge. It is not light enough to see the Rio Caballo below as she centers herself in the middle of the bridge. The woman leans on the rail of the bridge and listens in the darkness. The slightest of breeze whispers through the trusses of the supporting structure of the bridge below Casey Baxter's feet. If it was light enough and one could see Casey's face, you would see tears streaming down her cheeks. The eastern sky slowly adds a hint of pink to the gray gloom.

A half hour passes with only a single car traversing the bridge. The first vendor has set up shop just off the bridge approach in a graveled area used by the tourists to park and walk out on the bridge. A pickup truck bearing the logo of Laramie Engineering on its door parks near the early morning vendor. Patrick Ruiz emerges from his vehicle and ambles toward the bridge. He gives a silent nod and wave to a vendor unfolding the legs of a portable table in order to display his wares. The vendor nods back in the faint light.

Patrick approaches Casey standing at the rail of the bridge, leaning her elbows on the railing and staring out at the abyss of the Rio Caballo Gorge below. "Stop right there," Casey calls out without even looking toward Patrick.

Casey straightens and pushes herself to a straddling position onto the heavy steel railing of the bridge. She swings her leg over and she is now on the unprotected side of the bridge, hands gripping the rail. "Whoa!" Patrick hollers and begins to rush toward Casey.

"I said stop! Stay back!" Casey cries as she turns her head toward Patrick.

Patrick stops a good thirty feet away but continues to inch toward Casey. "Case, what are you doin'?" Patrick calls out as calmly as he can.

"Thanks for coming, Pat," Casey replies in a monotone.

"Come on, Casey. Let's go home. I'm really sorry about our fight last night. Everything's going to be fine. We got it all worked out."

Casey exhales deeply. She leans out into the emptiness of the gorge, her hands holding the rail behind her with her feet firmly on the bridge deck. "No…it's not."

"You wouldn't have called me if you really wanted to go through with this," Patrick insists, his voice gaining strength.

Casey manages a weak smile as she shakes her head from side to side, "I wanted you to deliver a message for me."

"Come on, Case," Patrick says as he edges forward.

"Just stay where you are, Pat," Casey re-grips the rail. "This little scheme and fling of ours…it's ruined lives. Too many lives; people have died…for what? Our personal aspirations for power? It's just plain stupid."

"And your jumping does what?" Patrick counters, "It doesn't fix anything."

"That's where you're wrong," Casey insists. "It spares me, and my family, additional shame."

"What about your family?" Patrick pleads. "Your husband? Your kids? What's going to happen to them without you?"

"They're young. They'll bounce back and move on," Casey calmly justifies her actions. "I can't face them. My insurance, investments, and other benefits will take better care of them with me dead than alive."

Patrick's voice cracks, "What about me? What about us?"

"What about it?" Casey answers matter-of-factly. "We both got something from each other. It was a mutual benefit, but it was a mistake. We have hurt a lot of people, and more people are going to end up hurt. I'm stopping myself from continuing to hurt people right now."

Patrick's mouth moves as he tries to respond, but no words come. He is finally able to stop his head from spinning as he steps closer to Casey. "Casey, your jumping from this bridge…this is the ultimate hurt for your family."

"Promise me you'll tell my family I'm sorry. Please tell them."

"No. No, Casey, don't do this."

"Goodbye," is the last thing Casey utters as she lets go of the rail and plunges into the gorge as the sun peeks over the mountains. There is enough light for Patrick to see the speck that is the lifeless body of Casey

17

on the edge of the Rio Caballo below, battered and broken on the rocks along the river.

Patrick turns and races across the bridge returning to his truck as fast as his legs can carry his massive body. He passes the vendor who asks the puffing Patrick, "Did that person just jump?"

Patrick ignores the man and reaches his vehicle. He climbs inside and speeds out of the parking area, heading back towards Verde on U.S. Highway 164 and then south towards Capitol City. Tears fill Patrick's eyes and roll freely over his cheeks.

Chapter 1

The Dusty Giant

Three Months Previous...

Just three months before Casey committed suicide, Patrick was involved in another traumatic situation...probably more dramatic than traumatic. It might be hard to imagine what conclusion a passerby would make of a situation where two young men in the middle of the Southwestern desert stand over a monster of a man down on his knees, crying, and holding his finger. To take a snapshot of the absurd situation and run a contest for the best photo caption would probably provide hours of entertaining and comical labels. However, this was not funny at all. A physical confrontation between a consultant engineer from Laramie Engineering under contract to the State Department of Transportation, Patrick, and a United States Transportation Department employee, Gary, had just defied all tenets of logic in the civilized world of government bureaucracy.

The wind blows across the gravel parking lot in front of a generic trailer used as construction office where the man sobs on his hands and knees. A Laramie Engineering pickup and a Chevy sedan with U.S. Government plates are the only audience to the dust up. The fight, if you could even call it that, was over before it started. Patrick, agitated by fellow engineers critical of his work, started with an expletive-filled rant, which preceded his blunt, accusing finger-poking to Gary's chest.

Gary had been assaulted with words quite a few times in his career on the job. When dealing with angry construction contractors, it was not uncommon to have salty language directed at you, but this was a first. This incident was with a fellow engineer; this attack was first with words, then with repeated jabs of a finger to the chest...Gary was taken aback.

Maybe even more surprising for Gary was his own defensive reaction. Never trained in any martial arts, he grabbed Patrick's finger and jerked one way, then the other. Patrick was immediately on his knees blathering like a baby. Gary could not stifle his smile and he admired his handiwork a little longer than appropriate. But, who's to say what is an appropriate amount of admiration given the situation?

With Gary this afternoon was Bryan, a fellow engineer also from the office of the United States Department of Transportation. For Bryan, well…his eyes nearly popped out of their sockets, witnessing something like this. His short career so far had been nothing but boring engineering questions, but now, things were getting exciting.

As Bryan got behind the wheel of the Government sedan, the G-car, and Gary got in the passenger side, Bryan made sure to spin the tires leaving a cloud of dust. The haze of gray, powdery earth surrounded the fallen giant, Patrick, still on his knees in the gravel parking lot. Patrick was left alone, moaning and wondering what had just happened. A poor start to a hot afternoon on his construction project. In between the jolts of pain radiating like electric shocks up his arm, the embarrassing thoughts of what his co-workers might think of him turned his stomach in knots. Worse yet was the idea of what his uncle would say. His uncle had helped Patrick rise to Vice President of Construction for Laramie Engineering, LLC. Patrick had a very important project to manage for the State Highway Department. But, now, Pat was on his knees in the dusty parking lot crying, a position Patrick's uncle would surely find disgusting.

Chapter 2

Modern Day Train Robbery

On an uneventful summer day, Gary Hillmann and his coworker, Bryan Baker, drive from their Capitol City office, south down Interstate 11 in the ninety degree heat of the afternoon to take a look at a construction project. Both Gary and Bryan were brought to the Southwest by their chosen occupation as engineers for the United States Transportation Department, the USTD.

The USTD, as the name would imply, is an arm of the Federal government that works in transportation with the major elements of its work consisting of the highways connecting the cities and towns of this country. The USTD has a small office in every state, and they work to oversee the billions of dollars handed out by the federal government to the state highway departments. In simplest terms, the USTD holds state highway departments accountable. The USTD assures that the money for highways is spent on highways; that the highways are built to specifications, and the taxpayer is getting his money's worth.

First and foremost on the watch list for the USDT is the interest of the Interstate System. The USDT personnel are charged with making sure the Interstate system functions as specified by Congress nearly 60 years ago. It was primarily established as a network of highways for the defense of the country in order to transport our military quickly across our large nation. The secondary function of moving goods and people has become the obvious and dominant use, but the original idea brought back to the United States by General Dwight D. Eisenhower after World War II was to have a strategic defense network of highways. Our Interstate system is a direct descendent of the German Autobahn.

Billions of dollars each year are redistributed by Congress to the states based on a formula involving factors such as population, miles of highway, vehicle miles traveled, and a myriad of other lesser criteria. This Southwestern state gets about $450 million each year from the federal government for its highways.

Each state USTD office, often referred to as the Division Office, has a small staff of about 15 employees for smaller states and maybe even 80 to 90 employees for bigger, more populated states like Texas or California. Ultimately, it is up to the USTD to administer the millions of dollars of federal funding for highways through the state highway department. The bureaucracy is always present in every governmental capacity; the USTD watches the state DOT, the state DOT, watches the local governments as well as the contractors they hire. The Office of Inspector General, the OIG, watches everyone, as the taxpayer dollars are managed and spent as efficiently as possible.

Gary Hillmann, one of the USTD engineers in this Division Office, hails from South Dakota. A real G-man, G MANN; taking his first initial "G" and the last four letters of his last name, "Mann," Gary was dubbed in high school "The G Mann." Now, he works for the government, a government man, G-man. Gary spent the first dozen years of his Federal Government service bouncing around the Midwest and Texas working for the USTD. He laughs at the thought of being voted "most likely to succeed" by his high school senior classmates, a group numbering forty kids that graduated with him from good old Reedville, South Dakota High School.

Gary's light skin, brown hair, and hazel eyes quickly identify him as an Anglo down in the Southwest where the majority population is Hispanic. The Hillmann name being of German heritage common to the Midwest is simplified by the natives…he is a Gringo. Gary may have it easier than most others given that humans make a quick judgment on appearance. It is probably safe to say that the old adage, "Don't judge a book by its cover," is thrown out the window by 99% of the people.

The remaining 1% are blind. Gary has been blessed with an appealing, some would even say handsome look, put together on an athletic, six-foot tall frame. Gary's attractive, non-threatening appearance has opened some doors more easily than otherwise might be available, but more than looks, Gary is able to connect with the people he works with by being more of a "common man." A humble Midwest upbringing provides that background for many people originating from the Dakotas, Iowa, Nebraska, and even Minnesota. Gary has always considered himself to be lucky that he grew up in South Dakota, although he may have been a little anxious to leave the harsh winters behind. He has found a spot in the Southwest that suits him.

The circumstances that lead Gary to his position as second in command of the USTD Division Office are a story in itself. A mere two years after arriving in the state, he was promoted to his Deputy Director position because of the mysterious death of the previous deputy. An internal corruption investigation, and the subsequent dismissal of his own team leader paved the path for Gary to climb the career ladder a little more expeditiously than most Division Office Deputy Directors.

So, here Gary is at 35-years old, second in command of assuring the $450 million a year for highways is used appropriately by the State Highway Department. Gary knows he's a lucky man to be able to live and work in the Rocky Mountains, finally fulfilling a lifetime dream. Here he finds the hunting and fishing are spectacular, the weather has four mild seasons, and the West is still a little wild.

Bryan Baker is Gary's right hand man from the operations stand point of the office. Bryan was raised in a small community in the hotbed of Ohio high school football. He was an undersized offensive lineman, and he still wears this chip on his shoulder nearly ten years after ending his high school football playing days. Bryan is another Gringo; an average White male of English-Russian heritage, he stands five feet nine inches, but his dedication to his workout schedule has continued, and he weighs a solidly-muscled 200 pounds with the biceps to show it.

Bryan started in the office a few weeks after Gary arrived. He was fresh off the highway engineer training program, and he witnessed the internal turmoil of the office and the rise to power of his friend, Gary. He respected Gary's demeanor and approach to their business from the beginning, but after the death of the previous Deputy Director, Bryan appreciated Gary's efforts even more.

$$*\quad *\quad *\quad *\quad *$$

On this day, Bryan and Gary drive their government sedan to a State Highway Department project that impacts Interstate 11. Bryan is behind the wheel of the new G-car, a Chevy Malibu. "So, what do you think?" Bryan turns to Gary posing a vague question.

Gary shrugs, "Mmmm. I guess it's ok. It's way better than those horrible compact cars we used to get. Did you ever drive a Dodge Stratus?"

"I'm not asking about the stupid car! I'm asking about the stupid train!" Bryan retorts. "Were you listening to me?"

"I'm sorry. I guess I was thinking about the weekend," Gary responds as he turns from viewing the open Interstate Highway to look at Bryan. "You want to come along this weekend? You can bring Ashley with."

Bryan shakes his head, "Ashley's mad at me again."

"Now what did you do?"

"Nothing!" Bryan exclaims defensively.

"Seriously, what did you do?"

"Well, I may have hinted that she should work out a little more."

Gary laughs loudly as he tries to cover his mouth to keep from snorting, "You basically called her fat."

Bryan's head wobbles on his shoulders as he rolls his eyes in disgust, "That pretty much sums up what she said that I said."

"Wow, I thought I didn't know much about women; you apparently know even less."

Bryan resumes his defensive tone as he looks for his exit off of the Interstate, "You know I like to workout and stay in shape."

"Yeah."

"Well, I said we should workout together, and boom. She goes right to her 'you think I'm fat' speech."

Gary laughs.

Bryan shakes his head and finishes explaining, "She didn't let me complete my thought. I wanted to emphasize to her that we could spend some more time together if we worked out with each other!"

Gary shrugs, "Live and learn I guess."

"Long story, short," Bryan flips his hand up in the air off of the steering wheel, "I think Ashley and I are on a break."

Gary glances over at Bryan and back to the road rising in front of the car, "That's too bad. My brother is coming to Allentown for some pharmacy convention, and we're going out. I get to introduce Katrina to my brother."

"Yeah, yeah," Bryan says with impatience, "You told me. You're going to see Texas Country Music star, Kevin Fowler at the Twilight Rodeo Bar, blah, blah, blah." Bryan glares over at Gary, "I can't stand that twangy, country crap."

Gary smiles, "Take it easy."

"Sorry," Bryan sighs and continues, "I can't stand this project and the project manager, Patrick Ruiz. I can't believe that the Deputy Chief Engineer for the Department assigned *him* to this project. Patrick is such a dick."

"I know," Gary nods in agreement. "Out of all the consultant engineers they could have chosen, they picked him. He must be solidly politically connected."

"Yeah. Oh well, thanks for coming with me to this meeting," Bryan says as he smiles and calms down a bit, "Pat just gets my goat. He knows how to push my buttons."

"No problem," Gary reassures, "It's just nice to get out of the office." Gary pauses and nods his head. "You know what the key is? The key is to remain calm and even-keeled, like Diego."

"How, in the name of all that is holy, can the Highway Department be spending this kind of money on a stupid commuter train? They don't have the cash!" Bryan's voice breaks a bit as his agitation continues, and he winds back up.

"Calm down," Gary urges, "You know our position, and Diego has made it clear, our job is to make sure that the Interstate Highway integrity is maintained."

"I know!" Bryan shouts. "But why do they have to put the stupid train in the Interstate median? My God, they will probably only have about 500 riders each day. For the amount of money being spent on this stupid thing, we could buy each of those riders a new hybrid electric vehicle!"

"I said, calm down already," Gary reiterates as he raises his palms toward Bryan. "Here's our exit."

Bryan steers the car down the exit ramp toward the Interstate interchange, under the bridge and down a small country highway to a cloud of dust that is the commuter train's project area.

Bryan smiles as he glances at Gary, who is now messing with the radio volume and bobbing his head to the music. Gary excitedly proclaims, "Hey, it's Kevin Fowler's song on the radio! I didn't even know they played his stuff around here."

Kevin Fowler's ballad, "Hard Man to Love" blares on the radio a good thirty seconds before Bryan cries out in pain, "Aurrrgh! I can't take it!"

Bryan pokes the radio power button, turning the radio off with extreme prejudice.

"Hey," Gary whines, "I was enjoying that."

"I can't stand that stupid twangy crap. Stupid love song," Bryan growls.

Gary snickers, "There, there, I know you're hurting. Ashley will forgive you."

"It's not just that; it's all this stuff," Bryan grouses, "I just can't accept that our ridiculous governor can spend $500 million on a stupid worthless train…Just so he can be a Presidential candidate!"

Gary shakes his head, "Hey, it's the politics around here; you know that by now."

"I know, but where I come from this bullshit wouldn't happen. Capitol City High Schools have a graduation rate of less than 50%, and yet here this douche bag of a governor spends money hand over fist on a…a romanticized Old West train!"

Gary chimes in, "Everyone knows it's a joke, but nobody will say a word against him. It's the old emperor has no clothes situation. Trains

25

don't work unless you have the population densities like New York, Chicago…"

Bryan picks up Gary's thought and continues, "Washington, D.C., Philly. Those are places where commuter rail works. Psssh, that ridiculous study that they put together showing how crucial this train was…now that's an embarrassment. Why in the Hell did you and Diego approve that?"

Gary narrows his eyes at the accusation, "Now that's unfair, and you know it. We approved the use of the Interstate median for the train location. None of the money they are spending is federal cash. If it were, it would be a different story on the analysis."

"I know, I know," Bryan nods and turns to Gary, "Someone should do something."

"The Governor was elected by the voters; he sets the policies and priorities; what would you suggest we do?"

Bryan sneers, "We should get smarter voters. Like I said, we got a bunch of high school dropouts in this backwards patronage system."

Gary laughs out loud, "I know what you're saying. It's amazing to me that this carpet bagger governor can come in here from Florida with his Hispanic name and Ivy League education, speak a little Spanish to the people and be like a rock star."

Bryan pounds the steering wheel with the palm of his hand, "See, it's the stupid education system. You got all these ignorant people voting style over substance. I'll tell you what. If graduation rates were like this back home where I grew up, heads would roll."

*   *   *   *   *

The government sedan approaches the end of the paved road. A small portable trailer sits in the distance surrounded by a few scraggly juniper trees and a few yuccas. The high desert view is in full glory from this position. Below is a deep canyon. The reds, browns, and greens of the desert colors explode in the midday sun. Mountains in the background loom dark, covered in their coniferous cloak. The heat of the day refracts some of the images, giving a wavy, shaky vibe to objects in view.

In the foreground is a low-end, generic-looking, manufactured home. The trailer marks the end of the line for progress in the state. Instead, a modern form of train robbery is taking place. Managed out of an anonymous looking travel trailer, taxpayer dollars are siphoned off of needed highway transportation projects to prop up a Presidential campaign of an egomaniacal politician. The largest transportation infrastructure project ever to be considered in the state is underway, and $500 million in railroad construction is being run through this trailer. The USTD calls a project of $500 million or more a "Mega Project"; people that are familiar with this particular effort just call it stupid. There's something to be said about the Ol' West train robberies and the brash idea that a gang of ne'er do-wells would steal money out in the open in broad daylight with masks and guns versus the kind of thieving that is done today under the guise of politics and policy.

Gregory L. Heitmann

Chapter 3

Finger Pointing

The gray, non-descript, government sedan approaches a trailer in the middle of nowhere; a cloud of dust roils in the breeze a few hundred yards away. The vehicle's approach stirs up its own miniature dust storm. The gravel lot in front of the trailer is empty except for a Laramie Engineering pickup truck. The two men from the United States Transportation Department have arrived at the construction site. Bryan places the government car in park and exits simultaneously from the driver's side as, Gary, slips from the passenger side. Gary and Bryan move towards the trailer. Gary taps Bryan on the shoulder and points to a sign fixed on the door of the trailer. The sign reads: "T'rrain Trekker, another quality project from the State Highway Department and Governor Stuart Reid-Salazar."

Bryan bursts out laughing, "Can you believe the balls on this guy? The governor acts like the Highway Department is his own personal construction company."

Before Gary can respond the trailer door swings open and a hulking figure moves through the doorway and down the stairs. The massive man extends his hand to Gary as he descends the last step. He is Patrick Ruiz, the consultant engineer in charge of managing this project for the Highway Department. He was handpicked by the governor and responsible for the commuter rail project. Gary shakes Pat's hand. He releases Pat's chubby paw and points with a smile to the sign on the trailer, "T'rrain Trekker, eh?"

Pat's jowls ripple as a broad grin stretches his face, "You like it? I think it's pretty clever."

"Your idea?" Gary inquires.

"I wish," Patrick responds with a grin. "Nope, that's all to Casey's credit."

Pat extends his hand to Bryan as he still smiles at Gary. Bryan shakes Pat's hand. Without looking at Bryan, Pat says, "Hi, Bryan, how's it going?"

Bryan shrugs, "Good."

Patrick Ruiz is a significantly overweight man in his late forties. His breathing is labored from descending the five stairs out of the construction trailer, the head quarters of the operation. His husky voice has a recognizable East Coast inflection. Patrick uses his hand to smooth his slicked-back, fine, sandy-brown hair as he hikes up his blue jeans above his belly, thwarting the trousers' on-going battle with gravity. "What do you say, guys? Should we go look at the operation? It's just over the edge of the hill where all that dust is." Pat gives a nod in the direction of a brown cloud a mile a way. "We can drive down the road just a piece and look at things while staying out of the way of the equipment."

"Sounds good," Gary says.

Bryan chimes in, "We'll follow you."

Patrick climbs in his Laramie Engineering truck and adjusts himself in the seat with a shove off the steering wheel. The truck rocks and groans under his massive three-hundred-pounds-plus weight.

Gary and Bryan get back in their vehicle and follow Patrick to the edge of the canyon overlooking the construction. The canyon is part of a natural drainage area that has provided the easiest grade for train tracks. The construction has now extended the natural arroyo, or dry river bed, into the median of the Interstate highway. The men exit their vehicles and look down into the construction area. Dozers, scrapers, earth movers, and water trucks cruise in coordinated movements a few hundred yards below and to the north of where they stand.

Bryan speaks first, "How are things progressing, Pat?"

"Good, real good," Pat responds in a serious tone. Patrick points to a line of orange flags encircling an irregular diamond-shaped area of about 4 acres. "You see those orange flags?"

"Yeah," Gary responds as he nods along with Bryan as they shield their eyes from the sun and look across to the opposite side of the canyon.

"What is it?" Bryan asks.

Patrick smiles crookedly, "That's one of our most controversial environmental commitments. That is the prairie dog town we're relocating. I'm sure you can appreciate the effort."

Bryan grimaces a bit, "Hardly, I'm not a huge fan of the rodents."

Patrick looks with solemnity at Bryan and back to Gary before speaking, "I just wanted to point out that we are following all processes, plans, and procedures."

Gary looks at Pat, "Yeah, about that, the reason we came out to see you, Pat, is that we have some serious safety concerns on the operation. Your own Highway Department District Office called to complain to Diego about the traffic control as you work to get the train tracks into the Interstate median."

"Really?" A truly surprised Pat cocks his head. "What's the problem?"

"Sheesh," Bryan emotes in disgust. "You seriously don't see a problem?"

Pat shakes his head, "No, what's going on?"

Bryan throws his hands up in the air. Gary looks to Bryan and holds up a hand to try to calm him. Gary responds as he lists items of concern on his fingers, "Well, first off, you gotta get this area protected. We have the traveling public on Interstate at risk coming through the work zone. You can't leave this hole wide open; it's gotta be protected. We need some concrete barrier in place along the highway to provide a positive barrier. We just can't have an errant vehicle careening off the highway."

Patrick interrupts, "I disagree. This has worked for us so far. You shouldn't worry about it."

"Pshhh," scoffs Bryan. "Listen, we don't like the idea of a stray vehicle hitting the barrier, but it's better than a vehicle crashing down the slope a couple hundred feet below and into the construction equipment."

The men watch as construction workers swarm the area where a short tunnel is being built so that the train can enter and exit the Interstate median underneath the north bound Interstate 11 traffic lanes. Steel rebar rises from the previously poured concrete foundations and sidewalls. Carpenters and laborers work on scaffolding to form the next stage of concrete placement for the tunnel. A construction zone has temporarily moved traffic away from the area, squeezing four lanes of traffic to two lanes in each direction, precariously close together. The hum of traffic in the distance is masked by a gust of wind that blows through the construction area, lifting dust in a whirlwind across the barren slopes. The steep slope below the men's work boot-clad feet looks menacing as they stand in silence staring down the slope as equipment races below them. The construction vehicles look like ants near an ant hill racing here and there in a pattern only the workers themselves can understand, kicking dust in intricate clouds every which way until the wind grabs hold of the dirty phantoms and directs their apparition-like forms in a uniform manner eastward across the desert sky.

Patrick stews as he takes a pad and pen from his pocket and takes notes.

"The second thing," Gary points out, "is the dust. You gotta get more water trucks out there. I see you have some watering operations, but it's not enough."

Patrick is getting irritated, "Really, now you're worried about water?"

"It's not the water; it's the dust, Pat," Bryan says.

"Uhg, I…" Patrick stammers, "You're kidding me with this stuff, right?" Patrick responds in a huff. "We're working out here just fine. Why are you so worried about this all of a sudden?"

Bryan sweeps his hand across the view of the construction area from the Interstate traffic to the construction equipment below, "What the hell, Pat? This is all that we worry about, the safety of the traveling public…the safety of the construction workers. When somebody gets killed? Is that when you want to start doing things right?"

The wind gusts again as the men silently watch the dust race through the construction area before Bryan continues, "I reviewed the plans. Your traffic control is not within specifications shown in the plan sheets."

"Bryan…" Patrick tries to interject.

"Don't interrupt me, Pat," Bryan says as he grits his teeth. The chip on his shoulder from his high school football days re-emerges as he clenches his fists. He will never let his underdog attitude wither. The drive of being an under-appreciated, middle class, average, White Boy from Ohio, where football is king, has carried him a long way. Bryan wants to prove this point as much as ever. He wants to show Gary that he can be counted on.

Patrick makes a note in his pad, "Come on, Bryan." Patrick looks to Gary, "Gary?"

Patrick sighs loudly, "Listen guys, we are on a tight schedule here…the Governor wants this done, and he wants it done yesterday."

Gary folds his arms as he looks to Patrick, "Answer the question, Pat. When do you want to start doing things the right way? Does somebody have to die?"

Bryan quickly adds, "Well, let me put it this way. We can shut the whole thing down if you don't get the operation back into compliance with the specifications. Start with fixing the traffic control and go from there."

Patrick is getting angry. He mashes the pad and pen into his back pocket. He steps forward into Gary's personal space. He wags his finger in his fellow engineer's face as Gary lazily leans against the government sedan and cocks his head at Patrick's angry display.

"Alright, Mr. Bureaucrat, you need to get your lackey under control. Nobody comes out to my project and talks to me this way!" Patrick's words spit through clenched teeth. Saliva literally sprays from his mouth.

Bryan laughs at the exhibition from Patrick. Patrick snaps his head in the direction of Bryan's laughter and is even more aggravated as Bryan questions, "Patrick, what are you doing?"

Patrick holds his finger in front of Gary's face as he has turned away and locked eyes with Bryan, who just smiles at the scowling man. Gary wipes his face of the spittle Patrick has spewed. He still leans against the car as he refolds his arms.

Bryan holds his hands out and shrugs, "What are you doing, Pat?"

"Uh, Patrick," Gary intones, "I suggest you take your finger out of my face."

"Oh, yeah," Patrick says sarcastically.

"Patrick, you already spit on me, now I'm asking you nicely to take your finger out of my face."

Patrick grins an evil, tobacco stained smile, "Really, Gary?" The fat man points his finger at Bryan, "I suggest you take your little monkey-boy over there, and get the hell off my project."

Patrick gets nose-to-nose with Gary. He winds up and forcefully pokes Gary in the chest with his finger as he yells, "Now get out!"

Bryan's eyes widen to saucer size, and he murmurs, "Uh-oh."

In the blink of an eye, Patrick is on his knees, crying, rocking back and forth as he holds his finger. The index finger he used to poke Gary in the chest with is now capable of pointing to the north and to the east simultaneously. Gary has taken matters to a physical level, very much against his nature.

Patrick snuffles and sobs; he looks up from his knees and meets Gary's eyes, "Why?" he cries between deep, breathy sobs.

Gary looks down at Patrick with a pitiful expression. He gives a slight shake of his head and turns to Bryan who steps closer.

"Geez, Patrick. What the hell are you doing?" Bryan shouts in surprise. "It looked to me like you assaulted a federal official. Luckily, Gary was able to defend himself."

Gary shakes his head and steps away from the car leaving Patrick still down on his knees.

Bryan continues, "You ok, Gary?"

"Sure, let's go, Bryan," Gary quietly says as he steps around to the passenger side of the car.

Bryan leans down over Patrick, "Gosh, Patrick, didn't your mom ever teach you that it's not polite to point?" Bryan opens the driver's side door, and it swings near Patrick's face, where Bryan catches it before it hits him. "Uh, careful there, Patrick."

Patrick gasps as he breathes, still not able to look up from holding his mangled finger. Bryan gets in the car and closes the door. He rolls down the window, starts the car, and leans out the window. "Pat, remember to get that traffic control fixed and to take care of the other stuff we talked about." Bryan smiles, "Hey, remember, safety first!"

Bryan puts the car in reverse, steps on the gas and spreads a cloud of dust around the kneeling Patrick. The G-car spins its wheels, shifts gears into drive, and speeds away, leaving a dusty, fat man, with dirty streaks of tears across his cheeks wondering what just happened.

Chapter 4

Post Fight Analysis

"Jesus Christ," Bryan whispers as he takes a deep breath; he looks over to Gary in the passenger seat and shakes his head.

His breathing is still shallow and rapid as adrenaline courses through his body. He slows the car as they move from the gravel road to the paved county highway heading back to the Interstate Highway. Bryan continues to look back and forth between the road and Gary. Gary sits calmly in the passenger seat and brushes dust from his blue jeans as he straightens the tongue of his boot.

"What the hell are you doing?" Bryan asks as he watches Gary brush something from his polo shirt.

"I was just brushing some lint or some thistle seed off my shirt."

"That's not what I'm talking about! How can you sit there so calmly?" Bryan manages to squeak. "I'm wound up to the max over here. I got so much adrenaline, I don't know if I can keep the car on the road."

Gary shrugs, "You want me to drive?"

"No!" Bryan shouts. "Seriously, what the hell did you do that for? Diego is going to flip when he finds out."

Gary fixes his eyes on Bryan, "What was I supposed to do? Patrick was…well, who knows what he was going to do. I was just defending myself, like you said."

"Good Lord!" Bryan rolls his eyes, "We are doomed!"

"Nothing's going to happen. You wait and see. Like any bully, you stand up to them and they crumble. There won't be a word from Patrick."

The government sedan approaches the Interstate 11 Interchange Exit 67, and Bryan follows the signs pointing toward Capitol City.

A smile flashes across Bryan's face, and he chuckles. He nods his head in agreement, "I know you're right. I'm just jealous that I wasn't the one that brought that fat-ass to his knees. It was awesome! If only I would have it on my cell phone camera. Priceless!"

The men ride in silence for a few moments.

"What are we going to do now?" Bryan asks.

"Well, I'd say we better talk to Diego. I want him to hear about it from me first."

Bryan smiles and hits the steering wheel with the palm of his hand, "This story is going to go through the highway department like a wildfire! I'm so glad I was there to witness it first hand."

Chapter 5

From A-Town to Cap-City

The Sangre de Sustantivo Mountains raise the observer's eye line and view of the horizon to the north of Capitol City. This is probably an appropriate moniker for the peaks given the dominance of the Catholic religion in the area dating back 500 years, when the Spanish Conquistadors moved into North America. Capitol City, the "Holy Sanctuary" of the Southwest but more likely referred to by the locals as "The Santuario," sits at an elevation of 6800 feet above sea level, nestled in at the foot of the Sangre de Sustantivos. Bare Mountain, not to be confused with Bear Mountain, is the highest peak looming over the city at just under 13,000 feet. The "Old Bare" is so named for its barren pinnacle, covered in rock and lacking vegetation; snow shows up in contrast with the pine covered slopes surrounding the area, and when there is no snow, the brownish gray rock contrasts against the clear blue sky. Elevation of the mountains provides that difference in temperature and precipitation that allows for the vegetation change from the scrub desert sage, chamisa, cacti, and junipers to the ponderosa pines, spruce, and aspens typically found above 8,000 feet. It is a beautiful dichotomy.

Some would argue to their last breath that the southwestern desert is ugly. "How can you stand living in a dirty desert?" Those would question.

It brings a smile to the people of the Southwest when they hear people denigrate the desert. "Just bring your money, visit, get back to your home, and leave us in peace."

"Less is more," when it comes to the population as most who live here would say. For people used to the lush green grass and leafy trees of the Midwest and East Coast, the desert can be strange and scary. Strange is often frightening for people. But, some people are transplanted by jobs, marriage, or even health issues; a few of these people fall in love with the desert and prefer it to staying "home." There is a statistic that reports that half the people live within 50 miles of where they were born…then there is the other half.

The City Santuario is the capitol of the state. It has remained under the influence of art, culture, and religion since its founding. It is caught in a virtual time warp. Capitol City is more or less thought of as a tourist destination, and that is probably appropriate. Sixty miles straight south on Interstate 11 you will find the modern city of Allentown. Allentown is at the crossroads of Interstate Highway 11, the north-south route, and Interstate Highway 14, the east-west route. The short, physical distance of 60 miles between Capitol City and Allentown is the antithesis of the distance between the cities' growth into the modern days. Allentown has seen unprecedented growth in its population, approaching seven times the population of Capitol City's metro area population of 100,000 citizens. Allentown, the city with a common name, is the real center of the state; Capitol City may be the seat of government, but Allentown surpassed the elite tourist city many years ago. Allentown was originally named in honor of a royal aristocrat in Spain, the Duke de Plata, with the hopes of being looked upon favorably by the Spanish monarchy. Four hundred years later, the city was renamed for an 1800's ranching family, the Allens. Allentown spurted to success after World War II. Spurred on by the war's secret atomic age efforts to the north in the Cactus Range and the Jack Pine Proving Grounds, and to the south, the Salida Range Site, where some of the first nuclear bombs were detonated, Allentown has thrived ever since. Today a modest downtown skyline exists. Besides the State University, a Double A minor league baseball team, the "Miners," enjoy the desert. The Rio Caballo, the Horse River, bisects the sprawling city, and to the north, upstream and away from the Rio Caballo, Capitol City continues its sleepy existence with virtually no growth, in stark contrast to Allentown. Its growth is virtually flat except for fabulously wealthy retirees and the intermittent movie star that acquires a foothill residence along the base of the Sangre de Sustantivos.

The exclusive zip code that is Capitol City with its bloated real estate prices forces a majority of its middle class labor force, mostly state government workers, to commute the hour drive from Allentown. The morning and evening commute is filled with many an employee of state government seeking the refuge of affordable housing in the Allentown metro area. Interstate 11 from Capitol City to Allentown can be referred to as the Desert NASCAR during the weekday commuting hours as thousands race to or away from work.

Over time, a number of "high thinking" politicians have proposed a remedy for commuter traffic. The idea for a solution has come around again; this time by an ambitious new governor in the state capitol. The time has come, according to the governor, to turn back the clock to a romantic time when the train tamed the Wild West.

Interstate 11 from Allentown to Capitol City can be a somewhat forgettable drive in many respects. Often times, people have no appreciation for what they can see immediately in front of them along the route. The Durazno Mountains rise out of nowhere to the immediate east side of Allentown, a result of unspeakable geological events. The highway passes through Enclaves, Indian settlements, Native American settlements to be more politically correct, recognized by the federal government. Two Tribes have casinos immediately adjacent to the Interstate. Saint Tomas Enclave, an Indian Settlement trying to shed the roots of its conquered name, now known as Toyabo, which loosely translated in their native tongue means "the people," does not have gaming. It has focused on the travel business with lower gas prices for the commuter and Interstate traveler. A large filling station attracts a steady stream of vehicles maneuvering to and from home to work via the highway to the gasoline pumps and back again.

The trip starting north out of Allentown and passing through the Enclaves will bring you to La Bajada. La Bajada, or "descent" when translated, is the steep slope up the escarpment to a crest that finds you looking down into Capitol City and the surrounding valley resting at the feet of the Sangre de Sustantivo Mountains. At the crest of the hill, on the Capitol City side, Interstate 11 provides a rest area for the traveler. Free coffee is provided along with restrooms and parking for the weary driver. Another 20 miles or so north from here you will find the Interstate skirting the southeast side of the City Santuario.

Allentown is a lesser known member of the "mile high city" brotherhood. It sits in the Rocky Mountains along with its famous high altitude partners of Denver, Colorado; Flagstaff, Arizona; and even Cheyenne, Wyoming. The total time for a typical highway trip from downtown Allentown to downtown Capitol City, at an even more oxygen-starved altitude of about 7,000 feet, is about an hour. As mentioned, the casual observer probably doesn't see anything but the wide skies and distant mountains, although the multi-colored soils along the roadside and in the eroded ditches can be equally interesting when you notice the intricate patterns carved into the earth by the sparse rainfall runoff. If a traveler takes the time to look around, he will find the trip memorable.

Gregory L. Heitmann

Chapter 6

Confession

Gary and Bryan arrive back in Capitol City and proceed to the USTD office just off Corral Road on the south side of the city. A densely configured office court is home to the federal transportation office. As Bryan parks in front of the office building, he turns to Gary to say something. Bryan is pale. His adrenaline rush has subsided, and he slouches over the steering wheel. "I don't want to go in," Bryan declares.

"Don't worry about it," Gary says as he opens his door. "You don't have to say a word. I'll explain to Diego what happened."

Bryan nods and exits the vehicle. The men enter the building. The USTD office building is a traditional pueblo-style, single story, stucco building. It rests along an arroyo that may run with water once or twice a year. The business office court is relatively new, built only after a rezoning of the floodplain in which it lies. The neighboring buildings house an insurance company, a county fire inspection agency, and a state therapeutic (massage, acupuncture, etc.) licensing agency. They pass by Sylvia's desk in the reception area of the office. Sylvia Wells is an Air Force veteran serving out the rest of her government service time working as the office manager for the USTD office. She is an African American living in Capitol City, having been transplanted from her native Texas to Samuels Air Force Base in Allentown fifteen years ago. Retiring from military service and coming to the USTD, the fifty-plus year old, mother and grandmother, keeps the office in order.

"What mischief have you two been up to?" Sylvia questions.

Bryan's eyes widen, and he points at Gary.

Gary smiles, "Nothing much. Is Diego back in his office?"

Sylvia laughs, "I guess from Bryan's reaction, you guys are in trouble."

"A bit," Gary replies as he holds his finger and thumb up separated by a half an inch, "poco." Gary laughs and looks at Bryan who is pale and sickly.

Sylvia shakes her head and waves the two away as she states, "Good luck."

Bryan marches to the back of the building and Diego's office as a man would march to the electric chair. Gary sticks his head into Diego's office, "Gotta minute?"

Diego looks up from reading some papers on his desk with a grin, "Sure."

Gary enters the office followed by Bryan. Diego arches an eyebrow, "Wait a minute; I didn't know Bryan was with you. What did you do?"

Diego Santana is the boss. The director of the state's Division Office for the USTD, he is responsible for nearly $450 million in federal money annually spent on highways within the state. It's a big responsibility for a "local boy that makes good."

Diego is a native of Allentown, a former basketball star at the University of Nevada Las Vegas after an all-state career at Allentown Preparatory School in the late 1960's. His career at the Department of State traveling the world with ambassadors prepared him for some intricate negotiations before joining the USTD ten years ago and getting his appointment back in his home state. Diego has the unshakeable quality of the head of a mob family along with a dark look that goes with it. Always dressed in a dark suit and tie, he sports the latest fashions including the trendiest eyeglass frames.

Diego smiles, "I'm just kidding, relax, Bryan. You look like you've seen a ghost. Have a seat, guys."

Bryan and Gary sit at a small table in the corner of Diego's large office. Diego stashes the papers on his desk in a drawer, leaving a clean work area as he moves over to the table to join the two men. "Why so serious?" Diego inquires brushing his lapel and smoothing his tie as he sits.

Gary sighs as he thinks back to when Diego hired him as the deputy director a few months ago. It had been a troubling year leading up to this time and now things seemed to continue spiraling downhill.

Gary had been ready to leave his federal job under the mounting pressure of a hostile work environment. The hostility was in the form of a team leader, Daniel Perez, who was corrupt and seemingly immune from Diego and the then deputy director, Tammy Martin. When the process finally played out, the team leader resigned under the threat of being fired for corruption. What happened next still weighs on the minds of the Division Office employees and the state highway department. Tammy was shot to death one evening as she left the office and the corrupt team leader, Daniel Perez, was arrested for the murder.

Diego offered the job as the new deputy to Gary and here we are. Gary snaps back to the present as he hears Diego ask again, "Well, I'm waiting. What happened?"

Gary again inhales deeply and sighs as he looks to Bryan, and then back to Diego. "Let me first say Bryan had nothing to do with it."

Diego nods and folds his hands on the table in front of him, "I see."

Gary continues his explanation as he recounts the visit to see Patrick Ruiz at the project site as Diego listens in silence without interrupting. When Gary finishes, Diego nods removing his glasses and wiping them with the prescribed soft rag from his glasses case. He replaces his glasses and almost imperceptibly waves his index finger to the door as he calmly and quietly speaks, "Bryan, you're excused. Please close the door on your way out."

Bryan springs to his feet and leaves without a word as he shuts the door with a click of the knob.

Diego rubs his chin as he gathers his thoughts and looks out the window a moment. Gary nervously waits. He takes a look around Diego's sparsely decorated office. A black and white poster of Diego's basketball playing days graces one wall, Colin Powell's biography sits on a shelf. A red and black Michael Jordan collectible basketball sits next to a red and grey Ohio State University football on a shelf near Diego's computer screen. Gary grits his teeth as Diego folds his hands again on the table and leans forward and meets Gary's eyes.

"What do you think you accomplished?" Diego asks.

"I'm going to stick with 'defending myself' if there are any questions."

Diego nods. He sits quietly for a full minute reading Gary's face and posture before continuing, "That's not what I asked, but I'll make a phone call."

Gary's shoulders sag as he breathes after unconsciously holding his breath.

"You need to realize this is unacceptable," Diego quietly lectures. "When I hired you as Deputy, you said you wanted to make a difference."

Gary cocks his head wondering where Diego was headed with this discussion.

"You have a lot of responsibility in your position, and I expect you will hold yourself and this office to a higher standard."

Gary shifts uncomfortably in his chair.

"Gary, you cannot try to exact revenge for some petty offense you think you may have suffered now or previously. I want you to leave this office tonight, and I want you to take the day off tomorrow and really think about whether you can do this job. I believe you can, but you have to believe in yourself. You can't fake this job. You have to execute. There are no two ways about this."

Diego points to the basketball on the shelf, "I know you played a little ball in high school. Don't you remember that you had to execute? There was no half-speed. You go all out, or you get whipped. It's the same translation to this job."

Diego purses his lips and looks again out the window gathering his last thoughts. "Learn from this. Talk to Bryan about it and teach him. People are human. They make mistakes." Diego gives a nod to the door, "Go."

Gary finally nods. "I'm sorry, Diego. I've put you in a bad position. I was wrong. Patrick was wrong. And two wrongs don't make a right." Gary stands and moves to the doorway. He turns back to Diego, "You have my word. I will do better."

Chapter 7

Rio Ragma

Governor Stuart Reid-Salazar was seemingly born and raised to be a politician with virtually no limit on what office he could reach. The only child of a Florida businessman, Carson Reid and Maria Salazar, Stuart was raised in both the Anglo and Hispanic worlds. His mother, Maria was the daughter of a wealthy Mexican commodity importer-exporter while his father Carson made money the old fashioned way; he inherited it from his father's car dealerships in Florida. Stuart was born at the family compound in Florida but spent his pre-school days and his summers during his school years at the Salazar villa outside Mexico City.

Stuart could pass as an Anglo, but his impeccable fluency in Spanish and English was a key in communicating to the Hispanic voters in the state. The finest prep schools and an Ivy League education opened the door to internships and eventually the high levels of federal service inside the Beltway. After spending those token amounts of time in government appointed positions in Washington, D.C., Stuart targeted the Hispanic state's governorship by resigning his Deputy Secretary of Interior post and taking a job with a private forestry company's executive board. Here he quietly raised money for office and made the local political contacts two years before the term-limited governor would relinquish his post and a wide open governor's race would occur. Tired of eight years of Republican rule in the Governor's office, the voters put Reid-Salazar in place with a comfortable ten percentage point victory. This was phase one of Reid-Salazar's secret ambition of becoming the first serious Hispanic candidate for President of the United States and possibly the first Hispanic President.

At fifty years old, Governor Stu was a little paunchy, but his charisma and communication skills had never been more polished coming into a political season. On this night, the governor sits in the upscale Rio Ragma Restaurant in Capitol City, enjoying a late dinner with two members of his staff. The Rio Ragma is just a stone's throw from the capitol building and is the center of the universe for the who's who in the state's political circles.

Rio meaning river, of course, but Ragma is not so easily defined. The accepted explanation of the word "ragma" is probably a Spanish approximation of the name of an ancient Toyabo Enclave located in the north central region of the state. "Rugma" was the likely original term influenced by the Spanish word "rama", generally thought of as meaning "branch." It finally evolved as "ragma" due to its connection as a tributary flowing into the Rio Caballo. So, a few hundred years later, we have a restaurant named in honor of a river, the Rio Ragma. The posh restaurant is located off the downtown plaza across from one of the oldest churches in North America, est. 1618, as documented by friars that traveled with the Conquistadors. There is history here in Capitol City that keeps life rather slow but attracts the faster pace of tourism. The restaurant clientele is rather elite. Tourists directed by hotel staff and guidebooks mix in with the locals. The food and ambience are at the high end, along with prices.

Tonight the governor sits unmolested in a dark, back corner of the establishment finishing dinner with a drink, sharing the company of his Chief of Staff, Curt Summers, and the Secretary of Public Safety, Jeremy Montoya; both men are friends of the governor since childhood, riding the coattails of their political pal. Jeremy Montoya has been a friend of Stuart's in fits and spurts. His mother's second marriage to a Philadelphia businessman in the waste management industry allowed Jeremy to get experiences in the not-so-glamorous side of the "influence trade" of politics. Jeremy's time in waste management partnered him with his own kin, his nephew, Patrick. Patrick Ruiz was Jeremy's sister's son. Patrick was a sharp kid that parlayed his wits into an engineering degree and steady job as technical advisor to the family's interest in landfills, a requirement in the familial operation. When the opportunity arose for Jeremy to move to the Southwest as part of the future governor's inner circle, he brought his own trusted advisor, Patrick, with him and got him an engineering job with Laramie Engineering, one of the big boys in the consultant engineer world of the Southwest. A reduction in pay for Patrick, but the benefits were nice. The groundwork for the planned political power grab was years in the making. Patrick had been in place with Laramie Engineering, consultants to the state highway department, for a dozen years. He had risen to a post of Vice President of Construction and been assigned the T'rrain Trekker Project for a reason.

The third member of the governor's staff at dinner on this night approaches the table. Dontrell Antonio, another longtime member of the governor's inner circle of advisors, and now, chief of the governor's security detail gives Governor Stuart a nod, "Sir, the two guests are here to see you."

The Governor finishes a sip of his cocktail, sets the glass down, and waves his finger to Dontrell as he says, "Show them in."

The Governor stands along with the rest of his staff as Casey Baxter and Patrick Ruiz are shown to the table. The ties for the men at the table have been put away for the evening, but they adjust their suit jackets as the governor greets them. "Patrick. Casey. Good to see you. You know everyone here, I believe."

Governor Stuart shakes Casey's hand and gives her a quick hug and kiss to the cheek, then repeats the same gesture for Patrick sans kiss. The rest of the men exchange hand shakes with the guests. Patrick gives a wide smile to his Uncle Jeremy when they shake hands, but there is no fuss over their kinship. Once the greetings are completed, the governor directs his hands to the chairs, "Please, let's sit."

Two additional chairs for Patrick and Casey have materialized from an impeccable wait staff and they sit. Additional waiters clear dishes and another wave of servers provide coffee with notable choreography in their maneuvers.

Governor Stu leans on the table and smiles as he casts his gaze back and forth between Patrick and Casey. He leans back with his coffee cup in hand and says, "So, how're my favorite highway engineer and my favorite public works director?"

Casey forces a smile. She is uncomfortable and feels underdressed in the company of the men in suit jackets, wearing a frilly-collared blouse and slacks. Casey nods, "I'm fine, Governor."

"Please, at this table, I'm just Stu," Governor Stuart interjects as he tries to wave away his title.

Casey Baxter falls into a category that would be considered "over achiever". Bucking the man's world, she has risen to power in the male dominated field of public works. She's in her early 40's with rusty-brown, shoulder length hair. She could easily pass for being in her early 30's. Her petite five foot frame belies her strength, and the men at the table notice her attractive figure and pretty face. Casey has climbed the career ladder in the Allentown Public Works Department and now has reached the magnanimous title of Director of Regional Planning.

Casey manages a smile as she relaxes ever so slightly, "Will do, Gov…I mean Stuart."

The men at the table manage a forced laugh at Casey's stumble. Everyone is all smiles. The governor turns to Patrick and addresses him, "Patrick, I do say, man, we got to get out on the golf course again. I see your name in the paper all the time in these local tournaments."

Patrick glows as he blurts out, "Sure thing! Say when and where."

The governor sighs, "You know how it is. The campaign never stops." Governor Stu frowns for a moment but quickly smiles again. "I'm so glad you could meet tonight. I was just having dinner with the brain trust here." Governor Stu waves his hand around the table at his staff. "Sounds like there's a lot going on."

Governor Stuart drains the last of his coffee, and a waiter sweeps in to take the cup and saucer as another waiter drops a glass of whiskey on the rocks in front of him. The governor turns to the server and says, "Thank you," as he picks up the glass and sips.

The governor continues to sip a couple more small tastes from his glass before taking a swallow in earnest. He sets his glass down on the napkin in front of him and straightens it. He looks back and forth between Patrick and Casey and points as he laughs, "You two crack me up. I keep seeing you on the TV news coverage, and once in awhile you finish each other's sentences. And I never see one of you without the other side by side. I can't help but think of you guys as Laurel and Hardy."

Casey and Patrick beam with pride at this recognition from the governor. Patrick rolls his eyes and offers, "Let me guess; I'm the fat one, Oliver Hardy?"

Casey laughs, "That makes me Stan Laurel."

"Seriously, a very attractive Stan." The Governor continues, "You guys are doing some good work on the train. I appreciate it." He cocks his head as he looks at Patrick and points to his own finger, "What's up with the bandaged finger, Pat?"

Patrick shakes his head from side to side, "Oh, nothing, just a work mishap."

Governor Stuart laughs, "You have to be more careful. You're one of my top guys. Plus, I don't want Laramie Engineering to have a big workmen's comp claim from you." The governor laughs some more at his own joke. "But, most importantly, you don't want it screwing up your golf game."

The governor catches a nod from Dontrell out of the corner of his eye. He looks to the doorway and sees another member of the security team at the entry way. The governor leans back in his chair and sighs, "I am sorry," he says as he nods toward the doorway, "I have to run. My staff would like to talk to you some more though."

The governor drains the rest of his whiskey and excuses himself. Everyone stands, shakes the governor's hand and sits as Dontrell escorts Governor Reid-Salazar to his car waiting outside.

Chapter 8

A Favor…Quid

Politics ends up boiling down to the simplest of economic formulas, in this case a barter system. Trading. Quid pro Quo, this for that. When Curt Summers, the governor's Chief of Staff, the "make-it-happen-guy" and Jeremy Montoya sat alone with Patrick and Casey, the negotiations were finished before they started. The governor had stroked the egos of Patrick and Casey to such a point they were putty in his hands. What could they do? They are human, susceptible to the basic psychology of wanting to be wanted; a feeling of making a difference.

Curt scoots his chair close to the table and eyes Casey and Patrick. The two lean forward in their chairs naturally drawn to this man and his presence of authority. Curt nods his head and speaks, "The governor asked that we have a conversation about getting the train up and running as quickly as possible. He would consider it a special favor."

Curt Summers is one of "those guys," the traditional power behind the throne. The lifelong friend of the governor was educated at an Ivy League school separate from his friend Stuart Reid-Salazar, but in constant contact and able to step back into Stuart's life and assist him on anything and everything. Curt is 50-ish, with a physically fit build. His salt and pepper hair and non-threatening facial features served him well when competing for positions on corporate advisory boards. His vast experience over the years in the world of business has served him well, also. He is the trusted counsel of the governor. Curt's $3,000 suit is out of place anywhere but Wall Street, even without his tie as he sits at the table.

Curt leans back as Casey steals a look out of the corner of her eye at Patrick. Casey's ears pricked up when she heard the term "special favor." Her many years of experience in public service has tuned her listening skills toward a sharp awareness for when a politician asks a favor, but at the same time, isn't asking for a favor.

Jeremy Montoya, the Secretary of Public Safety, sits for a moment, arms folded. Jeremy Montoya is a friend of the governor from a different world. Jeremiah Alfonso Montoya was from the wrong side of the tracks in Mexico City. As fate would have it, Stuart's summers spent in a baseball league as a child crossed Jeremy's path on the field. Each was the best player on his respective team, and they became fast friends enjoying the competitive spirit. The Reid family virtually adopted Jeremy. As they grew older, Stuart did everything he could to convince Jeremy to come work for him. He helped Jeremy with his U.S. citizenship and education at the University of Arizona, even teaching Jeremy English. The investment in their friendship has paid dividends in ten fold. Jeremy has more than once saved Stuart's skin whether it be in foolish gambling, foolish carousing, or just plain all-around foolishness. Jeremy is the voice of reason for the governor to bounce ideas off and to attempt to understand the "common man's" perspective.

Jeremy has made the best of his defined Hispanic look. The jet black hair, the dark skin, the relative diminutiveness, all lend credibility to any Hispanic observing the governor's relationship with Jeremy. Jeremy is truly one of them, and he is a powerful advisor to the governor, a coup for the Hispanics.

Jeremy chimes into the conversation with his typical, up-beat, sing-songy manner, "The governor's campaigning on this commuter train. This is a major investment, for him and for the state. I hate to say this, but it's become too big too fail. With the amount of money invested in the T'rrain Trekker, and with the train as the pivot point of his Presidential campaign, it has to be done. And it has to be done quickly."

Curt follows up immediately picking up where Jeremy leaves off, "I'll let you in on some behind the scenes campaign stuff...the governor is going to make this train the focal point of his arguments at the Presidential debate later this week. It's a metaphor for his leadership, a locomotive moving forward."

Curt counts off on his fingers the points behind the train, "It's about energy policy. It's about serving the underserved. It's about doing big things with big ideas. But, most of all, it's an example of what leadership can bring, demonstrated at a state level."

Patrick is on the verge of breaking into a round of applause, "Oh, for sure! He can count on us!"

Curt leans back and nods satisfactorily, "That's great to hear. We just want to make sure that everyone's clear on this. This train is the top priority."

Curt emphatically raps his index finger down on the table and pronounces, "Top priority!"

Patrick is overwhelmed by the inclusion in the governor's plans, "What do you need me to do? We're expediting things as much as we can. Isn't that right, Casey?"

Casey shrugs, "Sure."

"Good. Good," Curt resonates the positive vibe. "Listen, you guys go ahead and finish your coffee, have a drink. Get something to eat. Stick around as long as you like. It's all on the tab."

Curt and Jeremy stand; Patrick springs to his feet and signals for Casey to stand.

"Well, Jeremy and I have to take off," Curt says through a forced, tired smile. "It's chaos on the campaign trail. Take it easy, guys."

Hand shakes are exchanged and Curt and Jeremy exit as Casey and Patrick sit back down at the table.

*   *   *   *   *

Patrick and Casey sit in silence alone at their table. They look at each other and sip their coffee without saying a word. They are still awestruck. Finally, Patrick can contain himself no longer. He shakes his head and speaks, "Isn't this cool? The governor treating us to dinner? He remembers us. He's watches us on TV!"

Patrick picks up his coffee cup again and sips as Casey puts her cup on its saucer, "Geez, take it easy, Pat. There's always a catch. Who do you think is treating us to dinner? I'm guessing the tax payers."

"What are you talking about?" Patrick blanches. "You gotta lighten up and enjoy life a little."

Patrick picks up his coffee cup and drains the rest with a satisfied, "Ah."

He sets the cup back on its saucer and continues, "Let me put it this way, we're just doing our jobs. We just happen to do them very well."

Casey's face scrunches with a puzzled look as she shakes her head side to side, "Try not to let it go to your head."

Patrick laughs, "Yeah, whatever, Case. Come on!" Patrick reaches over and grabs Casey's shoulder with his hand and rubs it for a moment, "Enjoy life…just a little."

They both lean back in their chairs and size each other up in silence. A minute goes by before a smile creeps across Patrick's face followed by a mirrored smile from Casey. Patrick nods in affirmation, "That's the spirit. Let's get some food."

Patrick signals to the waiter and menus are brought to the table.

Gregory L. Heitmann

Chapter 9

Bike Trail of Tears

Gary walks along the bicycle/pedestrian trail that parallels the ancient railroad grade on the edge of his residential neighborhood. He strolls with Katrina Del Carmen, his girlfriend. In front of them, in the distance, the setting sun casts a purple hue on the Sangre de Sustantivo Mountains. Single family homes line the trail and train tracks providing a nice buffer between neighbors' backyards.

Katrina and Gary walk in silence lost in their own thoughts. Katrina is a thirty-year old native of Allentown. She could pass as a twenty-year old; her straight, jet black hair falls neatly to her shoulders and minimal make up lets her natural beauty radiate.

The couple met through their work where Katrina is employed by the State Highway Department as a biologist. They have a fountain of topics for discussion as their daily tasks often cross paths.

Gary hums along to Kevin Fowler's tune "Hard Man to Love" as they walk. Katrina breaks the conversation silence, "Really, you're just going to keep humming that song forever?"

"I can't help it!" Gary says defensively, "It's taken hold of my brain…and I can't wait to go see him live this weekend."

Katrina rolls her eyes and sighs. They walk in silence as Gary stops humming. Katrina breaks the long silence again as they continue walking undisturbed by anyone on the trail, "I hate the license plate on your truck."

"What?" Gary cries out in surprise and stops walking. "Where is this unprovoked attack coming from?"

Katrina stops. She shrugs her shoulders, "I don't know. It just bothers me."

Gary scoffs, "But, I am the G MANN, Gary Hillmann. G for Gary and MANN for the last part of Hillmann." Gary lowers his voice as if sharing a secret, he looks over his shoulder suspiciously, "It also has a double meaning because I'm a federal government man."

"Uh, I knoooowww," Katrina rebuts as she puts her hands on her hips. She makes a face of disgust and continues, "But that doesn't mean I have to like the way you draw all this unnecessary attention to yourself."

They begin walking again. Gary nods and says, "Ah, I see. I'll take your comments under advisement."

Katrina scoffs, "Yeah, I know what that means. You will ignore them."

Gary cocks his head to think for a moment before responding, "Probably."

Katrina playfully slaps Gary on the shoulder.

Gary growls, "Owww. No hitting. We've talked about this."

"Sorry," Katrina offers.

Gary grabs Katrina's hand, "You're beautiful when you're angry."

Katrina throws his hand down, "What is with you? I am not angry!"

Gary laughs, "I'm just teasing you. You are beautiful all the time!"

"I know."

Gary laughs again, "Yes, your modesty is also one of your most attractive qualities."

"Shush," Katrina scolds.

They walk until they reach St. Thomas Drive, a main business thoroughfare. They turn and continue their evening stroll along the sidewalk headed towards Gary's house.

"Did you hear anything this week about a confrontation with Patrick Ruiz?" Gary inquires.

"No. Why?"

Bryan and I were out at the T'rrain Trekker project for a site visit, and there was a heated discussion."

"Hmmm," Katrina shakes her head, "I never heard a word."

"Uh, never mind then."

Gary's face lights up even as darkness falls, "So we're still on to see Kevin Fowler this weekend, right?"

"Yes! My God, we're going! That's all you've talked about for the last month."

"Sorry," Gary offers. "First of all, I need this break; second of all, you know nothing about Texas Country Music." Gary throws his hands in the air. "You are a virtual neighbor to Texas and you act like it doesn't exist. There's nothing wrong with Texas and I guarantee you'll like the music…guarantee."

The walk takes them by Kmart and the Lowell's Grocery Store. Katrina puts her arm around Gary's waist, "I'm sorry. I know you need this break. It's been a hectic six months since Tammy was killed."

They turn their walk down the last two blocks headed to Gary's house. They walk through a cozy residential neighborhood holding hands. Katrina continues, "It's hard for me to comprehend your having to step into your boss's shoes. And on top of it all, she was murdered. It's just weird…and creepy."

"Yeah, that's an understatement," Gary adds. "Just think; I've gone from a low-level bureaucrat all the way up to a mid-level bureaucrat."

Katrina laughs, "That's got to be stressful."

They walk quietly, approaching the final street back to Gary's house. "It's still weird to think about Tammy being dead. But, hey, let's not talk about her; let's talk about going to see Kevin Fowler!"

"Oh, for the love of Pete!" Katrina howls as they reach Gary's driveway, "Enough about Fowler!

Chapter 10

Follow the Process

Another meeting for the T'rrain Trekker is on the agenda, this time at the Capitol City Municipal Building. Bryan and Gary arrive fashionably late in the government sedan. They sit inside the car for a moment to discuss the emergency meeting.

"So," says Gary, "What did you want me to say when we go in? Anything in particular?"

Bryan rolls his eyes, "Nah. I just thought there would be safety in numbers. I'm so sick of Patrick Ruiz I could puke. He's got to be the biggest douche bag in the state. That says a lot in this state."

"Just do our jobs. That's all we can do."

Bryan is frustrated, "He's treating this project like the transportation budget is his own personal treasury. Where does that prick get his arrogance? He thinks he's the smoothest player on earth. He's just a fat, jackass that's turned into a political yes-man, go-getter. How did the highway department lose control of this project? They've basically handed everything over to him!" Bryan rubs his temples with his fingers trying to massage away a tension headache. "Long story, short; I need you here to keep me from doing or saying something I might regret."

"Gotcha," Gary acknowledges with a nod. "I'm counting on you, Bryan. It's a little different now that I'm 'management'." Gary makes finger quotes around the word management. "Especially since our last little incident."

Bryan lets out a loud laugh, "How can I ever forget?"

The men exit the vehicle and head to the building. Gary turns to Bryan, "Do you think Pat's still going to be pissed about his finger?"

"I've said it before, and I will say it again, whoever said that fat people are jolly, i.e. Santa Claus, is a liar; yes Fat Pat's probably going to have a slight grudge against you."

Gary opens the door to the Municipal Building, and they proceed down the empty hallway to a conference room full of people. Gary and

Bryan ease quietly into the back of the room and observe Patrick Ruiz preaching from his soapbox.

"We need these rail stations built!" Patrick pleads, "What good is the train if nobody can get on and off the train?"

Patrick paces back and forth in front of a large plan sheet and aerial photo of the train's route. A group of men and women sit around a large conference table in the generically decorated conference room. Bryan and Gary stand against the back wall amongst some other meeting attendees without seats at the table.

Patrick stops pacing and points his index finger encased in its protective splint at the Interstate 11 median. He raps on the map with the splint. "Right here. Can anybody tell me the status of the Interstate station here in the median?"

A large logo of the T'rrain Trekker with its familiar, wavy blue and purple lines in the shape of the Sangre de Sustantivo Mountain skyline takes a prominent position on the map. Leaders drawn from the logo are connected to proposed station locations along the rail line.

"Please," Patrick pleads, "can somebody provide some positive information?"

Consultant design engineers, city personnel from Capitol City and Allentown, along with the construction contractors sit quietly in the room.

Patrick shrugs, "Nobody can tell me anything? No status on approving the locations?" Patrick heaves a big sigh. "We are on a schedule, people" he whines. "I have a construction contractor," Patrick points to the construction contractor foreman at the table, "ready to go, and we're sitting here practically discussing the color of the drapes!"

Bryan speaks up from the back of the room, "Drapes? Patrick, what are you talking about?"

Gary elbows Bryan in the ribs, but it's too late, the words are out of Bryan's mouth before Gary can intervene.

A frustrated Patrick ignores Bryan and continues, "The T'rrain Trekker is not going to wait! This commuter rail project is the most important transportation proposal I have ever worked on as an engineer in my twenty years of service! We need decisions, and we need them now!" Patrick folds his arms dramatically and heaves a sigh. He taps his foot for effect.

From the back of the room a hand goes up and Patrick cranes to see who it is. He shrinks back a bit when he sees it's Bryan attached to the hand and stepping forward. Patrick manages to mumble, "Yes, Bryan, what is it?"

"Hi, Patrick," Bryan announces as he drops his hand, "I'm still confused by the drapes reference."

Patrick smiles the best he can, "You know what I mean. We need decisions. We need locations. We need to be able to serve the people riding the train with stops. We can't let details slow us down!"

People in the room fidget uncomfortably but remain silent as they try to not make eye contact with anyone. The tension builds. Bryan shrugs nonchalantly, "Well, why the hell didn't you put in these stations when you originally let the contract?"

Patrick tries to hold it together the best he can, "We didn't want to hold up all construction while the neighborhoods fought over station locations, all right?"

Bryan moves to the front of the room next to Patrick, "Who is this 'we' you keep referring to? 'We' need to do this. 'We' need to do that. Who is 'we'?"

"Come on, Bryan," Patrick says quietly. "You know what I mean."

"Yeah, I do, unfortunately," Bryan acknowledges as he frowns. "The governor has his own agenda while he is running for President. Listen, we all know the stations are going to be built...maybe not as fast you want them, but they are going to be built."

Patrick's shoulders slump a little, "Come on, Bryan," Patrick whimpers. "We're just trying to keep a schedule. You put us off five days before you would even meet with us."

Gary speaks up from the back of the room, "Patrick, take it easy. You know there is a process to follow. And I think you know that this is not the only project in the entire state. We have oversight of many projects."

Casey Baxter speaks up from her seat at the table, "Guys, please. Can't you help us out? You gotta understand the pressure on this."

"I'm sorry, Casey," Gary shrugs with his palms up, "What do you want us to do, cut corners? That's not going to happen. Like we have been telling you, the stations are coming, but there is a process."

Bryan pipes back up, "Public input is part of the process. Public meetings are going on; we know that. I hate to be the cynic, but I just as soon keep the politics and influence out of this as much as possible. I'd hate to see stations go only to property owners who happened to be large contributors to the governor's campaigns."

"Ok, what do you want us to do?" Casey inquires.

Bryan counts off on his fingers, "Step one, follow the process. Step two, follow the process. Step three, follow the process..."

Casey turns her appeal to Gary, "Gary?"

"We'll help you out with expedited reviews," Gary replies. "But, that's all we can do. We don't want to get involved in the appearance of granting special treatment."

Bryan continues his hard line commentary, "Those are the rules, buddy. There's no special treatment. We work for the federal government and the *nation's* taxpayers; we don't answer to the state governor."

Casey looks at Bryan and shakes her head pitifully.

The meeting continues and outlines a plan of action for determining station locations and how to go forward. Everyone is minimally satisfied, and the meeting is adjourned.

* * * * *

The meeting is over. Casey and Patrick remain in the room. The two are alone and remove the maps and aerial photos taped to the wall for display. The large, ten feet long and four feet wide sheets of paper are placed on the table, rolled, and bound with rubber bands.

Patrick finally explodes in a rage, "God damn it, Casey! I have obligations to keep!" Patrick leans on the table, his hands are in fists, and he rests his weight on the table scowling at Casey.

Casey continues to roll up a map and fix the roll in place with a rubber band. She sets the rolled up paper on the table and locks eyes with Patrick, "What do you want me to do?"

Patrick straightens to his full height and puts his hands on his hips, "I want you to call in some political favors. Use any clout you might have. Make a phone call or two. We have to move on this. You and I have friends that are counting on us."

Casey stares blankly at Patrick, "What does that even mean?"

Patrick throws his hands up in the air in a fit, "Don't give me that! You know exactly what it means."

Casey holds Patrick's gaze for a bit longer as she leans resting one hand on the table holding the rolled up maps. She finally drops her eyes to the maps, drums her fingers on the table, and fidgets with the rolls of paper, straightening them. She stammers quietly, "Y-y-you're right. I guess I just wish I didn't know what it meant." Casey's lip quivers a bit.

Patrick cocks his head, "Hey, don't worry," realizing he has hurt Casey. Patrick moves around to the same side of the table as Casey. He moves in front of Casey and places a massive hand on her shoulder and looks at her. Casey won't look up from the table. "Come on now, it's going to be ok. Look at me."

Casey reluctantly turns her face to look Patrick in the eye. Patrick pulls her close, enveloping Casey's waif-like body in his mass, and whispers soothingly, "I'll take care of everything."

* * * * *

In the parking lot outside the windows of the municipal building's conference room, Gary and Bryan observe Patrick and Casey from the comfort of the G-car. Undetected by Patrick or Casey, they see the muted scene play out, puzzled by the actions they witness.

Bryan initially notices the pair inside before he even starts the car, "Dude, check it out. Looks like they're arguing."

On the other side of the windows, Patrick can be seen waving his arms wildly in anger; pointing at Casey. Casey cowers like a scolded puppy.

Gary and Bryan watch as the soundless scene plays out before them. Bryan narrates a bit more, "Wait a minute; Patrick is going around the table, now he's grabbing her shoulders! Do you see this?"

Gary laughs, "Yes, I see it."

Bryan's face twists in confusion, "What the heck is going on in there? I just don't know what's more disgusting to me, Pat, the fat slob, or the pathetic Casey."

They watch as Patrick holds Casey's shoulders. Patrick's mouth moves, and he gives Casey's shoulders a squeeze. Casey finally looks Patrick in the face.

Bryan's voice squeaks as he questions, "A lover's quarrel and now they are making up? Is that what we're seeing? Oh my God, he's going to kiss her."

Bryan and Gary watch as Patrick and Casey embrace. Bryan starts the car, "I can't watch this."

Gary laughs, "What's the matter with you?"

Bryan pulls the car out of the parking lot onto a narrow city street, still worked up over what he has witnessed, "Are you kidding me? You think those two are having an affair? Aren't they both married with kids?"

Gary shrugs, "Yeah, I think so. They are married, but not to each other!" Gary laughs heartily at his own joke.

Bryan smiles, "Capitol City diversity, God bless it."

"What do you care?" Gary questions.

"I don't! It's just that you think you know people, but you never really do."

That's true," Gary nods in agreement.

"I guess it makes sense…opposites attract. Casey is good looking and thin, Patrick is fat and hideous."

Gary chuckles as Bryan continues to rant, "Seriously, how did I miss this? It's just…it's…"

"Just what?"

"Casey and Patrick? Patrick is a slob! How could they be, you know…"

"A couple?" Gary inquires.

"Yeah."

"It takes all kinds to make the world go 'round," Gary shrugs.

Chapter 11

Long and Winding Trail

In the humble home of Gary Hillmann, the walls are crowded with a collection of his passion: hunting and the outdoors. The taxidermy mounts of four deer heads line the walls of the living room and den, two in each room. The small house is jammed with wildlife prints and wooden duck decoys on shelves. Gary's house is located in an older neighborhood in the vicinity of Capitol City High School. It is a pueblo-style, three bedroom, 1,400 square foot home in a middle class neighborhood. The modestly decorated home has but one luxury item, a top of the line flat screen TV for sports viewing.

Supper is over and Gary and Katrina don their walking shoes preparing for an evening stroll around the neighborhood. Gary punches the volume button over and over again on his remote bringing the stereo system to a deafening level as the radio plays Kevin Fowler's song "*Hard Man to Love*."

The song tells the story of a man behaving badly, and a woman, even with no reason to stick around, puts up with him. The lyrical references to a crippled kitchen table, barbed wire man, silky-soft woman, and a dog-house rose blare through the room.

Katrina looks up from tying her tennis shoe and scowls at Gary. She mouths some words, and Gary smiles and puts his hand to his ear. He shakes his head indicating he can't hear what she is saying.

Katrina takes a deep breath and shouts, "Are you ready…"

Before she can finish her sentence that is being drowned out by the radio, Gary cuts the power to the stereo, leaving Katrina to scream into the silence, "…to go for a walk!"

Gary puts on his best look of innocence, "You don't have to yell."

Katrina approaches Gary with her hands poised, ready to choke him, she wraps her hands around his neck and pretends to squeeze, "Let's go!" she commands.

"You bet!"

The couple departs the house and walks to the sidewalk as the garage door closes behind them. "The usual route?" Gary inquires.

"Yup."

"So, are you ready to see Fowler this weekend?"

"Jesus, Joseph, and Mary! How many times do I have to affirm your plan? I said we are going! Stop trying to sell me on the idea!"

Gary smiles and nods in a childlike fashion, "It's going to be awesome! I can't believe you'd never heard of Fowler before you met me."

"Oh, shucks," Katrina drawls in a mocking southern accent. "Leave it to a weirdo from South Dakota, to come to my state, and introduce me to Texas Country Music."

Gary ignores the sarcasm, "Pretty neat, huh? I'd say it's almost cool. We're nearly a mixed race couple. I'm a Midwestern White boy and you're a..."

Gary pauses and puts his finger to his lips. He pretends to think as they walk down the street. He leans back to try to imply he's taking a wider view of his girlfriend.

Katrina has all she can stand; she swings her hip into Gary, knocking him sideways. "Hispanic!" she shouts as she finishes Gary's evaluation for him.

Gary shrugs, "So you say."

Katrina shakes her head, rolls her eyes, looks skyward, and mouths the words, "Help me, Lord."

They walk in silence for a block as they reach Hill Street. At the connection of Hill Street and the rail trail, they turn and stroll down their familiar walking route.

"You'll never guess what I saw today," Gary finally says.

"What?"

"Bryan and I went to the T'rrain Trekker meeting, and afterwards, when we were in our car and leaving, we could see Casey and Patrick hugging and then they kissed."

"So?" Katrina scoffs.

"So, nothing. It was just weird."

The walk continues down the hill toward St. Thomas Drive. "Speaking of seeing things; guess who I saw at the grocery store?" Katrina queries.

"Oprah! No, Gene Hackman?"

Katrina scrunches her face, puzzled by the response, "The movie star, Gene Hackman? That's your answer?"

"He lives here, doesn't he?"

"Gene Hackman? I don't know! That's not who I saw."

Gary shrugs, "I don't know; just tell me."

"My ex-husband."

"No kidding?"

Katrina shakes her head with a frown firmly in place, "He was with his skanky new wife, who, by the way, looks like a stripper."

"He's remarried already?"

"Yes, the man is a child."

Gary shrugs, "You would know. You were married to him."

Katrina winds up and punches Gary in the shoulder.

Gary howls, "Ouch! Damn it! Why did you hit me? You were married to him! It's a fact!"

Gary rubs his shoulder as they continue to walk the trail.

Katrina turns her face to Gary and narrows her eyes, "Yeah, but you don't have to use that tone."

Gary scrunches his face and frowns, puzzled, "Tone?"

The couple walks in silence as they approach the trail's intersection with St. Thomas Drive. Gary flashes a smile as he is hit with an idea, "You know what you should do? You should actually become a stripper. That would show him."

Katrina rolls her eyes and forces a laugh, "Oh, ha-ha, you're always so full of useful suggestions."

"I try," Gary acknowledges.

Katrina can't hold back her smile. She reaches for Gary's hand as they walk past the Burger Coral. Gary does his best to whistle the chorus of Kevin Fowler's song, *Hard Man to Love*."

Gregory L. Heitmann

Chapter 12

Coffee Worship

Off of Coral Road, technically this is State Highway 14, near the sprawling commercial shopping area a few miles away from downtown and the Capitol Building, sits a grocery story. The grocery store is Albertson's, and it adjoins Target; across the street is a Best Buy. Target and Albertson's share a large parking lot with Panda Express and Dominos Pizza. Inside Albertsons is a Starbucks coffee shop. On a sunny and pleasant summer morning Gary waits in line for coffee. Beside him is Sarah Liriano, a longtime, loyal friend. They both examine the coffee menu posted above the serving area. They silently examine other options posted in multiple colors written on a chalkboard next to the cash register.

Sarah and Gary spent a lot of time together working highway projects, prior to each of their respective promotions. Sarah worked projects in the field as a right of way acquisition agent before her promotion to supervisor at the state highway department. Gary, prior to his promotion to deputy director, worked with Sarah on numerous projects certifying environmental and right of way requirements for individual projects. Now, both Gary and Sarah work at a management level, removed from the day to day details, but still maintaining awareness of projects…especially problem projects.

Sarah is a native of the Southwest. She just recently celebrated her big five-oh, fiftieth birthday. Gary and Katrina attended the surprise party that was hosted by her husband. Numerous high level personalities were in attendance at the party, including local news anchor celebrities, movie stars, priests, bishops, and maybe even a Cardinal. Sarah and her husband are each products of large Catholic families, and extended family ties intermingle their connections to every segment of society, but none more so than the connections with the "ruling class" of the Capitol City patrons.

Sarah is small, standing about five feet tall even with the two-inch heels of her summer sandals boosting her height. She has wavy, black hair with a hint of red highlights. Her pretty blue eyes contrast the dark hair and complexion of her Hispanic heritage.

When it's time for Gary and Sarah to order, they both choose a variation of ice coffees in order to combat the heat of the summer morning. They wait in line to pay; "I'm buying," Gary states as their total is rung up at the register.

"Thank you," Sarah acknowledges.

"Thank you for meeting me," Gary counters as he grabs the drinks and hands Sarah her beverage.

"No problem. Long time, no see," Sarah nods as she receives her coffee.

They move to a small table and sit as they sip their frappuccinos. "Ah, delicious," Gary casually comments.

"Mmm-hmm," Sarah concurs as she sips through her straw.

"So," Gary leans back in his chair, "Tell me, how's the family? Still got multiple kids in college?"

Sarah groans a bit, "Don't remind me."

Gary laughs as Sarah takes another sip of coffee before she continues, "Nobody's dropped out yet." Sarah giggles at her own comment. She stifles herself and her habit of laughing...her unique way of laughing at anything and everything; it's a bit of a nervous habit, but more of an indication of her enjoyment of life and living.

"Well, at least you got a bit of a pay bump with the promotion," Gary raises his coffee cup in a toast, meeting Sarah's coffee cup with a squeak of Styrofoam.

"Yeah, I'm not complaining...much."

Gary sets his coffee down and holds his hands up as he looks Sarah up and down, "How could you even have one child in college? You look as young and beautiful as ever."

"Stop it. All this flattery...free coffee...what is it? What do you want?"

Gary laughs, "Busted."

Sarah continues to laugh easily and at everything; she lets go of a cackle that turns heads at the grocery store. Gary covers his mouth trying to hold back from reacting at her outrageous laugh. After a moment they both regain enough composure to continue their conversation. "Tell me," Gary questions, "How about your right-of-way office? Are you buying property for the train stations?"

Sarah nods in affirmation as she sips from her coffee. She sets the cup down and folds her arms with a look of disgust, "You better believe it. Let me put it this way; the orders have come down and offers are being made as fast as possible."

"How is it possible to make offers? They haven't even finalized the locations," Gary counters.

Sarah shrugs as she unfolds her arms and wraps her hands around her coffee cup, "Tell that to your buddy, Pat. He's in our office every day breathing down somebody's neck asking for status updates."

"Yeah, my buddy, Patrick," Gary scoffs. "Let me guess; all the parcels you are acquiring are the *'pay to play'* land development buddies of the governor. And, I bet they all have nice highly developable chunks of land adjacent to the train's stations. How convenient."

"Pay to play?" Sarah asks with a puzzled expression.

"You haven't heard that? 'Pay to play' is the term that some reporter coined, and the media is using. These guys make some campaign donations, and the governor makes sure he dedicates time for them and whatever cause they support."

"Well, your guess would be correct, sir. It's weird though. The department is covering itself with all these additional "rescission of offer clauses," just in case some locations aren't selected. Are the Feds going to do anything?"

Gary sighs, "What can we do? We have no funding in this project. Believe me, if I had any say at all, we wouldn't have just plowed forward willy-nilly."

"What's Diego say about all this?"

Gary shakes his head side to side, "Nothing. We've talked about it, but it's not federally funded."

Sarah nods understandingly, "That's too bad. Changing the subject a bit, I heard you might have had a run in with your buddy, Fat-Pat."

"Oh, God," Gary whispers as his face reddens with embarrassment. "What did you hear?"

"Well, I heard you two had a fist fight; that's how Patrick broke his finger."

Gary smiles, "That's pretty much the gist of it, but it wasn't a big deal. We mostly exchanged words. As you can see from my handsome face," Gary frames his hands around his face. "He didn't land any punches."

Sarah and Gary both lean back in their chairs and relax a bit as they sip their coffee. Gary's discomfort talking about his confrontation with Patrick eases.

Sarah breaks the silence, "Do you think Patrick's somehow involved in the 'pay to play' stuff?"

"That's funny you should ask that; I was just going to ask you the same thing."

"I'll ask around," Sarah offers.

"Good Lord, I can't stand that guy," Gary emphatically states, his voice rising. "He's nothing but a fat, sloppy, wheezing idiot."

Sarah frowns, "I wish you wouldn't use the Lord's name in vain."

Gary smiles, "It always comes back to religion with you, doesn't' it?

"What do you mean?" Sarah retorts defensively. "You...you always somehow bring religion up!"

Gary and Sarah laugh again together drawing looks from surrounding customers. Gary sighs loudly again as he takes another sip of coffee, "I have one for you. What is up with Hispanic Catholics naming their kids Jesus?"

Sarah's face scrunches with a look of bewilderment, "It's not Jesus; it's *Heh-soos*."

Gary shakes his head side to side, "Same thing, Jesus, *Hay-zoos*. Doesn't that seem odd to you? No other religious group names its children after their Messiah. What do you think the Jewish people at that time thought of the name *Jesus*?"

"What do the Jews have to do with Jesus?"

"Hello, Jesus was Jewish, before he invented Christianity."

Sarah laughs loudly, "You're right!"

Gary pushes Sarah on the point, "Any thoughts?"

"About what? Jesus inventing Christianity? That's funny how you put that."

"Don't you think," Gary continues, "that it's a touch arrogant to give a child a name of the Savior? At the minimum, it seems like a lot of pressure on that poor kid. There's no way he could live up to the name."

Sarah shakes her head and stares at Gary a moment, "You seem pretty sensitive about all this for somebody who doesn't really practice much religion."

"I like to discuss the philosophical side of things."

"Oh yeah? I just thought of this," Sarah offers smugly, "...what about all the Muslims named Mohamed? How do you explain that?"

"Hmm," Gary is momentarily silenced, "Interesting...although Mohamed was a prophet and was not proclaimed as the son of God, i.e. Jesus."

Sarah laughs with an expression of disbelief, "Where do you come up with this stuff, you weirdo?"

"I don't know. I guess it just comes to me."

Sarah picks up her cup and takes a sip of her coffee. With her other hand, she playfully points a finger at Gary, "Well, I think you are going to hell. All this skeptical talk about religion."

Gary feigns shock and indignation, "What?!?!"

Sarah laughs, "I'm just teasing you."

"You are probably right, but come on; can't we at least enjoy our coffee before I have to go…back…to the office, not to hell?"

Sarah cackles, again turning the heads of surrounding customers.

Chapter 13

Fire in the Hole

On a quiet Friday afternoon when most of the United States Transportation Department employees had called it a week, Gary is catching up on his emails. The typical emails have piled up as they always do. The USTD Headquarters in Washington, D.C., loves to pretend they are busy. The powers that be constantly send emails alerting the Division Office of the important work they perform and recording their performance and its greatness throughout the week with a constant barrage of email notices. The prolific amount of email produced by HQ is comparable to those sent by spammers regarding wonder drugs available without prescriptions. Today Gary is noting the National Transportation Secretary delivered two speeches during the week. No less than twenty-five emails litter Gary's inbox regarding these speeches, and their supposedly far reaching impact and monumental success.

"Holy cow," Gary mutters to himself as he clicks away highlighting and deleting numerous, worthless emails.

The light overhead flickers, the computer screen on his desk winks, and suddenly electricity is lost. From down the hallway at the front door, Gary hears a scream. Sylvia is still in the office.

"Help!" Gary can hear Sylvia cry out from her area. "Fire!"

Gary can smell the smoke as he bolts from his desk toward the cries. He runs down the hallway and stops to grab a fire extinguisher. He approaches Sylvia's cubicle and sees smoke rolling out from the open doorway leading to the computer server room. Sylvia coughs and gasps as she futilely swats at the smoke billowing from the door. She pushes the door open for Gary, and he charges into the six foot by eight foot room that holds the computer equipment. Gary spots the trouble and flashes the extinguisher in direction of a smoldering mass of nylon. A few flames reach up again, but they surrender to the contents of the extinguisher. A half dozen nylon, laptop computer cases are a gooey mess. The bags are wrapped in a jumble of extension cords plugged into a power strip overloaded with plugs.

Gary and Sylvia back out of the server room as they gasp and cough to catch their breath. Chuck Roland enters the office, coughing as the smoke hits him in the face. "What's going on?" Chuck manages to ask between coughs.

Chuck is a transplanted Chicagoan. In his mid-thirties, he is the Information Technology Specialist, the IT guy. The computer guy. He is wiry, some would say emaciated. His blond hair is closely cropped in a crew cut.

"Everybody out!" Gary yells, "Get out in the fresh air! Sylvia, dial 911 and get the fire department over here. I don't want the fire to flare back up!"

Sylvia grabs her cell phone and calls as they move outside.

"Was there anyone else here, besides the three of us?" Gary asks.

Sylvia shakes her head side to side as she looks at Gary, waiting for the 911 operator to pick up, "We were the last ones for the week."

Gary turns to Chuck, "God damn it, Chuck! What were you doing in the server room?"

Chuck puts his hands up in fear, "Nothing!"

"You had extension cords and power strips plugged into everything and anything in there! I'm sure that's what caused the fire."

Chuck loses all color in his face realizing his mistake, "I-I-uh, I was just running some diagnostics with a couple laptops. I had them plugged in and running. It was going to take a few minutes, so I stepped out for a smoke."

"Jesus," Gary growls as he rolls his eyes in disgust. "You are lucky you didn't burn the whole place down!"

"I'm sorry, Gary," Chuck pleads. "Please don't fire me. I need this job. I have to pay child support."

Gary sighs, "You explain that to Diego on Monday. You'll get your chance to make your case to him then. You are lucky you are a contract employee. If it were solely up to me, I'd call your boss and have him send over a replacement right now. You get this fixed up over the weekend, and you'll get your chance to convince Diego to spare you."

"Oh, Gary, thanks, man. I'll get it fixed up. Don't worry."

Sirens from emergency vehicles get closer.

"You ok, Sylvia?" Gary inquires.

"I think so." She responds.

"Just go home. Chuck and I will handle the rest of the day."

Sylvia grabs her stuff and waves goodbye as she escapes the chaos of the parking lot full of emergency vehicles.

"Chuck, get with the building manage when he gets here. Make sure we get power right away. I want the servers up and running on Monday before everyone shows up for work."

"Yes, sir," Chuck salutes Gary and jogs to the neighboring office building that holds the business complex's management office.

Fire trucks encircle the area, and firemen head into the smoky building to inspect the damage.

Chapter 14

Twilight Rodeo

It is the night of the Kevin Fowler concert. Gary and Katrina arrive at the Allentown Marriott Pyramid North near the intersection of Interstate 11 and Paseo del Sol. The hotel resembles a cross between an Egyptian Pyramid and the Southwestern style adobe building. The Marriott Pyramid is hosting a pharmacy conference which Gary's younger brother, Glenn Hillmann, is attending for continuing education credits. Glenn's conference scheduling was carefully coordinated in order to combine Kevin Fowler's tour visit to Allentown. Glenn has enlisted some other pharmacy friends to help blow off some steam with a night on the town.

Gary calls Glenn on his cell phone as he and Katrina wait in the lobby of the hotel. Glenn picks up the call, and Gary notifies him of their arrival. Glenn makes his way to the lobby, calling his friends as he rides the elevator and telling them to meet in the lobby.

Gary informs Katrina, "They're on their way down."

Katrina nods, "You know what? I'll be the designated driver tonight."

"Are you sure?"

"Yup. You can have fun."

"Well, you are not going to get any argument from me, but to be clear on one thing, I don't need to get drunk to have fun…"

Katrina rolls her eyes as she finishes Gary's sentence, "Yeah, yeah, I know…but drinking sure adds to the enjoyment. Why must you always say that?"

"I wish I knew." Gary sees the elevator doors open and Glenn steps out. "Hey! Glenn's here!"

Glenn strolls over with a wide grin and a roundhouse wave of his hand. Gary welcomes him with a native handshake, a five on the side followed by a fist bump.

"Welcome," Gary says, "Glenn, this is my friend, Katrina Del Carmen. Katrina, this is Glenn, my brother."

Glenn extends his hand, and Katrina shakes it. She follows the handshake with a hug. "Nice to meet you. How was your trip?" Katrina inquires.

As Katrina and Glenn break their hug, Glenn responds, "Fine. No problems flying in." He looks at Katrina with a smile, "So, Katrina, eh? Like the hurricane that destroyed New Orleans?"

Katrina rolls her eyes, "Uhg. Like I've never heard that before," she says with a heartfelt mocking tone.

Glenn gives Gary a satisfied nod of approval, "Mean and sarcastic...I like her."

Gary shrugs.

"It's funny," Glenn continues, "that name is ruined because of the hurricane. It's kind of like O.J. and O.J. Simpson."

Katrina narrows her eyes as she stares at Glenn, "Thanks for comparing me to O.J. That's definitely something I don't hear every day."

Glenn stares back for a moment in awkward silence, "Hmmm," he looks over to Gary and back to Katrina, "Notice I didn't say 'nice to meet you'? There's a reason I haven't said it."

Katrina smiles and Glenn lets loose with a laugh, but cuts it short. Glenn frowns and looks toward the elevators, "Geez, these elevators are slow!"

"There's no rush," Gary offers.

"Yeah, but I have to be here all week for the conference, and it's torture to have to wait around for the stupid things."

The elevator doors open, "Uh, here they come. Finally!" Glenn waves his friends over, "Hey, everybody, this is my brother, Gary, and his friend, Katrina...you know, like the hurricane."

Katrina forces a smile, "Yes, still hilarious. That never gets old."

Glenn introduces his pharmacy friends, "This is Trisha, Beth, and Roger. They are also attending the pharmacy training session with me this week. Should be a good time."

Everyone exchanges handshakes and greetings as the introductions are completed.

Katrina stares at Glenn, and he picks up on her suspicious glance, "What?" Glenn says as he confronts her, "Stop looking at me!"

"I can't help it," Katrina replies defensively, "You and Gary look so much alike...except for your short haircut. You are the older brother, right?"

Glenn grabs his chest as if he is having a coronary, "How dare you?!?!" he shouts, "I am five years younger!"

Katrina blushes, "Oops, that's right. You are the Air Force pharmacist, my bad."

Gary speaks up, "What do you say? Should we roll out?"

Trisha peers down at her shirt and a look of horror comes over her face. She pulls her shirt out to look at it.

Glenn notices Trisha tugging on her shirt, "What's the matter, Trisha?"

Trisha stammers, "I-I-I forgot to put on my Fowler shirt!"

Trisha has a Rubenesque figure. She has a rounded cute face and sports an ample bosom and behind. She's not fat, maybe just on the chubby side, but still very attractive.

Trisha tugs at her shirt, "Do you guys mind if I go back upstairs and put on my Kevin Fowler shirt?"

Gary shrugs, "No, go ahead. We'll wait. What's your Fowler shirt say, 'Fat Bottom Girl'?"

Everyone turns and stares at Gary in stunned silence. Gary looks around meeting peoples' terror-filled eyes. "What? That's one of the songs that he sings. He does a cover of 'Fat Bottom Girl.' You know, it starts off, 'Are you gonna take me home tonight?'"

Katrina rears back and punches Gary on the shoulder, "How rude!" she yells at him.

"Owww!" Gary cries out and rubs his shoulder, "What was that for?"

"You know!" Katrina glares back at Gary.

"It was a legitimate question."

Trisha interrupts, "Ok, I'll be right back." She turns to walk away, stops, and looks back at everyone "The shirt says, 'Butterbean.'"

"Ah," Gary says looking around at everyone, "Yes, 'Butterbean,' that makes sense. That's one of his big songs for his live shows. Mmm-mmmh. I get it."

Trisha continues to the elevator.

"Sorry about that, everyone," Gary says. "Sorry," he waves his hand in shame. "It won't happen again."

*　　*　　*　　*　　*

There are a few minutes of idle chit chat among the group while waiting for Trisha return. The elevator doors open, and she emerges with a wide smile across her face, satisfied in her wardrobe. The lettering of the word "Butterbean" on the front of the skin tight shirt is deformed by her boobs trying to escape the clinging fabric. The group stares in stunned silence until Roger speaks, "Holy cow, Trisha, what size shirt do you have on, a child's extra small?'

The group laughs uneasily at Roger's joke until Trisha bursts out laughing. "It is a little tight, isn't it?" Trisha admits as she futilely pushes her boobs down. She smiles, shakes her head, and says, "Come on; let's go!"

"No rush everyone," Gary preaches as the gang moves out the automatic doors of the hotel. "Fowler won't even take the stage until after eleven, and it's only nine now. We got plenty of time."

*   *   *   *   *

The group loads up in Gary's extended cab pickup, wedging their way into three in the back and three in the front. Gary calls out as they settle in, "Be careful of my cowboy hat. Who's guarding it? Don't bend it!"

Glenn chimes in, "That's what she said! Don't bend it!"

Beth sighs with a huff and rolls her eyes from the middle position in the back seat, "Come on, Glenn, please don't start with that childish nonsense."

Glenn smiles as he looks at Beth, "Wet blanket, check!"

"I am not a wet blanket!" Beth shouts.

Katrina halts the conversation, "I got the stupid hat right here!"

"Good!" Gary slams his door and starts the truck, "Let's rock and roll!"

The truck pulls out from under the hotel entrance canopy as the sun sets and dusk casts its purple hue across Allentown. The violet shadows are diluted by the street lights coming to life. Gary points the truck south on Interstate 11 until he reaches Monterey Boulevard. They take the Monterey exit and travel east on the boulevard a few miles. The out of town travelers note the Durazno Mountains on the east side of Allentown with "oohs and ahhs."

The sunset reflects the pinkish hues of their namesake; durazno translated is peach in English. Many evenings as the sun sets, the mountains transition through the evening colors including variations of the familiar orange and pink hues of ripe peach skin. Tonight is one these nights. On the east side of Allentown, the crew finally arrives at the cowboy bar, the Twilight Rodeo, the cozy venue hosting Kevin Fowler this evening.

Gary puts the truck in park and cries out, "Woo-hoo! We made it! A Texas dancehall!"

Gary tosses the keys to Katrina who awkwardly fumbles them to the floor. "Be nice!" Katrina scolds.

The doors of the truck are flung open, and the group piles out of the truck.

"Nice try," Glenn corrects Gary. "We're only about, mmmmm, five hundred miles from Texas, but close enough to be called a Texas dancehall."

"Picky, picky," Gary rebuts, adjusting his cowboy hat as the group marches to the end of the line waiting to get tickets and get in the door. "How does my hat look?"
Everyone affirms and approves of the stylish straw hat. The mood is high, and there is excitement even in the parking lot. The bar door opens and closes as people get a ticket to enter, each time live music from the opening band spills from the building, blasting the parking lot with country music, but fading quickly as the door eases shut.

"Looks like a good crowd already," Gary notes.

"Typical Fowler...Kevin Fowler mania sweeping the nation!" Glenn adds as he leans out from the line to get a better look at their progress towards the entrance.

The sky is dark and night has settled over Allentown. Street lights and the lights of the parking lot provide harsh illumination and shadows on the crowd. Trisha is a big hit with her tight t-shirt as guys in line call out "Butterbean" when they see her. Trisha revels in the attention, as she pretends to wave off the interest of the cowboys in line.

The group finally gets their tickets and ventures inside the dimly lit bar. The full force of the band's music washes over them. The band covers a vintage Randy Travis song, "*Deeper Than the Holler*" and couples two-step across the dance floor, moving like a shadowy, lumpy, monster in the stage lights as bulbs rhythmically bounce to the music. Gary spots a small table with three stools and shouts above the music, "Let's take this table, it will be our base of operations. We don't have enough stools for everyone, but we can rotate sitting down."

Everyone agrees. Glenn steps forward and waves everyone close together. They all lean forward and in his loudest voice yells over the music, "Woo-hoo! Let's get this party started. Hands in everyone." The group puts their hands one on top of the other like a sports team breaking huddle after a timeout. Glenn yells out over the stack of hands, "Party on three...one, two, three."

"Party!" the group hollers out, pushing their hands down and breaking up their makeshift huddle.

Glenn shouts, "I'll get the first round. What does everyone want?"
Glenn gets the drink orders and heads off to the bar.

When Glenn returns with the drinks, a toast is made, and bottles of beer and glasses are clinked together officially kicking off the festivities. Gary and Katrina pair off and take a two-step around the dance floor, while

Roger and Trisha take a spin across the floor showing off their polished dance moves.

The waitress provides a second round of drinks as Gary and Katrina return to the table. The bar is at capacity and the opening band announces they have finished their set, and Fowler is up next. The house lights come up a bit revealing a packed house. Kevin Fowler's band sets up their equipment, and after twenty minutes a roar goes up from the crowd as Kevin Fowler is welcomed to the stage.

Gary elbows Katrina, "What time is it?

Katrina inspects her watch, "Ten minutes after eleven."

"I told you!" Gary yells out, "Fowler never starts before eleven. Right again, Gary!"

Katrina mocks Gary with dripping sarcasm, "Oh, Gary…You're soooo smart." She rubs Gary with her hands, leaning her head on his shoulder, fawning over him in false worship. "Thank you, thank you for being so smart!" She continues.

Gary returns the mockery with his best Texas drawl, "You're welcome, ma'am." He tips his hat to her as he puts his arm around her shoulder. Katrina bats her eyelashes in awe, continuing to play out the fun. "Care to accomp'ny me to the floor, missy?" Gary drawls.

Katrina, with the look of a love sick puppy, nods consent. They move to the edge of the dance floor turned mosh pit. The crowd has filled the floor leaving little room to dance. Fowler strikes the first chords of his hit song "*100% Texan*," and the crowd's roar practically drowns out the music.

Katrina bounces to the music as she is held in Gary's arms, and they inch their way through and around the edge of the dance floor, enjoying the music and each other. The band plays another upbeat song, and the couple stops attempting to fight the full capacity dance floor with their two-step, instead they hold each other and sway to the music.

Kevin Fowler banters with the crowd as the song ends and announces he is slowing it down a bit with his latest ballad, "*Hard Man to Love*."

Katrina squeezes Gary even more tightly in her arms as she cries out, "It's your song!"

The band plays the plaintive song perfectly matched with Kevin's husky, un-polished vocals. The crowd is hushed enjoying the rendition. Kevin announces, "Get your hankies out. Another ballad. This is from the *Beer, Bait, and Ammo* Album. *If These Old Walls Could Talk* is for y'all romantics in the crowd."

As the ballad finishes up, Kevin announces, "Let's turn it loose! One…Two…Three!"

The band kicks up with the country rocking "*Loose, Loud, & Crazy*."

"Let's get back to the table," Katrina suggests.

"Ok."

They pick their way through the crowd, back to the group enjoying themselves.

Gary exchanges high fives with Glenn and Roger. Roger lets loose with a deafening Rebel Yell, "Yeee-hawwww!"

Katrina tucks herself back under Gary's arm and raises her voice over the music, "He is good."

Gary raises his beer and replies, "I told you."

"Well, there is no doubt, you called this one right. Hey, I've got to hit the rest room."

Gary nods, "Me too. I'll use the can and pick up some beers on my way back."

Katrina kisses Gary, and they each wind their way to their respective destination.

Gregory L. Heitmann

Chapter 15

You Can't Un-See Things

The lavatory facilities at the packed dancehall are overwhelmed by the capacity crowd. Gary waits for his turn at the trough. The urinal is a trough running the entire length of the wall. Two stalls in the rest room manage other, more delicate operations. As Gary relieves himself, he reads the posters advertising what bands are booked for future dates. He notes that another Texas Country Music favorite, Cory Morrow is planning a concert in the upcoming months.

Gary moves to the sink to wash his hands. In the reflection of a highly polished piece of steel that acts as a mirror in the rest room, his eye catches something. He can't make out the dull images in the mirrored surface, so he looks over his shoulder and sees what he didn't want to see. A couple is locked in a kiss as they push their way into a stall. Gary's blood runs cold as he recognizes the people: Casey Baxter along with one of his least favorite people, Chuck Roland.

*   *   *   *   *

Gary's mind spins as he contemplates what he has just seen in the rest room. He walks, semi-dazed, through the crowd back to the table. Katrina and Gary reach the table at the same time. Katrina squints at Gary. She can see that something is wrong.

"Where are the drinks?" Katrina asks. She pauses a moment, "What's wrong?"

Gary is distracted. He winces and points with his thumb over his shoulder, "I saw something in the bathroom."

Katrina recoils, "Gross!"

"It's not what you think. Do you know Casey Baxter?"

Katrina contemplates the question, "I think so. Doesn't she work for the City of Allentown as a planner or something?"

"Yeah."

"So," Katrina plies for an explanation, "what about her?"

"I just saw her kissing our computer guy, Chuck, as they were heading into a restroom stall."

Katrina's eyes widen; she shoves Gary back, "Get out!" she yells as Gary steps back. "Good Lord, isn't she married with young kids?"

Gary straightens his cowboy hat, turned askew when Katrina shoved him, "I don't know. I just wish I could un-see it." Gary chuckles, "Oh, well, I guess now that's what could be expected...we're in a cheatin' honky tonk." Gary shakes his head, "Did I tell you that Chuck almost burned down our office?"

Katrina laughs, "Yeah. Whatever. Just forget about it. I'll go get us some drinks."

Gary nods, "Definitely!"

Katrina starts to walk away, but is hailed by Gary, "Hey, get some shots of tequila. I need something to erase those images burned into my brain."

Katrina gives a thumbs up, turns, and heads to the bar.

Gary shakes his head as he mutters to himself, "This is perfect. Now, every time we're in meetings together, I'll be reminded of that horrible image."

*   *   *   *   *

The night starts to wind down. Gary and Katrina hit the dance floor once more. It has cleared a little as some people have called it a night and others have retired to their drinks. Fowler rasps with his best Texas drawl, singing about "*All the Tequila in Tijuana.*" Gary and Katrina hold onto each other and two-step, circling the floor. Katrina breaks the silence, "I'm surprised."

"About what?" Gary inquires.

"Kevin Fowler...his performance is quite impressive."

Gary looks into Katrina's eyes and pulls her closer, "I'm trying to dance here. Less talking, more groping."

Katrina giggles and squirms from Gary.

Gary can't keep himself from laughing, "You're the designated driver, right?"

Katrina scoffs, "Yeah?"

"What are you so giggly for? You haven't been nipping on the down low?"

Katrina is indignant, "No!"

Katrina attempts to push away from Gary, feigning anger. Gary just holds her tighter. Gary's mischievous grin gets wider, "Why are you so giggly?"

"I'm just happy for the first time in quite awhile."

Gary is momentarily satisfied with the answer, and they dance for a beat or two before Gary follows up, "Glad I can help. But, let's back up a bit. Why do you always doubt me? You are surprised that Kevin Fowler, something I picked, is enjoyable and that you had a good time!"

"I don't doubt you! You just surprise me, and I can't believe that I can still be surprised by anything anymore."

Gary kisses Katrina, "How about you and I surprising everyone with a 'scene' on the dance floor."

Katrina pulls away from the kiss and wriggles free as she continues to giggle. The music changes up with a fast paced song. *"Butterbean"* is played, and Trisha hauls Glenn to the dance floor for a jitterbug as Gary and Katrina move to the edge of the dance floor and watch the fast moving choreography.

The music winds down, and Kevin Fowler announces that he is wrapping it up with a favorite Queen cover song, "Here's a musical question being asked by the single guys out there tonight."

Fowler belts out "Fat Bottomed Girls." The song summarizes the question of the single men and finding company for the evening afterwards.

Gary bursts out laughing. Katrina looks up at him quizzically, "What's your problem now?"

"No problem; isn't it a strange coincidence that he played, *'Butterbean'* and *'Fat Bottomed Girl'* back to back?"

Katrina joins Gary with a rousing laugh, "That is funny! It's like he knows Trisha!"

*　　*　　*　　*　　*

The night concludes. Katrina drives Gary's truck to drop the guests back at the Marriott Pyramid. Everyone departs, and goodbyes are exchanged. Gary hops in the passenger seat as Katrina points the truck north on Interstate 11, headed back to Capitol City.

"My God, I'm getting old," Gary offers holding his ears. "My ears are ringing."

"I hear you. My ears are ringing too."

"What!" Gary cries out holding his hand to his ear.

Katrina laughs as she looks over at Gary's smiling face, satisfied with the joke.

The radio softly plays in the background as KYOT, "Coyote" 103.7 Rock, provides some background for the decompressing ride home. The Scorpion's song *"Rock You Like a Hurricane"* echoes quietly from the speakers providing its recognizable guitar lick. Gary reaches for the volume knob and cranks it up, "Check it out!" Gary yells.

Gary waits it out until the chorus, bobbing his head with the beat. The chorus kicks in, and Gary provides his customized lyrics with the song:

'No one can, rock you like Katrina can
Come on, Come on, Come on, Come on!'

Katrina bursts out laughing, causing the truck to wander in the lane.

"Geez, watch where you are going!" Gary cries out, "It wasn't that funny!"

"Not to you, but to me that is classic, Gary…G MANN!"

Katrina reaches over and grabs Gary's hand as she drives.

Chapter 16

Un-Adult-erated Fun

The weekend is over, and Gary is back in his office. Blowing off some steam was a good time, but the fun is done, and the tension picks up where it left off after the Friday afternoon fire. Chuck has had power restored, and Gary boots up his computer, but is unable to log onto the server. "Gol dang it!" Gary yells at his computer, "Stupid machine!"

Gary stands up from his desk and mutters through his gritted teeth, "Chuck." He stomps out of his office down the hallway and into the open area of cubicles. He sees Chuck across the office in Shannon's cubicle, his butt parked on her desk. Shannon is a brand new trainee, a product of the USTD development program. She smiles as she devotes her full attention to Chuck's story. Her petite frame bounces her page-boy haircut as she nods along to the story. Her Asian heritage gives her an even younger appearance; she could pass for a twelve year old boy.

Gary watches from a distance as Chuck waves an imaginary stick in his hand. He simulates pounding the stick into his other open hand as a policeman would handle a billy club. Gary moves closer; he can hear Chuck's monologue, "It was awesome! I was an extra, a prison guard in a movie! They filmed it right out here at the old State Pen." Chuck points in the direction of the prison. "I still can't believe it. Tobey McGuire is in the movie…Spiderman himself!"

"Wow!" Shannon responds, genuinely in awe. "Do you think I could be an extra sometime?"

"Sure," Chuck replies. "I can put in a good word for you with the casting people."

Gary interrupts, "Chuck, can you come help get my computer working?"

"Yes, sir."

Gary walks back to his office, and Chuck waves goodbye to Shannon as he follows Gary. They get to Gary's office, and Chuck sits at Gary's desk and starts to type on the computer. He looks up at Gary with a smile, "Did you hear me saying I was an extra in a movie this weekend?"

Gary folds his arms and glares at Chuck, "Weren't you supposed to be in the office this weekend making sure the computers were up and running?"

The smile disappears from Chuck's face, "I-I-I'm sorry," Chuck stutters. "I needed assistance from Headquarters, and there was nobody available until this morning. Things are working now. You're the last one I needed to adjust." Chuck looks at the computer screen, "There, now you are on-line too."

Gary moves to his desk as Chuck stands. Gary sits at his computer and attempts to log onto the server. Chuck smiles, "Did you hear me say that Tobey McGuire was in the movie? Jake Gylenhaal is also in the movie." Chuck nods with self satisfaction, "I was a prison guard; I had to escort Tobey through the prison."

Gary shakes his head as he looks at the computer screen, "It's still not working."

Chuck is caught off guard, "Really? That's weird."

Gary stands and Chuck sits back down at Gary's desk and furiously types and clicks the mouse. "Huh. I'll have to go call the help desk. There might be a bad server cell here in the office still."

Chuck stands, "We filmed at the old abandoned part of the State Pen. Man, is that place creepy. You should go out there if you ever get the chance. We actually shot some scenes in the execution chamber where they used to have the electric chair. It was freaky."

Gary nods.

"Ok," Chuck heads out the door. "I'll work on your connection. I should have it up in a few minutes." He taps the doorway a couple times and gives an uncomfortable wave as Gary stares at him. Chuck walks away down the hall to the server room.

Gary heads out of his office over to Bryan's cubicle. "Hey, Bryan, what's going on?" Gary asks as he leans against Bryan's cubicle entrance.

The office cubicles are about ten feet by ten feet squares. They have fabric walls that stick up about six feet high under the twelve feet high ceilings. The interior of the building is mostly a giant open area with the exception of Diego's and Gary's offices.

Bryan leans back in his chair, "Morning. Nothing going on here."

"Is your computer working?"

Bryan scoffs, "Hell no!"

"Surprise, surprise," Gary says sarcastically, "Your boy was on the ball this weekend, I see."

Bryan laughs, "Yeah, I heard Chuck tried to burn the building down on Friday."

"Good Lord!" Gary grimaces, "He's just not that useful. Can't even burn the place down correctly, just like everything he does, half-assed."

Bryan laughs even harder, "Wasn't he supposed to come in over the weekend and make sure the computers were up and running?"

"What?" Gary says mockingly, "You haven't heard? I've heard Chuck tell the story three times already. Chuck was an extra in a movie over the weekend."

"That's right; he said he was a prison guard. Who would ever buy such an effeminate man would be a prison guard. That's just bad casting."

Gary nods, "For all we know, he was in some low budget, home-made, gay porn."

Bryan snorts as he laughs, "I can just picture it. He's a prison guard slapping his 'baton' around, sodomizing inmates." Bryan makes finger quotes around the word baton.

"You know what pisses me off even more?" Gary asks.

Bryan shrugs.

"This was the weekend of the Kevin Fowler concert and guess who I saw there? None other than Chuck. And get this, I saw him making out with our gal pal, Casey Baxter. They were heading into a bathroom stall in the men's room together."

Bryan's jaws hangs loose as he stares at Gary in disbelief.

Gary shakes his head, "I didn't tell him that I saw him there."

Bryan finally speaks, "Holy shit! Isn't Casey Baxter married? She's stepping out with that clown? Wow!"

"Yeah, Chuck's out partying and making movies when he was told to make sure the computers were fixed. If I were Diego," Gary says as he shakes his head, "I would fire his ass. We got ten people sitting around waiting for our computers to work."

"Well," Bryan wonders out loud, "You're management now; why don't you advise Diego to get rid of him?"

"Yeah, you're right."

Bryan shakes his head from side to side, "I never thought much of the old IT guy, Francisco, but Chuck makes Frankie look like Stephen Hawking."

"It's funny you should mention that," Gary starts to chuckle. "I heard Chuck make a reference recently about the great physicist, Sadie Hawkins."

Bryan slaps his knee and laughs silently, shoulders shaking. Gary smiles and continues, "Sadie Hawkins, the noted physicist that studied motion and momentum of bodies dancing."

Bryan catches his breath and wipes an eye that is filling with tears from trying to hold back his laughter, "Uh, that is too much."

"Well, on that note," Gary straightens his stance, "I'm outta here. I am going to see Sarah over at the Highway Department. I think she's got some info for me."

Bryan points across the office where Chuck is telling his movie story as indicated by his wild hand gestures imitating a camera swooping in for a shot. Bryan wants one more dig on Gary; he nods with a serious look on his face, "I am going to go over and see if Chuck will tell me the whole story about his acting one more time."

Gary can't hold back the grin spreading across his face as Bryan smiles. Gary shakes his head and starts back to his office, "Shut up!" he says over his shoulder as he points a finger of warning at Bryan, "Get some work done," he says with a laugh.

Chapter 17

Grow Like, Uh –A Weed?

Gary knocks on Sarah Liriano's door. Her office at the highway department is a small ten foot by twelve foot space; one entire wall is packed with reference books describing appraisals, negotiating, and history of real estate in the Southwest. Books of every size, color, and shape line the shelves covering the wall.

The exposed walls are painted a pale green and remain barren for the moment. A large window behind Sarah's desk features a nice view of the department parking lot. If one strains to look, he or she could make out some of the foothills of the Sangre de Sustantivo Mountains.

"Knock, knock," Gary calls out as he stands in the doorway of her office.

"Hey, there," Sarah replies, looking up from a small potted plant she is fussing with. "Come in! Have a seat."

Gary points to her name on the door, "Nice office, they even got your name spelled correctly." Gary comes in and sits down. "You got a window with a view, a whole library of books, a plant…what more could you want?"

Sarah laughs her resonating chuckle of delight, "I don't know about you."

Gary leans over to see around her desk. He spots a dozen or so framed pictures on the floor, leaning against the wall. He points to the photos, "What's more, you even have a bunch of wall space for displaying all the pictures of your kids." Gary sweeps his hand towards the barren wall.

Sarah laughs even more, "Yup, I got it made! If it weren't for the work that they make me do, this would be a perfect job!"

"You and me both," Gary nods in agreement.

"So, how are you, Gary?"

"Fair. What the heck are you doing?"

Sarah frowns, "This stupid plant that I just brought in is infested with bugs. I'm going to get rid of it."

"Just spray it."

"It's full of bugs! Just look at it!"

Sarah shoves the small plant into Gary's face. Gary ducks out of the way in an over dramatic gesture, "Take it easy with that thing! I can see the bugs just fine from here."

A few little bugs fly in circles and alight on the soil in the pot. Gary watches one fly near his face. He claps his hands together and opens them to observe the flattened bug. "Yup, I had these same bugs at my house. It happened when I repotted a plant. The soil was contaminated. I had purchased the soil at the Garden Depot."

Sarah's eyes widen and she exclaims, "That's where I got this plant!"

"Well, we got the source of the problem nailed down; now all you have to do is spray...like I had originally mentioned. It worked for me."

"Aurrrgh! I don't want to spray a bunch of chemicals in here. I'm just going to dump it out. I want to save the pot though. I like the pot...it was a gift."

Gary looks at Sarah quizzically. He cocks his head and narrows his eyes, "What did you just say? Did I hear you correctly? You like the pot? I knew it! You like to toke it up, don't you."

Gary razzes Sarah unmercifully; Sarah's eyes nearly pop out of her head when she realizes what she said. She doubles over in laughter, howling as Gary points an accusing finger at her. "No, sir! I don't do that!" Sarah cries out between laughs.

"But," Gary holds his palms up with a shrug, "and I quote, 'I like the pot,' end quote." Gary makes finger quotes in the air; his mouth twists in trying to keep a smile off his face, while remaining stoically judgmental.

Sarah throws her head back laughing. Her hair bounces rhythmically to her gasping laugh. She points to the pot, "The plant container, you know that's what I meant! Stop twisting my words!" She taps the glass pot with her finger.

Gary throws his hands up in surrender, "Hey, I'm just repeating what I heard. I sure hope this news doesn't leak out," Gary says with a wink and a nod. "That might be pretty damaging for a new supervisor."

Sarah sighs deeply with a flourishing huff. She feigns anger, standing with her hands on her hips, "Why are you here, anyway?"

"Oh, good Lord," now it's Gary's turn to sigh, "I had to get out of the office. My building is a joke today. Stupid, Chuck. You know Chuck, our IT guy?"

"Yeah?"

"Well, last Friday he about burned down the office. He had too many things plugged into a power strip; something malfunctioned, and a fire started. It burned up part of our server connected to Washington, D.C."

"Really?" Sarah questions, very interested in the story.

"Chuck was supposed to come in over the weekend and make sure everything was up and running…"

Sarah finishes Gary's sentence, "…but, alas, he didn't show up and now your computers are down."

"Of course, and get this; he's going around the office this morning telling everyone that he was an extra in a movie that was filming this weekend out at the State Pen."

"No kidding?" Sarah says, fascinated by the tale.

"Nice, huh?" Gary huffs. "Get this, Chuck was at the Kevin Fowler concert that I took Katrina to on Saturday night."

"When he should have been working," Sarah nods knowingly.

"Not only that," Gary whispers, "I saw Chuck and Casey Baxter making out and heading into a men's room stall."

Sarah gasps, "Casey Baxter, the nice lady planner from Allentown?"

"Yup," Gary says dejectedly. "She's married with two young kids."

"Come on; let's go outside and dump this plant," Sarah nods to the door as she moves from behind her desk. "Let's get some fresh air."

Gary and Sarah walk out of the right-of-way section and into a main hallway of the generic government building. They pass through a glass atrium connecting two pods of adjoining brick buildings, out the doors of the atrium to the outside, and down the sidewalk heading to the employee parking lot. They stop in the shade of a nice spruce tree. Beneath the tree, the shaded ground is bare and dusted with a few pine cones and needles from the evergreen.

"It's nice in the shade," Gary notes. "The breeze is nice," he continues, inhaling deeply.

Sarah loosens the soil in the pot and dumps the plant and the dirt on the ground. She smoothes out the clumps with her foot. She looks at Gary, "Tell me, why does this thing with Chuck bother you so much?"

Gary ponders for a moment, "That's a good question. I guess it comes down to responsibility. His actions are impacting everyone today. Nobody is able to use their computer because of him. It's one thing if it only affects him, but he has prevented fifteen people in our office from doing their job. And he couldn't care less!"

Gary stares down at Sarah's foot still smoothing the soil.

Sarah shrugs, "So, it's just a job."

"Yeah, but it's a symptom of today's society, and I don't want to just accept it. There is just less and less accountability in the world, and I'd like to see that trend go the other way."

Sarah shakes her head, "You can't control everything."

"That's true, but Diego and I can control who does our IT work. I'm going to meet with Diego about getting somebody new."

Sarah smiles, "I guess you miss Francisco?"

Gary meets Sarah's eyes, "Turns out he wasn't so bad. Maybe we can get him back?"

Sarah pats her foot down on the soil with a final effort of compaction. Gary looks down at the wilting plant mixed in with the discarded soil, "I can't help but think of Bob Marley and the Wailers...all your talk about pot and seeing the soil dumped out, maybe we should be hearing some reggae music, possibly *I Shot the Sheriff* or some *Stir It Up.*"

"Shush," Sarah fires back. "Can't you let that go?"

"Fine," Gary smiles, "I need to let it all go. Chuck...pot...the train...everything. My job is hard enough; I don't need somebody else making it more difficult, i.e. Chuck."

"Yup," Sarah nods, "let it go. Come on, let's go back inside."

Gary and Sarah return to the building, walking and talking. Sarah brings up Chuck again, "What is it with that guy? He seems pretty harmless. What's your take on him?"

"To tell you the truth, I don't have a take on him."

Sarah swipes her security key card for the door. Gary opens the door to the atrium and follows Sarah inside. Sarah stops in the glassed in area, "Seriously, he's not much of a man's man." Sarah leans in and whispers, "I thought he might be gay."

Gary pauses a moment remembering the image of Casey and Chuck moving into the bathroom stall. Gary shrugs, "He's got a daughter."

"That doesn't mean much," Sarah waves her hand and continues to walk down the hallway. "Maybe he's changed teams...discovered his true self."

Gary shakes his head, "I guess I just don't know him. I suppose that's part of my problem. If I knew people better, than maybe I'd understand what makes them tick and what makes them do what they do."

They reach Sarah's office. Sarah nods in agreement, "You're right. Just like me, we are both new to the supervising thing. It takes some work to look at people from a different perspective when you are a leader."

"Yup, more work." Gary pauses for a moment, "I guess I should be going," Gary sighs.

Gary turns to the door, but Sarah speaks up, "Say, are you and Katrina coming to the party?"

Gary turns back to face Sarah, "I think so. At least for a little while."

"Oh," Sarah gets serious for a moment, "It would mean so much to my sister. She's been going through so much lately." Sarah smiles, "She would really appreciate seeing both you and Katrina…she's going to have her new boyfriend there," Sarah bounces her eyebrows.

Gary twists his face with a puzzled look, "Isn't Betsy still married?

"Technically, yes. It's complicated," Sarah rolls her eyes. "Just show up, pretty please?"

"Yeah, yeah. I'm pretty sure we are a 'go' for the party. Don't worry about it."

Gary leans over and hugs Sarah, "See you later."

"Ok, bye."

Chapter 18

Party 'Til the Cops Show

Katrina and Gary pull up to the wrought iron fence, having arrived via Gary's truck. They have reached the gated community nestled into the Foothill Park section of Capitol City. Here the wealthy folks shield themselves from the commoners through gates, fences, and security patrols. Gary presses the buttons on the keypad, numbers given to him by Sarah. The speaker activates, and a "Hello" crackles through the intercom.

"Gary and Katrina here to see Betsy," Gary shouts into the intercom.

"Gary and Katrina!" shrieks the intercom's tinny speaker, "You made it! Let me buzz you through."

Gary and Katrina wait for the gate to open, and Gary pulls his truck through and winds his way up the mountain side, passing houses the likes he has never seen. "Yikes," Gary says, "I think I'm in over my head."

"Relax," Katrina advises. "It'll be fine. Betsy is just house-sitting for these people."

"Yeah, but does she have permission to throw a party? If the neighbors see my Chevy truck, they're going to be suspicious. Have you looked around? If it's not a Land Rover or a Mercedes, all the other cars are Cadillacs or BMWs."

"Relax!" Katrina orders.

They arrive at the hillside house and are welcomed at the door by Sarah. "Come in," she commands with a smile.

The pleasantries are exchanged, and Sarah leads them to the kitchen for a drink and hors d'oeuvres. Sarah whispers, "Just hang out in here for a moment. I'll come and get you in a minute."

Gary looks at Katrina suspiciously, eyes darting back and forth, "Okaaay?"

Gary waits with Katrina in the luxury kitchen as the door swings behind Sarah. The stainless steel appliances shine in the brightly lit, cavernous kitchen. "Wow," mutters Katrina, "this is my dream kitchen."

Gary glances around the room, "Yeah, keep dreamin'. What the heck? Why are we stuck in here?"

"Beats me. You know how Betsy and Sarah are," Katrina smiles wryly.

Gary spins his finger around, pointing to the side of his head.

"No!" Katrina yells. "Not crazy...ditzy, maybe, but not crazy!"

"Keep it down!" Gary whispers hoarsely.

The door swings back open and Sarah appears. "Ok," Sarah smiles, "Come with me." Sarah grabs Katrina's hand and tows her through the swinging kitchen door.

Gary follows Katrina and soon they are in the living room. People mingle in all corners of the sunken room. Every luxury item imaginable adorns the space. Expensive art hangs from the wall with special lighting illuminating top flight, oil paintings and bronze statues. Betsy stands with her arm interlocked with a man in an inexpensive suit. She smiles brightly and drops the man's arm as she throws herself at Katrina, who gracefully catchers her. "I'm so glad you made it," Betsy squeals. "Hi, Gary," she nods demurely.

Sarah makes the introductions. "Gary Hillmann and Katrina Del Carmen, this is Detective Quinton Navidad of the Capitol City Police Department."

Detective Navidad shakes Gary's hand and follows up with a light hug for Katrina. "Nice to meet you," he adds politely. "Nice place, huh?"

"No doubt," Gary acknowledges his eyes dancing across the enormous room.

"Only the best for my little sister," Sarah laughs.

Betsy Valdez is a near mirror image of Sarah, maybe an inch shorter, but it is hard to tell them apart; they could be twins, with the same styled shoulder length black hair.

"So, what do you guys do?" Detective Navidad asks Gary and Katrina.

Katrina responds, "I work for the state highway department. I'm a biologist with the environmental section. Bugs and bunnies, you know."

The detective nods.

Katrina continues, "Gary works for the federal government, the U.S. Transportation Department. He tells us, over at the highway department, what to do."

"I wouldn't say that," Gary rebuts.

"You're a G-man, eh?" Detective Navidad comments.

Gary's face lights up, "Yeah! You can call me G MANN. Since my name is Gary, the 'G' and MANN from Hillmann, *and* I work for the government!"

Katrina rolls her eyes and Gary notices her reaction as the Detective nods, "Cool."

"What's wrong with you?" Gary asks Katrina. "What's with the eye rolling?"

"Nothing, G MANN!" Katrina retorts sarcastically.

"How's the crime fightin', Detective?" Gary asks.

"Good."

"Good to hear," Gary nods. "Say, do you have a card? You never know when I might need some police help."

"Sure," Detective Navidad digs in his jacket pocket and pulls out a business card and hands it to Gary.

"Thanks," Gary says as he reviews the information on the card.

There is a bit of silence as everyone sips from their drinks. Katrina breaks the calm, "Gee, Sarah and Betsy, I swear, you two could be twins. You both look so young and pretty. I won't ask who is older."

"Oh, stop!" Betsy says, blushing and wrapping her arm back through Detective Navidad's.

"Thank you," Sarah adds, "You are too kind."

There is a bit more awkward silence and Gary looks around at everyone. He finally speaks up, "You know what's weird?" Gary holds up an hors d'oeuvres. "The words cocktail and wiener. First of all, the words are completely awkward to say. Cocktail, cocktail, wiener, wiener. Second, they are weird sexual innuendos. Finally you combine them into some sort of snack, and label it cocktail wiener. That's crazy!"

The group stares at Gary pitifully in silence. Gary continues after a sip of his drink, "I think those words should be retired from the English language."

Silence settles like a blanket over the group, completely shutting down the conversation. People look around the room uncomfortably. Katrina steps forward and grabs Gary's arm and leads him away, "Okaaay," Katrina says, "we're going to get some punch. Nice to see everyone."

Katrina leads Gary away from the group. She whispers, "Wow, could you be more awkward?"

"Hey, this stuff isn't my cup of tea."

"Yes," Katrina nods still towing Gary to the other side of the room where appetizers and drinks are located. "That is quite the understatement."

"I hate small talk."

Katrina smiles and turns Gary to face her, "And small talk apparently hates you. The rest of the night, you just stand by me and nod your head yes or no. I will talk. It will be less embarrassing for everyone. Especially me!"

"Fine!" Gary smiles and shrugs.

"Fine!" Katrina affirms with a nod.

Chapter 19

Splitsville

Gary works at his desk reviewing the electronic time cards of the employees in the office and approving the bi-weekly payroll submittal. He is engrossed in the task and barely notices Bryan shuffling along the short-cropped industrial carpet.

Gary looks up in time to see Bryan's slumped shoulders and frown before he flings himself into a chair in front of Gary's desk. Bryan sprawls in the chair; his head is back, and he stares at the ceiling. Gary studies Bryan for a moment, slouched like a wet dishrag over the chair, before making his observation, "What's with you, all hangdog, moping around?"

Bryan doesn't move but provides an answer, "Nothin'."

Folding his hands, Bryan rests them on his stomach. His feet stick out at the ends of stiff legs. His posture emulates a plank of wood leaning across a chair.

"Really?" Gary pries, "Are you sure? You don't look too comfortable."

"Just forget it." Bryan groans as he pulls himself out of the chair and shuffles out of the room.

"Whatever," Gary shrugs as he returns to the spreadsheet on his computer screen.

Bryan drags himself out the office, feet scuffling on the carpet. Gary hears something at his door, and it's Bryan appearing back in his door way. Gary looks up and offers, "What?"

Bryan frowns as he leans against the doorframe, "Ashley and I split."

"Oh, geez. Sorry to hear that."

"Yeah," Bryan offers as he moves into the room and sits on the edge of the chair.

"I apologize."

Gary flinches, "Apologize for what?"

103

"I'm sorry that I've been in a bad mood lately; it's probably affected my work."

Gary sweeps the comment away, "Don't worry about it."

"What do you think I should do?"

Gary is puzzled, "Do about what?"

"Ashley. What would you do?"

"I don't know," Gary shrugs, "Talk to her sister, she's kinda hot."

Bryan smiles ever so slightly, "Yeah, look at you. So helpful."

"You asked."

"Maybe just take a break," Gary tries to sound soothing. "You both get a few days away from each other, and maybe you'll see things aren't so bad…or you'll realize it was the best decision."

"Yeah, you're right," Bryan concedes with a nod.

"You know what you should do?" Gary asks.

"What?"

"Get on your new mountain bike and ride up and down that whole train project. You can do an inspection on bike. You know they're putting in a new bike trail with this construction…right parallel to the rails."

Bryan's face lights up, "That's right! That's about the only good thing to come out of this project. Miles of bike trails! I'll do it!"

"There you go. Bring a camera and take some pictures," Gary encourages further. "Let me know how it goes."

Bryan springs to his feet, "I'll go get ready right now!" Bryan bolts from the room with just a wave.

Gary yells down the hall at the disappearing Bryan, "See you later!"

Chapter 20

A Simple Fix

It was a long day of handling time cards on the computer and updating the SUR, the Status Update Reports, or the "sewer" reports as they are affectionately known. With the computers back on-line, Gary was able to plow through the daily requirements by the late afternoon. Chuck was now at Gary's door per his earlier encounter with him in the break room at lunch. Chuck knocks crisply on the door frame, "You beckoned?"

Gary looks up from the papers on his desk, "Come in."

Chuck ambles in and sits at the chair in front of Gary's desk. "What's up?" Chuck inquires.

"I need a favor."

Chuck purses his lips with a nod of his head, "Sure, buddy. What do you need?"

"First off, I'm glad you got the office computers up and running." Gary smiles, "It was a little touch and go for awhile, but you got it done. Good job."

"Thanks," Chuck acknowledges.

"I was wondering if you could take a look at my personal laptop?"

"Sure," Chuck shrugs.

"Off work hours, not here in the office. Just keep track of your hours, and I'll pay you. Is forty dollars an hour ok?"

"Bah," Chuck waves away the question of money. "If it's anything serious, you just give me twenty or thirty bucks. What's wrong with your computer? What's it doing?"

Gary reaches for his book bag and pulls out his laptop and sets in on his desk, "It might have a virus. It has been randomly shutting off."

"No problem. I'll check it over, and if it's something more serious, I'll talk to you before we do much else. You might be able to buy a new one cheaper than fixing it."

"Yeah, I'm mostly worried about getting some of my data off it. It won't stay powered up long enough to copy files to disk or thumb drive or anything. I got tax stuff on there I don't want to lose."

"I hear ya," Chuck nods. "When do you need it?"

"The sooner the better. That's my main computer at home."

Gary hands over the laptop to Chuck. Chuck points to the Minnesota Vikings sticker on the computer, "Hey, nice Vikings sticker. I'm a Bears fan."

"That's right," Gary nods, "You're from Chicago."

"Yes, sir, the Windy City," Chuck laughs, "I sure don't miss it...the wind and the cold winters. I like it here." Chuck stands and pulls the laptop to his side, "So, how quickly do you really need it back?"

"It's not a 'drop everything' situation, but timely would be nice; say a week?"

"You got it. Couple days; I'll have it back, hopefully fixed."

"Thanks, Chuck."

Chapter 21

Helmets Save Lives

When Bryan returned to his house after talking to Gary about inspecting the T'rrain Trekker project via his bike, he was pumped up. He immediately changed into his workout clothes, donned his helmet and climbed on his new bike. The excitement of the workout shot to exponential heights when he hit the wide open bike trail winding through his Tierra Madre neighborhood. As quickly as his adrenaline pumped through his legs from pedaling his bicycle, it reached a crescendo after a short five minutes in the form of a dog. A man, oblivious to the world, casually walked his feisty medium-sized mutt on one side of the hill; on the other side of the hill, Bryan raced his bicycle up the slope. The bicycle and dog had a rendezvous with destiny. It wasn't a pretty sight when the man, with a retractable leash, failed to control his pet, and met Bryan at the crest of the hill. The blind spot on the trail for both rider, walker, and dog was the point of convergence on that day.

Bryan did his best to swerve away from man and dog, but the leash was a different story, the leash would not be dodged. The leash lodged into the sprocket of the rear tire after springing from the ground and passing under the front tire. The dog-walker was no worse for the wear when the leash he held loosely in his hand just disappeared from his grip. The man watched helplessly as the split second crash played out. The taut line between the bike and dog whistled eerily as it whisked the dog through the air. The weight of the dog on the end of the frozen rear tire was more than Bryan could recover from as the bike fishtailed. For a moment he thought it was not going to be a problem. Bryan's momentum had thrown him forward on the bike, and he lost his grip on the handle bars and any chance to apply his brakes. As his instinct took over, he lowered his right foot already detached from the pedal of his toe clip. When he dug his foot into the dirt at the side of the trail, his foot caught firmly, sending him into a roll over and off his bike. The pain was there immediately, but not before Bryan, still in the process of rolling five or six times through yucca and cacti, watched the dog on the leash fly overhead giving the appearance of a weighted fly wheel on some bizarre machine.

Bryan remained on his back a moment or two before pushing himself off the ground to survey the damage to his brand new bike. The owner of the dog was still frozen in place, stunned. Bryan limped to the terrified dog straining and crying to be free of the bicycle, still entangled with the leash. Bryan released the clasp of the leash from the collar of the dog.

The cream-colored, shaggy mutt was a dirty brown color after being flung through the air and dragged through the soil, but seemingly intact and healthy. The mutt, tail between its legs, found its owner's side as the man snapped back to reality, "Y-Y-You ok?" he called out to Bryan.

"Yeah," Bryan groaned as he picked up the bike and ran the leash through the chain and sprocket. The gears spit out a ragged leash held together by just a few threads. "How's the dog?" Bryan asks.

"He seems ok, just scared," the man answers as he kneels down and strokes the shivering animal. The dog nuzzles and licks the man's hand and lunges to lick his face. He stands wiping his face, "I think he's fine."

"Good," Bryan responds as he tosses the battered leash to the man. "Looks like you need a new leash."

The man is stunned that Bryan is even on his feet nonetheless talking. He points to Bryan's helmet, where there is a dent and missing paint, "Good thing you had a helmet on; check it out."

Bryan takes off his helmet and sees the scuff; he looks on the ground and finds a rock with matching paint marks. He laughs, "Yup, helmets aren't just a fashion statement."

Bryan straps his helmet back on his head, dusts himself off, and climbs back on his bike. He turns to the man with a wry smile, "I guess I'll cut my ride short today."

Bryan pedals away and each time he pushes down on the pedal of his right foot he grimaces and cries out, "Ow, ow, ow, ow, ow…"

Bryan pedals slowly noting that his brand new bike is suffering from a severely bent frame that makes it look more like a crab as it moves down the trail. He shakes his head, "Isn't this just perfect?" he grumbles.

*　　*　　*　　*　　*

Gary received the phone call from Bryan at about 9:00 am the next morning. "Guess what?" Gary heard from the voice on the line.

"What?" Gary replied.

"This is Bryan," an amplified, slurred voice responded.

"Yes, hi, Bryan."

"I-I-I'm, I-I-I'll be out on six, I mean sick leave," Bryan stammered, emphasizing the word "Sick."

"What's wrong, Bryan? You sound weird."

Bryan answers slowly, enunciating each word carefully, "I broke my leg, thanks to you." He stretches the word "you" out a couple extra beats and laughs loudly.

"What?" Gary demands.

"I was all excited to ride my bike yesterday, and I hit a dog on the trail."

Gary laughs, "No kiddin'?"

"I swear it. The dog wasn't even hurt. I hit its leash and crashed."

"Oh, my God!" Gary offers, "How bad? Surgery?"

"They don't think so. I don't have a cast yet, but I go back tomorrow after the swelling goes down a bit."

"Sorry to hear this, man," Gary sympathizes.

"Don't worry; they give me some awesome painkillers. I'll be fine."

"Ok, then," Gary says, "I'll let everyone know you are out. Give me a call if you need some help. Hey, did you call Ashley and tell her? She'd probably be up for nursing you back to health."

"Hell no!" Bryan shouts into the phone, "We're on a break. I sure don't want her to think I owe her anything if she helps me."

Gary laughs, "Ok, fine. I'll talk to you later."

Chapter 22

Trailer Trashed

The sun is setting and shadows creep across the valley of the T'rrain Trekker tunnel construction site. Crews fire up generators to energize high powered mast illumination to continue their concrete placement and finishing work toiling into the night. Pouring concrete is better at night for the material and the men. A reprieve from the heat is welcomed by most of the labor force, and the heat from the chemical reaction of cement and water dissipates more quickly allowing the material to set more timely. Construction plows ahead. Wooden forms constructed by the carpenters during the day are now filled with the fluid mix of cement, sand, rock, and water by the concrete crews. The tunnel is beginning to take shape.

Patrick Ruiz remains in his construction manager's on-site trailer. Half the trailer is his office; the rest of the trailer is shared by the three lead construction inspectors for the state highway department. Tonight, as darkness falls, Patrick sits at his desk. He is sprawled in front of a laptop with a recognizable Minnesota Vikings sticker pasted to the case. Patrick scrolls and clicks the mouse as he inspects the computer's contents.

*   *   *   *   *

Casey provided Gary Hillmann's rogue laptop to Patrick's greedy hands. Casey received the laptop from Chuck who happened to mention, in casual conversation, Gary's request. Casey was thrilled to think that she might be able to motivate Gary to be a little more accommodating with regards to the T'rrain Trekker station construction. On the other hand, if Patrick knew how Casey came into possession of the laptop, he might not be so focused on his quest for the evening. The friendship of Casey and Chuck was in full blossom, while Patrick was oblivious to Casey pulling away from him. On this night, Patrick is looking for any information he could use as leverage to coerce or blackmail Mr. Hillmann. Patrick has taken the request from his friends at the governor's office to heart. From Patrick's point of view, Gary is holding the project back, and the only thing between success and failure is a stubborn federal government employee. There are peripheral benefits also; Patrick not only wants to move the project forward, but feels it might be nice to take Gary down a peg or two. He searches files and folders, confident that there is something on the computer that could embarrass Gary and make him see things differently.

Patrick was well into his second hour of staring at the screen, clicking, scrolling, and searching through photos, letters, anything that he could use as a persuader. Alas, there was nothing. His massive hand races the mouse around the desk; he is surprisingly quick and dexterous for a man of his size.

*   *   *   *   *

How did Patrick get Gary's computer? In this instance it was coincidence. Casey Baxter, civil servant, planning professional, and mother is also a woman of secrets. Maybe boredom drives a person to look for excitement, it was never clear why Casey carried on multiple lives and relationships, intertwined, but hidden from each other. Casey and Patrick had a long relationship as more than friends; secret to society, they were lovers enjoying one another's company for nearly twelve years. Their relationship was secret to everyone, family, friends, associates...no one knew or even suspected the two; each had a spouse and children while carrying on clandestine lifestyles. Not that an open marriage is new or surprising to the Capitol City, a diverse city, open to arts, culture, and liberal lifestyles. The amazing facet of Casey's and Patrick's relationship was that the secret had held for more than a decade.

Time goes by and relationships evolve. Casey is a woman that gives the appearance of a mild-mannered citizen, satisfied with her choices in life, but she was bored with her marriage and her lover. About the same time Patrick began making friends with the more powerful, elite, ruling class. Nearly a year passed, and Casey saw less and less of Patrick. Patrick caught a whiff of the power of the people he was introduced to and became completely obsessed with more...more for the State, more for the United States, and maybe a little more for himself. Patrick was introduced to Governor Reid-Salazar on the golf course at a charity event. At the event he met another man, the State House of Representatives Majority Leader, Calvin Hernandez. As Patrick golfed with these men and listened to their conversations, he knew that these men could do great things…making a difference in people's lives.

As Patrick and Casey drifted apart, Casey looked for something to fill the void left by Patrick's longer and more frequent absences. In a chance meeting, at a regional conference for the Parent Teachers Association, she met Charles. They hit it off as friends; each had a ten year old child. Chuck's marriage had melted down, and he divorced his wife, but retained joint custody of their daughter. They also had something else in common; they shared a common distaste for one, Gary Hillmann. Charles "Chuck" Roland had become a friend and secret lover of Casey's.

It was simple, when Chuck casually mentioned fixing Gary's laptop, Casey knew she had something to share with Patrick. Something that would very much please Patrick, as Casey still loved Patrick and would do virtually anything for him and vice versa.

*   *   *   *   *

Patrick's patience has worn thin after two hours of searching Gary's computer for any info that he can use as leverage. The windfall of the computer, a gift from Casey, has ended up as a bust.

"Come on, come on. Come on!" Patrick yells.

Patrick wipes a bead of sweat from his brow. Patrick shakes his head in disgust, "Damn it! Fuck you, Hillmann!"

Patrick stands, sending his chair crashing into wall. He extends his arm across the desk and sweeps the computer onto the floor. He grabs his hair and howls, "Arrrrrrrrgh!"

Patrick tears at his hair, beside himself with rage. His chest heaves as his breathing rasps loudly throughout the office. Rico Suarez, the swing shift, lead highway department inspector, turns the knob of the door and enters the trailer, witnessing the tantrum. Patrick's eyes meet Rico's. "Get out!" Patrick screams pointing his finger at Rico.

Rico pirouettes and hightails it back to his truck parked outside in the dark. A stunned Rico gets in his truck and sits wide-eyed trying to figure out what he just saw.

After a few moments, Patrick is able to regain his composure. His breathing returns to normal. He puts his hand to his chest, the twinge he has felt periodically throughout his life prickles at his chest. It quickly passes, and he puts his office back in order. He picks up the computer, places it on his desk and powers it down. Patrick sighs loudly, "Now what do I do?" he pathetically whines.

Gregory L. Heitmann

Chapter 23

Juanita's

Juanita's restaurant sits on the western edge of downtown Capitol City proper. The popular eatery is located inside one of the historic buildings of the former railroad depot for the long retired narrow gauge Corvair & Rio Caballo Railway, the "Pepper Line," running north out of Capitol City to just across border at Corvair. Dubbed the Pepper Line because of its consistent cargo of chili peppers, the tracks parallel the more navigable grade following the Rio Caballo, going north, but soon rise to the high desert plains, tracing its way to the border. The rail line, like most others of that era, has long since been retired. The only remnant of its once flourishing existence is a tourist train to the east, the Estrella & Norte Scenic Railroad operating between Corvair and San Luis. Maybe the last vestige of the Pepper Line in Capitol City is Juanita's, a popular eatery for locals and tourists alike. A virtual "must stop" on the tourist guides, it boasts a healthy and consistent crowd on nearly every night with overflowing crowds routinely waiting under the portal in the summer months.

Tonight, Gary and Katrina have ventured out amongst the tourists to patronize their favorite Mexican style cuisine at Juanita's. They put their name in with the hostess and move to the bar for a drink while they wait for their table. Santiago, "Santi," recognizes his regular customers, "Two swirls?" he asks, shaking their hands to welcome them.

"Need you even ask?" Katrina smiles.

The swirl is the staple of the restaurant. It is a frozen margarita injected with sangria. The sangria "swirls" into the icy mix, giving it a fancy flavor to match its color and moniker. Santi is back in a moment with the two yellow-green margarita drinks with a red stripe of sangria encircling the inside of the glass.

"Mmmmm, swirls," Katrina says, "Thank you, Santi."

Gary pays, and they move out of the way for other customers and stand in the lobby to wait and savor their drinks. Voices echo off the red brick interior of the ancient depot building. It is loud inside with the crowd of people chattering away.

* * * * *

Some people consider it a shortcoming; a character flaw. Gary never thought of it that way; to him it was a strength, although he recognized its potential weakness at the same time. How can wanting, even demanding accuracy be a bad thing? Gary probably has an over-developed sense of right and wrong that some psychologists would classify such behavior as some form of neuroses, but who is really to say?

So, if you hear somebody say something blatantly wrong, what is the harm in correcting them? Yes, tact is needed in order to minimize the person's embarrassment when they are corrected, but should you just let somebody go on and on being wrong about something in polite conversation? For instance, the one hundred dollar bill has a picture of Benjamin Franklin. If a person holding a hundred dollar bill makes a remark about what a great President Ben Franklin was, should you just let that go? There is no harm in just letting it pass. Or is there? What if in the future they are in a situation where they need to impress somebody, say a boss or someone they are dating? A one hundred dollar bill comes out and this person, who was never corrected, begins espousing his or her lack of knowledge about presidents, then what? They are embarrassed in a more critical situation and maybe looked upon differently, maybe never promoted; maybe that date never calls again.

It's a touchy situation no doubt. A good motto might be: "err on the side of education."

For Gary, a quote that has puzzled him throughout his adult life is "Lose the battle, but win the war." That always seemed ridiculous to him. If you win every battle, how could you possibly lose the war? The more appropriate quote is "Choose your battles wisely." Since if you don't battle, then there is no winner or loser. You should choose to battle only when you are positive you will win, per Sun Tzu's "The Art of War". Alas there is no guarantee that you will win, but stack your odds before you go into battle and you should win. All that said, Gary's war has consisted of battles of facts and setting the record straight. This "personality quirk" has been the source of trouble for Gary on more than one occasion. Tonight was no different.

As Katrina and Gary stand in the crowded waiting room, Gary reaches for a few strands of Katrina's hair and runs the back of his index finger over the locks, "You have very pretty hair."

"Why, thank you," Katrina strokes her hair and smiles.

"I like the straightness," Gary continues, "And black hair...it's just...mysterious to me. I like it."

Katrina stops stroking her hair and cocks her head at Gary, shooting a look of contempt, "My hair is brown, not black!"

"Hmmm," Gary contemplates as he sips his drink, "I'm looking at your hair right now, and it is black."

"Nooooo."

Gary puts his finger to his lips, "I'm assuming that's your natural hair color?

"Mmm-hmmm."

"You're Hispanic, correct?"

"Yes."

"I rest my case. Your hair is black."

"What!" Katrina rasps in an angry tone, but trying to keep the conversation private, "How do you make that leap...Hispanic means black hair?"

Gary shrugs, "Predominantly."

"Shush!" Katrina warns with a raised finger, "We've had this conversation before. Why do you insist on this black hair fetish?"

"Because I'm right!"

Katrina settles back on her heels a moment, "What color is your hair?"

"Brown, dark brown."

"Yes, and my hair is like yours!"

"I agree your hair is like mine...except your hair is black."

Katrina clenches her fist, "Aurrrrgh!"

Their table is ready and the pager vibrates in Gary's back pocket, "Uh, hold that thought; our table is ready." Gary reaches into his pocket and extracts the notifier that buzzes and flashes.

The hostess leads them past the autographed photo of President Bill Clinton, memorializing his visit to Juanita's. They move to the dining area designated as the Randy Travis Room. This dining area is named in honor of local resident and country music legend, Randy Travis, a frequent visitor to Juanita's. Randy even has his own special--The Randy Travis plate: pork chops and green chile, the menu indicates "Randy likes it!"

A useful endorsement if you indeed name a special after someone. Yes, the sanctioning party's endorsement is a critical element.

Gregory L. Heitmann

Gary and Katrina are seated by the hostess beneath a replica, framed platinum record album of Randy's, "Always & Forever." They review the menus. "What are you getting'?" Gary asks.

"Hmm, the usual, enchiladas with red chili," Katrina shrugs.

"I want fajitas, but I don't see them on the menu," Gary replies. "Do see them on here?"

"No."

"What? How can the premiere Mexican restaurant in town not have fajitas, and how come I never noticed this before?"

"Weird," Katrina concedes.

"Oh, well," Gary sighs. "I was thinking about the Randy Travis Plate, but I'll go with the chicken quesadilla and a tamale. You can't beat that."

They place their order and enjoy some chips, salsa, and their swirls. Gary's eyes light up, "Did I tell you about Bryan?"

"No, what?"

"He broke his leg."

"Seriously?"

Gary laughs, "Yeah. He hit a dog riding his bike."

Katrina laughs, "Is he going to be all right?"

"He was feeling no pain when I talked to him. I guess he's got some good drugs to ease his discomfort."

The food arrives and they dig in with a first bite. Gary looks up from his plate, through the doorway, outside the Randy Travis Room, in the main dining area, the hostess is seating Casey Baxter and Patrick Ruiz at a booth. "Are you kidding me?" Gary groans.

"Now what? Something wrong with the food?" Katrina inquires losing patience.

"I thought," Gary nods in the direction of Patrick, "I saw frickin' Casey Baxter and Patrick Ruiz sit down in a booth out there. Good Lord, I just can't get away from that guy."

Katrina casually looks behind her, holding her margarita and drinking a sip to see what Gary is looking at. Her eyes widen and she whispers in a hushed tone, "Oh my God; they're sitting on the same side of the booth!"

"Should we just leave?" Gary asks with a pained look.

"No! Geez, take it easy. Forget about them. I'm starved, and we just got our food."

Gary takes a bite of his food and looks at Patrick, "Look at that fat load. He's going to squish poor Casey. Why doesn't he sit on his own side?"

"Relax!" Katrina orders through gritted teeth.

They continue to eat in silence for a moment before Gary interjects, "I told you that Bryan and I had a run in with Patrick, didn't I?"

118

"Mmm-hmm," Katrina acknowledges, wiping her mouth with a napkin.

"You see that splint on Patrick's finger?" Gary nods toward Patrick.

Katrina turns and sees Patrick talking and gesturing with his hand. Katrina nods with a puzzled look and meets Gary's eyes. Gary sneers, "I broke his finger in our little 'confrontation' the other day."

"What?" Katrina shouts, drawing a few strange looks from neighboring diners. "That guy right over there. You broke his finger?"

"Yeah, that's the douche bag. I broke his finger."

Katrina shakes her head wide-eyed, "Are you crazy? Please tell me you are not serious."

"I'm not proud of it, but I can't say I didn't enjoy it. He was poking me in the chest with his finger." Gary pokes himself in the chest attempting to re-enact the incident.

Katrina stares at Gary slack-jawed. She throws her napkin down on her plate, "So, violence is the answer? Not to mention, you could be fired!"

Gary's voice goes higher in his defense, "He was poking me in the chest! Talk to Bryan, he was a witness. It was self defense."

"So, who do you think you are, Dirty Harry?"

Gary scoffs, "I'm just supposed to sit there and take his physically assaulting me?"

"You're a fool."

Gary flinches at the insult, "What?" Gary looks at Katrina in disbelief, "Are you seriously angry? This is ridiculous, he attacked me. I already squared it with Diego"

"Gary," Katrina's voice calms, "First, you go on attacking my hair color with this authoritarian complex. Now, I'm just finding out about an assault. It's bad enough you never even told me about it, but now you are relishing it."

Katrina folds her arm and glares at Gary. Gary stares back expressionless and shrugs, "I don't know what to say."

"You need some counseling," Katrina points a finger at Gary. "Again, how many times have we talked about your anger; you are angry all the time, at the littlest thing!"

"I don't want or need counseling," Gary shrugs.

"Well, I don't want to be here anymore," she shoves her chair back in a huff.

Gary looks at her, "Fine. We'll go then."

"No, I don't want to be here with you," Katrina grumbles as she digs money out of her purse, "I'll find my own way home."

"Seriously?" Gary stands and reaches for Katrina.

Katrina balks and puts her hands up to shield herself from Gary, "Just...just leave me alone." Katrina throws some cash on the table and leaves. Gary watches her walk out the door, and she disappears from view.

He does not follow and eventually notices the staring eyes and the silence in the room. He smiles uncomfortably and sits down trying to become invisible.

*　*　*　*　*

After ten minutes, Gary feels time has sufficiently erased the memories from the other diners. He gets the leftovers boxed and pays the bill. He slinks out the back door to his truck in the parking lot. He gets in and starts the truck. Kevin Fowler's song *Hard Man to Love* courses from the speakers. "Damn it," Gary yells out as he punches the "eject disc" button on his stereo. "Isn't this just fucking perfect?"

Chapter 24

Unsolicited Advice

Gary has ventured out alone to Patrick Ruiz's construction office on the commuter train construction site. Patrick invited Gary to a one-on-one discussion of the project progress and to ask a favor. Gary arrives in the early afternoon, just as it starts to heat up. He parks the G-car in the dusty gravel lot next to Patrick's Laramie Engineering truck, the only other vehicle around. Gary climbs the stairs to the trailer, knocks, and enters as he removes his sunglasses. He blinks as his eyes adjust from the blinding desert sunshine outside to the darkened trailer.

Patrick looks up from his desk and stands, "Hey, Gary, thanks for coming." He motions to a chair in front of his desk and sits down in his creaking chair, "Have a seat."

"No problem," Gary acknowledges, but before sitting, he extends his hand to Patrick, who provides his own, and they shake hands awkwardly, doing their best to avoid the splint on Patrick's finger. Gary lets go of Patrick's hand and points at the splint, "Sorry about the finger."

Patrick looks at his finger, "Uh-yeah…no, it was my fault. I started it; I guess you finished it."

The men size each other up in silence for a moment. Gary crosses his legs, "Did you hear about Bryan?"

Patrick raises an eyebrow, "No, what happened?"

"He crashed his bike and broke his leg."

Patrick laughs. He holds up his splinted finger, "Seems to be going around."

Gary laughs and silence blankets the room again. "So," Gary finally says uncrossing his legs and leaning forward in his chair, "Why did you want to see me so urgently?"

Patrick heaves a sigh and stares at Gary for a few moments. Gary shrugs before Patrick sighs again, "I don't know how to say this, so I just will. I need your help. That's the reason I wanted to talk to you. I know you care about getting things done, so I thought I'd just ask for your help to get this project rolling at full speed."

"I'm listening," Gary nods. "What can I do?"

"It's simple," Patrick leans back in his chair, and it creaks and groans under his massive frame, "We just need your support." He puts his hands behind his head, interlocking his fingers.

"Excuse me," Gary laughs the words.

"Your support," Patrick insists leaning forward. "You support the T'rrain Trekker amongst your office, and that'll do the trick."

Gary shakes his head in disagreement, "I'm flattered that you think I have that much influence, but you are mistaken. Haven't you heard, over and over again, people in our office say, 'we are going to do the right things, right'?"

Patrick sneers a bit and catches himself, turning his sneer into a smile, "Who's to say what is right? All I ask is that you sign off on the station locations, and we finish the construction. It's a win-win. The public gets mass transit access and we," Patrick signals with a pointed finger between the two men, "get credit!"

"Patrick, you know what's right. I'm positive you know the laws, regulations, and policies better than most at the highway department. Those things tell us what we have to do to stay in compliance. They steer us. If it feels wrong, then it's probably wrong. Listen, we will work with you and do everything in our power to help, but it has to be reasonable; within the regs."

Patrick frowns, "It's easy for you to sit on your high horse, answering to nobody. I have to answer to the authorities!"

Gary scoffs, "Don't give me that; I answer to one authority," Gary holds up one finger, "The taxpaying citizens. If they aren't getting what they are paying for, I am failing." Gary turns his extended finger to Patrick, "I understand that you answer to your company's shareholders, to making a profit, and to politicians, but I have to be accountable to the public."

"Oh, please," Patrick dismisses Gary with a wave of his hand, "Don't be so naïve. Politics has a huge grasp over you whether you want to acknowledge it or not."

Gary gets a pained expression on his face, "Patrick, I don't think you understand my role. I work for the federal government to administer the fuel tax money collected at the gas pumps…"

Patrick interrupts, "I know, I know…"

Gary holds up his hand, "Let me finish."

Patrick crosses his arms and has the look of an impatient child painted across his face.

"My job," Gary continues, "Also entails tempering the state and local political pressures and knee-jerk reactions. There is a higher calling than just what the state or what Capitol City wants. We have to consider a national interest."

Patrick holds up his palms in contrition, "I can't argue with you. But, there is a reality I have to deal with. That reality is politicians with aspirations of higher elected office."

"Does that make it right to cut corners?" Gary questions.

Patrick sits in silence. He drops his hands and shrugs.

Gary's eyes narrow, and he takes on a serious tone, "Let me give you a bit of unsolicited advice: Watch yourself. Don't put yourself into a compromising situation."

"Why would you say that?" Patrick counters hurtfully.

"I understand the political pressure. I just don't have any sympathy for people that cave into it."

Patrick chuckles, "I'll take it under advisement."

Gary smiles, "Good. One other thing, and I hope this isn't insulting, but it's a piece of advice that I take to heart. It's never the mistake that hurts you; it's the cover up that kills."

Patrick scrunches his face, puzzled, "Where is this all coming from? What are you implying?"

"Well," Gary settles back in his chair, "I refer in part to the property you bought from the Jensen Ranch right here, where this trailer sits. Everyone knows that there was a bust in negotiations."

Patrick is defensive, "But, we got right of entry!"

"At what cost!" Gary counters, "How in the world are you in a position to negotiate when you have a $500 million dollar investment sitting on the property you don't own?"

"We're going to acquire the property, don't worry," Patrick adamantly retorts.

"That is not the point. You are going to end up paying a premium on a piece of property that is virtually worthless without the railroad tracks crossing it."

"What have you got against this project?" Patrick poses as a question, but it comes out as a demand.

"I have nothing against the project; it's just the way it's been shoved down the public's throat. If this had been completely under the auspices of our office, there is no way on earth you would have started construction without having plans, right-of-way…everything in place."

Gary shakes his head and continues, "If you look at history, James Madison wrote in the Federalist Papers about making the government slow and deliberative. It was purposely done this way; a reaction to the previous rule of a king who could make decisions on a whim. That's why government is sometimes painstakingly slow. It was designed that way for a reason. I realize it doesn't jive with a lot of people who want the government reacting at a snap of fingers, but the founding fathers knew what they were doing. This was their attempt to thwart rash decision-making."

Patrick laughs breaking the building tension, "You know what, Gary? You and I just have a philosophical difference of opinion. You want everything in place before you move, and I want to make things happen now, clean up the details later. We are just different. There's nothing wrong with that."

Patrick extends his hand as he stands, "Thanks for meeting with me. I appreciate your efforts and perspective."

Gary shakes Patrick's hand, again, trying to be careful of the splinted finger. Gary leaves the trailer, and Patrick finally sits when he hears the vehicle driving away, and, from his window, he catches a view of the car's dust cloud chasing down the gravel road.

Patrick picks up the phone on his desk and dials a number from memory, "He won't play ball."

On the other end of the line is Patrick's uncle, the governor's secretary of public safety, "I'm sorry to hear that. I guess we take the next step. You wait until I contact you before doing anything. I'll make the preparations."

"Will do," Patrick simply responds before hanging up.

Chapter 25

Stationary

The music of Johnny Cash's *"Folsom Prison Blues"* echoes from the portable public address system. The song rings out with its familiar baritone, twangy, hear-the-train's-a-coming referenced lyrics.

The music fades, and Governor Stuart Reid-Salazar steps from the group of people on the platform to the podium in front of a small crowd of people gathered on this day to dedicate a new T'rrain Trekker commuter rail station. The governor waves and smiles to sporadic cheers from the crowd. A young man near the back of the crowd holds up a hand painted sign that reads, "What can Stu do for you? Reid-Salazar for President!"

Governor Reid-Salazar holds his hands up to quiet the crowd. He moves one hand to his ear, pretending to listen, "Do you hear that? Can you hear the train whistle? The T'rrain Trekker is almost ready for operation!"

The crowd cheers wildly, and the governor waits for the crowd to calm before continuing. He nods, satisfied with the turnout and the response. "Today is a milestone day for the state…," he begins.

Up on the platform behind the governor a dozen or so people stand in support of the politician as he lectures. Several state and local political operatives, along with some of the public works people, are among the representatives to cut the ribbon opening the station. Casey Baxter is on one side of the group; Patrick Ruiz is the bookend on the other side of the officials on the stage encircling the governor. Everything is perfect on this morning. The 10:00 am sun is not too hot, but lighting things well for the television news coverage. There is only the slightest breeze, not enough to move a strand on the governor's perfectly coiffed hair, but still a cooling breath of fresh air.

Governor Reid-Salazar continues, "There are a lot of people to thank for this accomplishment, and you can see many of them up here on the platform with me," the governor turns and sweeps his hands to each side, like a model from "The Price Is Right", and the crowd provides a round of applause for the officials on stage. In the curious, supportive crowd are Patrick's wife and daughter. In a separate area of the crowd, Casey's husband and two kids applaud for their mother and wife. As Casey proudly acknowledges her recognition from the governor and the crowd, she catches her husband's eye and gives him a wink.

The governor continues to speak, "We should be proud of the work we see in front of us today. This station is strategically located between several state agency offices. Many men and women will now have an opportunity to take the commuter train in the morning rather than fight the congestion on the highways and streets. Thousands of workers live in Allentown and commute each morning and evening to and from Capitol City, and this is one of several stations that will provide that critical transportation option for the working people of this state. In this time of rising energy prices, I'm proud to lead the fight against the grip that Middle East oil producers have on this country. This train station is a symbol of the options available in this great country. It is a symbol of what the government can do to assist the middle class workers." The governor's voice rises in excitement for his flourish, "It is a symbol of the progressive people of the Southwest."

The crowd cheers on cue. The young man holding his "Stu for President Sign" jumps up and down. The governor smiles and points in the man's direction, "I see you out there. Are you watching the Presidential debates? I hope I'm making y'all proud!"

Another cheer goes up from the crowd. On the platform Patrick watches Casey, he sees Casey wink at her husband and wave to her children. Patrick looks for his own wife smiling at him from the crowd of people. Patrick manages to smile back and give a wave to his wife and daughter as the governor continues to speak.

"The best of the Rio Caballo Valley," the governor shouts, "is here and coming down these tracks…"

From opposite sides of the stage, Patrick finally catches Casey's eye. They smile at each other in satisfied acknowledgement.

"Our work is not finished," the governor closes with a dramatic flair, "but, remember this day! Let's cut this ribbon and christen an historic part of our future!"

A red, white, and blue ribbon is stretched across the columns supporting the canopy of the open air station along the set of railroad tracks. The tracks extend about a hundred yards in each direction, but are not connected to anything. The station is being dedicated and will sit unused for a few more weeks or months while construction is being finished on the rail mainline, but the governor got what he wanted; a photo opportunity and some perfect television news sound bites for his Presidential campaign.

Over-sized scissors are handed to everyone on the stage, and each clips a portion of the ribbon to the cheers of the throng of people. The crowd mills around for a few minutes as the governor obliges the members of the mob with a few photos. The people begin to disperse. Casey finds her family, and they exchange hugs. They wait to get their photograph taken with the governor and then make their way to their car in the parking lot.

Patrick waits in line with his family for a photo with the governor. He looks over his shoulder and watches Casey walking toward the parking lot with her own family. Patrick sulks a bit as Casey never even bothered to say, "Hello or goodbye." She left Patrick with only a nod of her head as they stood on stage earlier.

Chapter 26

Supper Time

In the Allentown suburb of Rio Loma, the Baxter family gathers for supper. Casey Baxter's husband, Ken, dishes out a second helping to the kids; another round of scalloped potatoes and ham. He stands, scooping the food onto the children's plates. He turns, prepared to serve Casey, who stares off into space. "Would you like some more, Dear?" Ken asks.

Casey is oblivious.

"Honey, more ham?" he asks again.

Casey snaps back to reality, "Pardon?"

"What's the matter? You're a million miles away."

"Just work," Casey shrugs. "There's a lot going on."

Casey's mind races through thoughts of Patrick and Chuck. Patrick informed Casey of the futile attempt to extract useful information from Gary's computer. Now, Patrick's obsession with the train and Gary was reaching a new level of insanity. Every conversation they shared was about the train and that eventually lead to what Patrick saw as obstructionism by Gary. From there, the conversation always turned to the governor: "Did you hear what the governor said? Are you going to the fundraiser?" Patrick would constantly spout.

Casey wondered constantly how she could break off her friendship with Patrick. She didn't see a way out.

Ken rests his hand on his wife's shoulder, "I know you have a lot going on, but you're home now. You've been working too hard. That train eats all your time. The kids and I hardly see you."

Casey looks up at her husband and gives her best smile, "You're right. Thanks for cooking again, Honey. Great supper."

Casey puts her hand on top of Ken's and pats it. Ken smiles, sits back down, and resumes eating his supper. Forks clank against plates as the kids shovel food into their mouths. Casey looks across the table and is able to smile at her kids even as the day's ribbon cutting events play over and over in her head. The question of what to do next rattles through her brain, and she pinches the bridge of her nose as the tension headache is back. Ken notices his wife, "Your headache is back?"

Casey nods slightly. A tear slips from her eye and rolls down her cheek as she musters a whisper, "It's very stressful lately."

Ken pushes away from the table, "Let me get you the extra strength aspirin."

Casey whispers, "Thank you," trying not to disturb the family supper.

Chapter 27

Yoga, Yogi

At the Fort Randall Recreation Complex just north of downtown Capitol City, nestled between the foothill mansions and the Plaza, Katrina, Sarah, and Betsy wrap up their aerobics class with a few cool down yoga poses. The instructor leads the class of about twenty-five people in a triangle pose and finally moving into warrior pose. "Good workout," the instructor calls out. "See you next time."

The ladies retreat to the locker room, talking as they grab towels to dab sweat from their respective brows. "Katrina," Betsy calls out, "I can't thank you enough for coming by our little mixer the other night. Quinton thought Gary was hilarious."

"No problem," Katrina replies, "Did Quinton realize that Gary wasn't necessarily intentionally being funny?"

Betsy laughs, "Quinton was just as uncomfortable as Gary; that's what he told me later. He really appreciated seeing Gary, and not just a whole bunch of stuffed shirts."

Sarah chimes in, "What did you think of Betsy's new boyfriend? Don't you think he's cute?"

"Sure," Katrina nods in agreement with a smile. "To look at him, you wouldn't know he was a detective. Listen to you though; you have him as 'boyfriend' classification already...nice work."

Betsy and Sarah giggle. Sarah playfully elbows Katrina, "How about you and Gary? Any big news? Engagement announcement, maybe?"

Katrina heaves a sigh, "Not likely. We're not really talking at the moment; we're on a little break."

Sarah and Betsy gasp in unison. "What are you talking about?" Sarah hisses, gulping for breath, "What happened?"

"He's out of control! He's just been a complete jerk lately."

"Gary? I can't believe it," Sarah remarks dubiously.

"Believe it. I'm sure a lot of it is his stupid job. He just won't relax. By the way, have you seen Patrick Ruiz lately? He's got a splint on his finger."

"Yeah, that dipstick, Pat, is in my office everyday," Sarah grimaces.

"Gary did that to him. He broke his finger," Katrina whines.

"Are you kidding me? Pat jokingly said that he got in a fight, but later admitted that he got it caught in a door," Sarah says in disbelief.

The ladies reach the locker room and start digging through their bags to change clothes. "Nope," Katrina continues, "Gary told me that Pat was poking him in the chest, so he grabbed his finger and just snapped it."

Betsy sits on the locker room bench wide-eyed at the story, toweling off, "Wow. You guys have exciting lives."

Katrina turns to Betsy, "That's why Gary took the card from your detective boyfriend. He thinks he might need a friend in the police department."

Sarah shakes her head, "This is unbelievable."

"It gets worse," Katrina sighs. "I left him sitting in Juanita's the other night. He is just so mean sometimes. He just teases and teases…he goes too far."

Sarah smiles uncomfortably, "Yes, that sounds like the Gary we all know and love."

"Yeah," Katrina quips with sarcasm. "We're on a little hiatus."

Betsy frowns, "I'm sorry to hear that."

Katrina stops pulling clothes from her bag and puts her hand on her hip, "I wish he would come with me to do some yoga like this. Get rid of some of that stress."

"Gary? Not likely," Sarah laughs.

"Wishful thinking on my part, I know."

Betsy stands and takes off her sweaty shirt. She waves it away, "I'm sure you two will be fine."

Katrina nods with a faint smile, "Thanks."

Chapter 28

Rico

Gary sat at his desk, staring back and forth between his Outlook calendar on his computer and his monthly wall calendar. It was already that point in the summer when hunting licenses were drawn and plans needed to be made for going back to his home state of South Dakota to hunt deer and pheasants as well as set aside time for a local elk hunt in the Sangre de Sustantivo Mountains. Gary was in deep concentration and never heard Sylvia approach his office. She knocked, announcing herself, "Gary…"

Gary recoils in surprise, and Sylvia laughs.

"Holy cow, Sylvia. You scared the bejeezus out of me."

Sylvia continues to snicker as she reports, "There is a man from the state highway department here to see you."

Gary sits frozen in his desk. His mind races, trying to remember an appointment he might have made for the morning. He finally looks at his calendar, "Hmmm, I don't have anything on my calendar. Who is it?"

Sylvia shrugs, "I don't know Gary. I didn't recognize him. He just asked for you."

"Ok." Gary stands and follows Sylvia back to her desk, down the hall. They pass the generic walls of their government office. A few of the walls have some nicely framed photographs of scenic places in the Southwest providing a splash of color: Pike's Peak, the Grand Canyon, and the Golden Gate Bridge. Gary passes his favorite photo; it is a twenty-four inch by forty inch framed photo of hundreds of balloons launching at Balloon Fiesta in Albuquerque, New Mexico. It brings a smile to Gary's face as he approaches Sylvia's desk where a man is waiting.

"Hello," Gary says introducing himself and extending his hand, "I'm Gary Hillmann. Why don't we head back to my office?"

The man grabs Gary's hand with his own weathered and calloused hand and shakes it. "My name is Rico Suarez. I'm an inspector for the state highway department working on the T'rrain Trekker project."

"Ok," Gary nods as they move back down the hallway toward Gary's office. "Nice to meet you. Thanks, Sylvia," Gary gives Sylvia a wink as he turns and walks away.

They arrive at Gary's office where Gary removes some papers from a small table in the corner of his workspace opposite from his desk. Four chairs surround the table and the men sit. "What can I do for you, Mr. Suarez?"

Mr. Rico Suarez is a twenty-year veteran working for the highway department. Starting right out of high school, he is now thirty-eight years old; he looks somewhat older having spent all the years in the southwestern desert sun. Rico is dressed in clothes you'd expect a man working in the field to wear; faded Carhart jeans, a faded red t-shirt under a plaid flannel shirt with the sleeves rolled to the elbows, ready for work. Gary's first impression of the man would be the clichéd, strong silent type. Rico, built like a quick NFL tailback, appears to not have an ounce of fat on his body.

Rico Suarez looks at his arms and tightens the creases of the rolled up shirt sleeves. He meets Gary's eyes and looks back over his shoulder at the office door and back to Gary. "I need to speak to you privately…in confidence," Rico finally announces.

Gary points to the door and nods; he rises and shuts the door that latches closed with a click. Gary sits back down, rests his elbows on the table, and folds his hands.

Rico rubs his lip with his index finger searching for where to begin; he looks at the floor and runs his hands through his hair before meeting Gary's gaze. "What I'm about to tell you is something I very much regret." Rico pauses.

Gary sits patiently; he narrows his eyes, "What's this about?"

Rico sighs, "It's about the T'rrain Trekker and Patrick Ruiz."

"Oh," Gary says curtly, and he mimics Rico's sigh. "Would you mind if I bring Bryan Baker in to listen? The T'rrain Trekker is one of Bryan's projects. Do you know Bryan?"

"I know him like I know you. I have often heard Patrick refer to both you and him."

"If it's ok, I'd like to bring Bryan in."

"That's fine," Rico nods in agreement.

"Pardon me one moment," Gary excuses himself and exits his office.

Gary shakes his head as he moves down the hallway, concerned about what Rico has to present. Gary dreads having the finger-wrenching scenario brought out into the public light, but he realizes that he made that bed and may have to sleep in it, no matter how uncomfortable. Gary reaches Bryan's cubicle. Bryan is back at work sporting his fancy fiberglass cast. "Knock, knock," Gary calls out, stepping into the door of the cube, "Can you come with me?"

"Sure," Bryan does his best to spring up on his good foot and grab his crutches. "What's up?" Bryan asks as he crutches behind following Gary to his office.

"It's about the T'rrain Trekker."

"Ah, that's great. Good thing I took an extra pain pill this morning."

The two men reach Gary's office. Bryan introduces himself to Rico. "Yes, Bryan. I heard about your broken leg through the grapevine. You're feeling better, no?"

Gary shuts the door. Bryan shrugs as Gary gets in behind the table, and Bryan hops into position to sit at the table, "Yeah, they patched me up. Couple months in a cast…be as good as new."

The men are situated, and Gary nods to Rico. Rico shifts his gaze back and forth between Gary and Bryan, "I was just telling Gary that I had some troubling information on the T'rrain Trekker." Rico pauses and he shifts uncomfortably in his chair. "I will just try to explain the best I can. Please bear with me."

Gary and Bryan nod, so as not to interrupt, both curious on what the subject of the matter is.

Rico begins, "Mr. Ruiz has problems. The way he talks about you two guys…" Rico pauses and points back and forth between Gary and Bryan, his hand still resting on the table, finger twitching between the men. Bryan and Gary exchange puzzled glances.

Rico continues with a sigh, "It's not normal. It's like he is obsessed. The highway department culture is different. It is go along, get along…I'm not a perfect man. I have known and worked with Patrick Ruiz nearly my entire career, a good two dozen projects. There is something going on…"

Rico puts his elbow on the table. He rests his chin on his hand and taps his lip with his index finger. "The contractors are rushing to construct the rail line as fast as possible, and we have pushed the limits…"

Rico stands, "Do you mind if I stand?"

Bryan and Gary shake their heads and shrug no objection.

Rico sighs, "Patrick has falsified the concrete test results on the tunnel into the interstate median." Rico exhales deeply and looks away from Gary and Bryan. "I'm really sorry I didn't come immediately to your office. As an inspector, I knew…I knew the results were failing and I told, Patrick. He said he would take care of it."

Gary nods, "I see."

"The whole system is broken…it's corrupt! Everyone is afraid to say anything. They are pushing this project so hard. They want to finish early!"

"What's the main problem with the testing?" Bryan inquires.

"It's concrete. Water content. Slump. Entrained Air. One of the biggest problems was the trucks mixing on site and sitting and waiting in the heat. We were rejecting loads, and Patrick would overrule us. The mix was hot, unworkable, and they were adding water to it like crazy, just to be able to get it out of the truck. On top of that cure times were not followed…so we were pouring on top of uncured concrete. Cracks everywhere."

Rico throws his hands in the air. "They grouted the cracks and backfilled over them as if nothing was wrong…per Patrick's orders."

Bryan stares at Rico slack-jawed. He shakes his head and closes his mouth. "Y-y-you," he stammers, "You have proof of this?"

"I have the reports," Rico affirms with a nod. "I don't think Patrick realized we had some dual reporting on this project. Typically, everything is reported via the laptop computers, on the server…any changes would be noted in the history files."

"What do you mean?" Bryan asks.

"Well, I checked the inspection report files on the server; they show everything was fine. They don't show any history of changes or tampering…However, I have a laptop that crashed in the first week of the concrete pours; it showed the real inspection reports, before they were doctored. I had a buddy of mine, not with the highway department, look at that computer. He was able to get it running again. I looked at the history files along with their properties, and you can see the original entry dates for the inspection reports." Rico sits back down at the table.

"Ok…ok," Gary nods as he thinks. He exhales deeply, glad that his fear of the finger incident wasn't the reason for the visit from Rico, and at the same time, disgusted at the new news of corruption.

Rico shakes his head, "I had to tell…I have seen minor things before, but this…this train? Rushing to get done, cutting corners. Somebody is going to get killed. I don't want that on my conscience."

"I know. I know," Gary nods.

Bryan shakes his head in disgust, "I can't believe this. Why has this stupid train got people so bent out of shape?"

"The politics," Gary throws his hands in the air. "We weren't moving fast enough. This office has consistently said the train is going to happen…but, by the rules and procedures and they take time."

"So, this is all about the stupid campaign for President?" Bryan questions.

Gary shrugs, "What else could it be?"

Rico sits in his chair staring at his boots. He does not look up, "I'm thinking what you are thinking. I'm not proud to be a highway department employee at this time. The governor wants to be President. He will do anything, and he has the people to assist him to make it happen." Rico shakes his head slowly in disgust.

The men sit in silence for a moment or two, each contemplating what comes next. Bryan speaks first, "What do you want us to do?" he asks pointing back and forth between himself and Gary.

Rico meets Bryan's eyes, "I'm still not one hundred percent sure. I was hoping you would help me."

"Can we have the information…the computer you were talking about? It is something we will need. It's just best to have the original info. From there, this will be something for the United States Office of Inspector General to be brought in on."

"I have the computer in a safe place," Rico nods. "I can get it to you."

"That's the first step, contacting the OIG. They will investigate for any potential fraudulent acts and criminal activity to give to the U.S. Attorney," Gary continues.

"You know what?" Bryan interjects, "There is a pre-construction meeting in Mora next week. I will go up there with you to the meeting, and you can give me the laptop and anything else there is. No sense in drawing any attention to the situation. You'll just be giving poor old injured Bryan a ride." Bryan taps on his cast.

Rico smiles and nods, "I like that idea."

"Wait," Bryan adds. "Speaking of unwanted attention, does anybody know you're here talking to us?"

"No," Rico forces a smile, "I am at a doctor's appointment as far as my supervisor knows."

"Rico, you need to know that you are protected under the Whistleblower Act," Gary offers with a serious tone. "They can't fire you or retaliate against you even if this investigation does leak out early. You understand that, right?"

Rico nods.

"Once word gets out," Gary continues, "stuff's going to hit the fan. There will be fire and brimstone, but your job is protected."

"I understand. I just want things safe for the traveling public," Rico offers quietly.

"You're doing a very good thing here, Rico," Gary announces as he stands up. "It's not going to be easy, but you should be proud of yourself for standing up for the public and what's right."

Rico stands. He sighs deeply. Gary extends his hand and Rico shakes it. "Thank you again, Rico. I can walk you out."

"Thank you guys. I knew I could depend on you," Rico says swallowing hard.

Bryan eases out from behind the table, hopping on his good foot, and he grabs his crutches. He points to Rico with a crutch, "Give me a call, and we can arrange the details for going to Mora."

Rico nods and moves to Bryan to shake hands. Gary walks with Rico to the front desk and out to the parking lot. Bryan waits in Gary's office.

*   *   *   *   *

When Gary returns to his office, Bryan is fired up, "I knew it!" he shouts. "Fat Pat is dirtier than a pig in slop. I knew it! We're going to take him down!"

"Yeah," Gary agrees in a subdued tone. "It's sad though. It's so hard for me to believe how corrupt the politics are here."

"I know…up and down every aspect of government…corruption," Bryan shakes his head as he balances on his crutches. He smiles mischievously, "It just makes me so happy that Pat is going to get what's coming to him. He is a *bad* guy."

Gary exhales deeply, "Don't count your chickens before they hatch. This is just starting." Gary shakes his head in disgust, "It just makes me sick that this is going on."

"You and me both," Bryan grimaces. "I gotta go. I need to elevate my foot for awhile."

"All right," Gary smiles. "Speaking of your foot, I forgot to ask you earlier, but did you cry?"

Bryan looks incredulous, "What? What are you talking about?"

Gary smiles even more, "Your leg? When you broke it, did you cry?"

Bryan responds loudly, "No! Well…" Bryan pauses and frowns. "Not at first. Not when it happened."

"I knew it," Gary snickers. "I'm glad you're man enough to admit it."

Bryan finally smiles, "It flippin' hurt, buddy. You try snapping a bone in your ankle sometime."

"No, thanks," Gary quickly offers. "But seriously, I'm glad I got somebody to help me with this." Gary sighs, "I guess I better talk to management."

Bryan laughs, "What do you mean 'talk to management?' You are management!"

Gary smiles and hits his head lightly with the heel of his hand, "I keep forgetting. I should say, I'll talk to Diego when he gets in."

"That's more like it," Bryan concurs with a sharp nod of his head as he begins to crutch his way out of the office and down the hall.

Gregory L. Heitmann

Chapter 29

Diego

It was mid afternoon when Diego showed up at the office. Gary heard the rustling of papers in the adjoining office, signifying Diego was present. Gary knocked on the open door as Diego was removing his suit jacket. "Hey, man. What's up?" Diego calls out when he looks up and sees Gary in the doorway. "Come on in."

Gary moved into the office as Diego draped his jacket on the back of his chair and sat down behind his desk. "Sure gettin' hot out there," Diego says as he runs his hand through his hair, eventually adjusting the band holding a short ponytail binding his shoulder-length, salt and pepper locks.

"Oh, yeah?" Gary questions. "Well, get ready for more heat."

Diego's eyebrows go up and a crooked grin appears on his face, "What's up?"

"I wish I could say 'not much.'"

Diego signals Gary to sit. Gary sits and continues, "Bryan and I just talked to a highway department inspector, Rico Suarez; he says he has information on fraudulent inspection reports regarding the T'rrain Trekker."

Diego emits a low whistle as he brings his hands back behind his head and settles back in his chair. "Someone finally coming forward. I'm not familiar with the family name, what'd you say? Suarez? Hmm, Suarez. Suarez. Doesn't ring a bell. How about you? You know this guy?"

"Nope. Never met him until today."

Diego nods and releases his hands from the resting spot behind his head, "You think it's legitimate?"

"I have no reason not to believe him."

Diego smiles broadly, "A whistle blower, eh?" Diego pauses a long time. "Good! I wonder what took so long."

Gary sighs, "Oh, God."

Diego looks at Gary with a puzzled face, "What's wrong?"

"I just realized that this is going to be a lot more work."

"Hey, don't be complaining. You wanted to make a difference," Diego points an accusing finger at Gary. "Welcome to my world, one thing after another thrown onto the pile. It's going to be fun."

"Aurrrrgh," Gary growls. "There are not enough hours in the day! This is going to eat my lunch. Katrina's already mad enough at me. If I spend less time with her, it's not going to make it any better. Work life, home life, all the same," Gary slumps in his chair.

Diego laughs, "Take it easy. What does this Rico need from us?"

"Nothing really. He's going to get the information to Bryan. Rico is going to drive Bryan to a preconstruction meeting next week up in Mora. All the info is on a laptop. Apparently it had all the failed inspection reports before its hard drive crashed. Allegedly, Patrick Ruiz has doctored a bunch of the concrete testing reports; the computer shows contradictory info, a bunch of the reports before they were modified."

"Bueno," Diego nods in agreement. "Did you call the OIG?"

"Not yet. I wanted to talk to you first."

"I'll do it," Diego volunteers. "Let's plan on you and me talking more once we get the info."

Gary stands, "Sounds good. All right, I'm outta here."

Gary moves to the door, but Diego calls him back. "Hey!"

He stops in the doorway and turns around to see Diego pointing a finger at him, "Talk to Katrina. Try to separate work life and home life. She's a smart girl; she can appreciate the pressure of your job."

Gary gives thumbs up to Diego, "Will do."

Gary moves back to his office where he finds Chuck sitting in his chair, "Hey, Chuck, what's going on?"

Chuck hits a final click on the mouse, "I'm just going around granting permission on the browser update. You shouldn't get that error message anymore when you get on the web…at least until they have their next update."

"Thanks, Chuck."

"No problem," Chuck gets up from the computer and starts to leave.

Gary stops him in the doorway, "Hey, about my laptop? Any word, or is it a goner?"

"Oh, man," Chuck flinches as he remembers that Casey "borrowed" Gary's repaired computer. He lies without difficulty, "I haven't gotten to it. I'll get to it and let you know in the next couple days."

"No problem. Just let me know."

"You got it, buddy," Chuck replies firmly.

Chapter 30

Shopping

Bryan Baker has a secret passion. He loves food. He loves to cook and eat. His biggest obsession is shopping for groceries. A broken leg was not going to deter Bryan from a favorite past time. He made it to one of his favorite grocery stores after only a couple days of kicking back. He literally hopped onto one of the electric carts, stowed his crutches, and tooled up and down the aisles. To be more precise, Bryan looks at food, he doesn't necessarily buy much, but he enjoys looking at ingredients in packaged food and then buying fresh, what he needs to mimic the processed food. Today, a box of Stove Top stuffing is being evaluated. Bryan wants to spice up the usual chicken breast prepared on the grill. As Bryan stares at the ingredients, memorizing and imagining proportions and ratios of herbs and spices, a familiar, but not-so-friendly face playfully bangs his shopping cart into Bryan's scooter. "Hey, Bry," Patrick Ruiz calls out, towering over Bryan.

Bryan zones into the present, his mind still jumbled with random herbs needed for a homemade dressing recipe. Bryan stares up at Patrick, "Patrick, what's up?"

"Oh, man! I'm sorry about your foot. Are you doing ok?"

Bryan shrugs, "Yeah, look at me. How awesome is it that I get to shop from this cool cart?"

Patrick smiles half heartedly, "Say, I was wondering if you had a chance to talk to Gary? He and I had a good conversation about a week ago. I thought we might be all in agreement. Any word?"

Bryan shakes his head with a blank look on his face, "He sure didn't say anything to me."

Patrick leans down, resting his arms folded across the handle of the shopping cart, "Well, you tell him that there's a lot we can do for each other. You too, Bryan. There are benefits for you as well."

Bryan laughs incredulously, "What are you talking about?" his voice rising in a near falsetto. "Are you trying to influence a federal official? Some might consider your tone borderline bribery."

"Take it easy, Bryan. Open your mind. See the big picture. This is national...Presidential, if I may say!"

"Are you out of your mind?" Bryan retorts. "Seriously, what are you getting out of this deal?"

"Deal?" Patrick straightens, offended by an implied accusation. "There is no deal. I do my job out of a sense of duty and honor!"

Bryan exaggerates a mocking salute, "What are you, some sort of bizarre form of Marine? Semper Fi!" Bryan shakes his head, "You work for a consultant engineering firm; your loyalty is to profit unless I'm mistaken."

Patrick laughs a fake, forced laugh, "Yeah, you're hilarious. I care about this state and having good highways and trains. This is a big deal, Bryan. Think about what I'm telling you."

Bryan shakes his head dismissively, "There's that word again, 'deal.' You really like that word." Bryan points at Patrick, "Listen, I don't want any 'deal' from you or any of your cronies. Don't include me in the governor's pay to play scheme."

Patrick throws his hands up in the air, "I got ya," he states shrilly. "I'll make sure the message is passed on." Patrick spins his cart around and walks away.

Bryan yells at Patrick's back, "Yeah, you make sure you do that!"

* * * * *

Bryan returns to his box of stuffing, muttering to himself and unable to concentrate as his rage simmers. After a bit, a smile curls Bryan's lips as he thinks about the future jail time Patrick may soon be seeing.

Chapter 31

Getting Better

As Gary ascended the stairs to Katrina's office, he tried to gather himself. He rehearsed his apology in his head a final time before opening the building door. He wandered through the maze of cubicles in the small building. Katrina's office was located in an annex, detached from the main campus of the highway department offices; the environmental section of the agency considered themselves the ugly stepchild of the administration, at least that's the way they felt they were treated. "Exiled" away from everyone else in the department, they did have at least one perk, a decent building with an almost entire glass exterior allowing plentiful natural light for its occupants.

In Gary's head, he could hear Diego telling him to make it right with Katrina. That's what he was doing on this midday foray away from the office, an unannounced visit to apologize. He hummed Kevin Fowler's song *Hard Man To Love* as he moved through the building, smiling to himself at the fun weekend concert memory. He returned a few nods and waves as people recognized him. Nearly everyone was familiar with the relationship between Gary and Katrina; it was likely the worst kept secret in the highway department.

Gary arrived at Katrina's cubicle and stood in the opening for a moment. Katrina was engrossed in reading a report. She was leaning forward in her chair, resting her elbow on her desk and her forehead resting on her hand. Gary watched her a moment or two, thinking to himself how beautiful she really was. "Hey," Gary finally said. "You got a minute?"

Katrina's shoulders twitch as she is startled. She turns to face Gary, a puzzled look crosses her face a moment but is replaced by a dimpled smile. Gary smiles a crooked smile, "Sorry to come over unannounced. I have a statement; we don't really need a long talk. In fact you can just listen. I just have an apology. No flowers. No candy. No card. Nothing but a speech."

Katrina cocks her head and shoots a bemused look at Gary. This does not help Gary; he's already nervous, and the strange look from Katrina blows away his entire rehearsed apology. He begins to ramble, "It's weird though; I told myself on the way over I should stop and get some flowers. I thought, 'the grocery store is right down the block; they have good flowers,' but then I got to rehearsing my apology in my head and drove right past the store. I was still rehearsing the apology as I climbed the steps when it dawned on me that I forgot the flowers. I just said, 'forget it' at that point."

Katrina gives an ever so slight shake of her head.

Gary's eyes widen as he realizes he hasn't apologized. He clears his throat, "I don't..." he stops trying to remember how he planned to keep it short and sweet. "No excuses..."

Gary grabs his hair with his hand; he narrows his eyes racking his brain trying to remember his eloquent apology that was, just moments ago, flowing like a stream in his head. The silence is deafening. The long awkward pause lingers on and on.

"Please," Gary finally begins again. "Hear me out on this. I know this is my fault, and I would like to put this behind us."

Katrina enjoys Gary's discomfort. She looks up at him from her chair, sits back, folds her arms, and smiles.

"Umm," Gary is beside himself with embarrassment. "The point is...well, I'm not exactly sure what my point is. The thing is...you are right, I am wrong."

Katrina and Gary stare at each other a long time. Neither one breaking eye contact. Thirty seconds go by before Katrina nods ever so slightly, "I accept," she announces triumphantly.

"Hmmm?" Gary inquires.

"I accept your apology," Katrina says definitively. "Even as pathetic as it was. I never even heard the words 'I'm sorry.'"

"Good," Gary laughs uncomfortably, still trying to recover his bearing. "Mmmmm, do you want to hug?"

Katrina stands. With a shrug she extends her arms, "Ok."

They hug each other tightly and seal the deal with a kiss. Gary pushes in for an extended passionate kiss but is rebuffed. "Ahem," Katrina whispers, "I'm at work. Aren't you supposed to be working too?"

Gary laughs, "Yeah." He sighs deeply. "Ok then. Yes, that's settled."

"Good," Katrina nods, satisfied, "Well, I'm trying to finish this report, then Colleen and I are going out to your favorite project."

Gary starts backing up slowly, as if he is moving away from a precariously balanced stack of Jenga blocks, "Ok. I…will…leave. Yes, I will leave!" He inches away, not turning his back on Katrina, "I will call you later."

"Ok, see you later," Katrina gives a wave.

Gary, still backing away, bumps into Colleen coming to retrieve Katrina for their project visit. "Oops," Gary jumps forward trying not to crash into Colleen, "I'm sorry. Oh, hi, Colleen."

"Hi, Gary," Colleen sweetly intones. Colleen is in her mid forties and still saving the world. She stands barely five feet tall, but is tough. Her short curly hair with streaks of red and white indicate she is still rebelling against something. Her designer glasses contrast with her simple clothes, blue jeans, and t-shirt. Her left-wing tendencies and constant liberal dialog are like finger nails on a chalkboard for Gary. Colleen is one of Katrina's closest friends. They both started at the department almost ten years ago and have worked on many projects. The train project is their latest work together.

"We're going out to work on the T'rrain Trekker," Colleen coos like a child. "I love trains," she continues while holding her hand over her heart. "Trains fight global warming and are the way of the future."

Gary's eyes roll around his head as he tries to bite his tongue.

Colleen continues, "I know of no other project in my lifetime more important to this state than this commuter rail. It will help the poor struggling people in the middle class."

Colleen sighs, "Governor Reid-Salazar is such an insightful man, a real leader." Colleen is lost in her own dialog as her thoughts float orgasmically around her brain. She is absorbed in her ideas of helping save the planet and people.

Gary makes eye contact with Katrina; he makes a feigned frightened expression. Katrina scowls back at him.

"Anyway," Colleen finishes. "We are making sure the prairie dogs have all been relocated. Can't have train tracks squashing the poor, innocent prairie dogs." She smiles a wide smile, looking at Gary then Katrina. Satisfied by her performance, she reverts to a strictly business attitude.

Gary gives an irritated shake of his head, but again catches a glare from Katrina. He smiles and winks at Katrina, "Ok, be careful out there, bye."

With a wave from Katrina and a salute from Colleen, Gary departs.

Gregory L. Heitmann

Chapter 32

Prairie Dog Scourge

Katrina caught a ride with her best friend, Colleen Davison, in the highway department sedan on their way to the T'rrain Trekker project. The task for the late afternoon and into the evening is to verify a report submitted by a biology sub-consultant. This report and verification is regarding an environmentally sensitive issue in and around Capitol City, prairie dogs. To be clear, the prairie dogs in question are not rare. Populations are not threatened; in fact, they are thriving. Some kind-hearted, trust-fund laden, old ladies, it seems, wanted a new and unique cause to support…lo and behold somebody suggested adopting the cute little prairie dog. This came about mostly to the fact that developers were plowing over prairie dog towns, burying the poor critters alive, without a blink of an eye. Well, this was too much for a group of wealthy retired ladies with time on their hands. The next thing people knew…the Capitol City as well as Kingman County had passed laws protecting the flea bitten rodents with the friendly sounding name, the prairie dog.

Colleen was in charge of making sure that relocation efforts had moved the prairie dog town that was adjacent to, and in the area, where ground disturbing work was required for the commuter railroad track construction. Katrina was along today to stake out the area, providing another pair of eyes to scope out the rodent community for any stray prairie dogs that weren't captured by traps and taken to their new home, a ranch and wildlife preserve, twenty-five miles from this location.

On the drive to the project Katrina questions Colleen, "Why in the world do you say things to Gary like, 'I love the train'? He thinks you are the most bleeding heart liberal in the world!"

Colleen laughs as she steers the car down the highway, "Because it's so funny to watch him react. He cannot take any teasing whatsoever."

"Tell me about it," Katrina groans. "He teases and teases, but tease him back, and he goes crazy."

"I know I shouldn't push his buttons," Colleen shrugs. "I'll try to lay off in the future."

"Thanks, it would be doing me a favor. He's wound tight enough already; he doesn't need any more prodding from you. I know you can't stand the governor, yet there you were, praising him!"

Colleen snorts a laugh, "I know! That was hilarious, the look on Gary's face."

Colleen pulls the highway department vehicle off the road through a recently bladed ditch and onto a long bench carved into the side of the mesa. Empty prairie is situated along the shelf adjacent to an area of pasture, grazed to virtually nothing from the hungry prairie dogs and a few head of cattle from the Jensen Ranch.

A couple thousand feet above Katrina and Colleen, a mining operation digging fill material for use on the railroad grade is in full swing. Giant loaders and haul vehicles are slowly, mechanically eroding the mesa. Taking soil from the top, they haul it a few hundred yards away where the train tracks will eventually be placed. The women are out of the way of the activities and stealthily hike a quarter mile from their vehicle right to the edge of the prairie dog town. They set their gear down and unfold chairs as a few whisps of shade from the passing clouds rolls over them. In another hour, the sun will be making its last efforts of the day before disappearing behind the adjoining mesa and finally receding behind the Tohono Mountains in the distance. This should be the prime time for any straggling prairie dogs to make a feeding run. If there are any leftover dogs, Colleen and Katrina can note them for the report; if not, they will verify the documents, and construction work can commence on the abandoned prairie dog town. It's only a matter of time before steel rails and railroad ties criss-cross the abandoned dog town.

Time passed and the shadows elongated in the desert. The light breeze that was present died. The whines and groans of the working vehicles high on the mesa dominated the ambient noise. Neither Colleen nor Katrina had noted a prairie dog, and they were contemplating when to call it "good." It was eventually decided, purely by chance, that Colleen would walk back and get the vehicle, and Katrina would stay on the lookout. Colleen had driven the department sedan, and she still had the keys in her pack. She was going to go back to the vehicle and, in the mean time, Katrina was going to stand vigilant with a flashlight to see if any final prairie dog would poke its head up from a burrow into the darkness.

Colleen trudged through the desert about a hundred yards, dodging chamisa, yuccas, and a few prickly pear cacti, before she reached the two rut trail that she could drive the sedan down and eventually pick up Katrina along with the gear they had carried. That was part of the strategy. Why carry everything back? Walk back to the car empty handed and then drive over and pick it up. It was different than their earlier approach to the prairie dog town. They wanted stealth when they arrived. They had to sneak into the area so as not surprise a potential wandering prairie dog. Now, it was load up and get back home.

It got dark quickly, miles away from the city lights, but above, on the mesa the machinery rolled, and headlights flashed and bounced. Katrina noticed the lights of the sedan illuminate, an indication that Colleen had made it to the vehicle. An odd stillness came over the mesa; Katrina looked to the top of the hill where the mining operation seemed to have suddenly ceased. It caught her attention. A shrill squeal of metal on metal, or metal on rock, pierced the air. Katrina squinted in the darkness towards the top of the hill. She could see nothing. Voices very far away, but carrying in her direction, seemed to indicate a commotion, and it sounded like yelling.

A thumping noise in the darkness grew louder, and the sound of stones cascading could be heard intermittently. Katrina cocked an ear in the direction of the thumps. The steady thumping was above her, but angled in a direction toward Colleen. The darkness allowed for no visibility. Katrina gave one last sweep of her flashlight over the prairie dog town as she stood and directed her full attention to the thumping noise. She reached her full height and stared in the direction of the sedan. The car's light shone in the darkness. Katrina flinched when the headlights flipped and rolled. The crashing noise of the sedan shook Katrina. She stood frozen and shuddering upon seeing the rolling lights and hearing the crunch of metal. The headlights momentarily shone in her eyes before completing another, and final, revolution. A muffled scream and gasps followed the echoing crash. An eerie silence settled before the headlights on the car eerily dimmed and disappeared. Katrina was frozen only for a moment before her feet began running. The beam of the flashlight bounced before her, and she screamed, "Colleen!"

Katrina's legs carried her as fast as she could ever remember running. What had happened? Her mind raced with no answers. She called out again, "Colleen!"

No answer; she slowed as the flashlight finally illuminated a mangled, mess of twisted metal that was the sedan. The vehicle was sitting back on its wheels, but a massive truck tire was imbedded in the driver's side door and roof. Katrina moved closer to the vehicle and could see the blood seeping from where the driver's compartment was. "Help!" Katrina cried barely audible at first. She yelled louder and louder as she dug for her phone and pressed the digits of 911 summoning emergency responders.

Katrina was not aware that workers from the mesa above were already at her side when the 911 operator answered. A construction worker took the phone from Katrina's hand and provided information to emergency services as she collapsed to her knees and the flashlight revealed a crushed arm and leg beneath the giant tire. Colleen was dead.

*   *   *   *   *

Gary was puzzled when Katrina never answered her phone, and later, she never returned his phone message. Immediately he thought that she had decided to rescind her acceptance of his apology. This is what dogged Gary's mind for an hour or two after the sun had set. He went for a walk in the dark, passing by the familiar stores of his neighborhood in the strip mall, including Kmart. Gary returned home. When the phone finally rang, Gary relaxed when he saw the caller ID indicating Katrina on the line. He fumbled the phone in his hands, but recovered it to hear a strange man's voice telling him that there had been an accident. Katrina had asked the first responders and fire crew to call him. She was in no condition to drive after witnessing a horrific scene. Gary grabbed his keys and made for the door. The messenger had said the crash had been near the T'rrain Trekker tunnel construction area.

*   *   *   *   *

Gary made a beeline for the project site as fast as his truck would take him down the Interstate. He made the twenty miles in 15 minutes. The scene was a flashing mass of chaos. Emergency vehicle lights blinked red and blue; the lights strobed in rhythm to the steady thumping of rotors from a news helicopter hovering overhead.

Gary parked as close as the police would allow. He hustled to what seemed like the command center and found Katrina in the back of an EMS vehicle covered in a blanket. She looked as small as Gary could ever recall; she trembled as she stared at the ground. "Katrina!" Gary called out.

Katrina's head came up slowly, and she recognized Gary. Gary moved quickly to her as she stood from the bench inside the EMS vehicle, the blanket falling from her shoulders. Gary reached up and Katrina fell into his arms, burying her face in his shoulder as she sobbed. "She's dead. She's dead," the words were muffled by Gary's shoulder as he gripped her in his arms.

"I know," Gary whispered, "Are you all right?"

"Colleen…she's gone," the sobs continued.

"What about you? Are you ok?" Gary pleaded for an answer.

"I-I-I think so…but," Katrina shuddered, "Colleen's gone,"

"There was nothing you could do," Gary comforts as he rocks her in his arms. "Thank God, you are ok," he whispers. "You'll be ok. I'm here."

Chapter 33

Summoned

Patrick Ruiz was still at his construction trailer office, directly across from the location of the prairie dog town, on the opposite side of the canyon. Darkness had fallen, but through his window Patrick could see the glowing lights of gathering vehicles. The intensity of lights outside his window was growing, and when the first cherry red emergency lights flickered together with the adjoining blue strobes, he was motivated to investigate.

Patrick was in his truck and moving slowly down the temporary construction road along the grade line when he received the first telephone call. It was James "Corky" Wilson, the superintendent of the construction contractor. Corky was always a gruff man, and tonight was no exception, "Pat, you better get over here," Corky drawled.

"I'm halfway there. What happened?"

"You're going to have to see it to believe," Corky sighed. "One of the transports sheared a wheel. It rolled down the hill and drilled one of the highway department's cars. There was a woman inside, killed."

"Holy shit!" Patrick yells into the phone. "You got to be kidding me!"

"No, sir. Just get over here," Corky orders, disconnecting the call.

The short drive for Patrick from the trailer to the accident scene only took three or four minutes, but in that time, the number of vehicles responding seemed to have doubled. Patrick parked his Laramie Engineering truck about a hundred yards from the crushed sedan with the giant transport tire still embedded. From Patrick's slightly elevated vantage point, he could see that there was no urgency from medical staff or anyone. Away from the wreckage, he noticed another woman in the back of an EMS vehicle. She was sitting, slumped-shouldered, covered with a blanket, and medical staff seemed to be talking to her. Patrick remembered that the environmental people were coming out to review the prairie dog recovery work. It finally dawned on him; these were biologists from the highway department caught in a freak accident. It was Colleen he had spoken to earlier that morning. She had wanted to make sure it was ok to come out and that they wouldn't be in the way. Patrick had assured her it was fine. In fact, he couldn't wait to get that clearance box checked for the prairie dog recovery operation. It was holding up some work, and they wanted to get going as soon as possible. He had often worked with Colleen on many projects in the last few years; she had always been pleasant to work with he remembered. Patrick exhaled as he took in the scene further. He contemplated that the shadowed woman in the EMS vehicle had long hair, it wasn't Colleen...Colleen had short hair; was Colleen dead?

Patrick's phone attached to his hip buzzed and played a light-hearted tune, jolting him from his thoughts of Colleen. He answered the phone, not recognizing the number, "Hello, this is Ruiz."

The thumping of a helicopter rotor broke away for a moment as it repositioned. The threshold of hearing returned momentarily about the same time Patrick heard the governor's voice in a controlled fury over the phone, "This is Stuart. Get yourself to the governor's mansion, now!"

Patrick's body straightened in attention. He stood rigidly and answered, "Yes, sir. Right away, Governor."

The helicopter hovered overhead, and Patrick watched it for a moment, still trying to understand the chaotic scene unfolding below him. Temporary mast lights for construction had been brought in from the top of the mesa mining area and were now fired up and illuminating the scene with bright, harsh light.

Patrick climbed into his truck with a shake of his head, still feeling numb. He pulled away from the scene slowly, careful to avoid any emergency vehicles and the gathering news media vans. His attention caught a speeding truck come to a sliding stop near the yellow police tape barrier. He swore the man running from the truck looked like Gary Hillmann, but Patrick couldn't imagine why Gary would be on the accident scene this quickly.

*   *   *   *   *

Patrick had never been to the governor's mansion. He wasn't sure where he was going, but a quick call to Casey provided the directions through downtown Capitol City and past Fort Randall Park into the foothills and right to the edge of the gated communities of the city's elite neighborhoods. A security officer was waiting for Patrick in the driveway when he arrived about 45 minutes after receiving the call. It was just after 10:00 pm, and Patrick was feeling the long day in his bones. His joints ached from carrying his massive body around; he felt grimy and dirty after a full day on the dusty project, plus he was still haunted by the images of the carnage he saw at the wreck. He had seen people killed on construction sites before in his nearly three decade career; five or six men had died under his watch. This was the first woman killed on his project.

Patrick was escorted by a large man, a security officer casually dressed in khakis and a polo shirt. He was delivered to the mansion's gymnasium where he was left alone with the governor. Governor Stuart Reid-Salazar was walking steadily on a treadmill. He was watching live coverage of the wreckage at the T'rrain Trekker site. KLTW's Dick Forsine, from channel 13 TV was conversing with a reporter getting the details of the breaking story. Closed captions rolled across the screen as the sound was muted. The governor was looking to be in decent shape, having slimmed down considerably for the Presidential campaign on top of a recent heart arrhythmia and orders from his doctor to lose some weight. He played the medical condition to his benefit, surprising many of the political pundits. Reid-Salazar talked publicly about his love of Mexican food and excessive eating. He pointed out that he was like most Americans out there, a bit over weight, and he was going to muster some discipline and work to curtail his appetites. The declaration had bumped his poll number a solid point and half.

Patrick noted to himself how sharp the Governor looked in the flowing silky sweat suit and perfectly styled hair, even during a workout. Governor Reid-Salazar had not been in public the last three days, and he sported a mustache and goatee. Patrick was impressed at how real this man appeared.

The governor hit a button on the treadmill, and the machine returned to level, down from a six percent incline. He hit another button, and the machine slowed to a stop. Governor Reid-Salazar playfully rode the conveyor belt to the edge of the machine, delivering him right in front of Patrick. "Ah, the best part of exercising, riding off the machine, signifying the workout is over," the governor states satisfactorily, smiling. The smile disappears quickly as he addresses Patrick, "Hello, Patrick."

"Governor," Patrick nods in reply.

"Listen to me, and listen to me good, Patrick," Governor Reid-Salazar points a finger in Patrick's face, but backs away to grab a towel and blot sweat from his forehead while regaining his bearing.

"Gov…" Patrick begins but is cut off immediately.

The governor raises a finger at Patrick, "Do not interrupt me," he growls through gritted teeth. He takes a drink of water and motions a hand offering a bottle of water to Patrick. Patrick declines with a wave.

The governor stares at Patrick while Patrick averts his eyes and steals only quick looks to the governor, not maintaining eye contact. Patrick has no idea what to say or do. He tries to speak again, "Can I just…"

Governor Reid-Salazar raises his voice, "Don't you dare! I am doing the talking; you are doing the listening."

One of the longest minutes of Patrick's life ticks by as the governor stares at him, toweling off and drinking water. Finally the governor speaks, "I'm having drinks with some supporters later tonight. I needed to burn some calories with a workout; those drinks, they add up to some worthless pounds." The governor finishes off his water bottle. "It's important to hydrate. We live in a desert; dehydration sneaks up on you."

The governor grabs another bottle of water and tosses it to Patrick, "Drink it." The governor grabs another bottle for himself and drinks again as Patrick fumbles with the cap and nervously takes a swallow.

The governor fixes his gaze on Patrick, "This death on the job site…can we survive this?"

Patrick gives the slightest of nods, and the governor continues, "I'm not covering for you or anyone. If you need to tell me something, tell me now; otherwise, we're getting out in front of this." The governor looks away and exhales deeply, "This is on you, Patrick! Jiminy Christmas! We were just all over the press with positive momentum on the station ribbon cutting, now this!"

Patrick holds up his hands in defense, but doesn't speak. The governor continues, "When I said get things done…" he pauses and shakes his head, "I'm in the campaign of my life!" The governor takes another swallow of water and breathes in through his nose and out through his mouth in exaggerated fashion. He smiles, "Patrick, the Presidential campaign is going good. I've already been told by the two frontrunners that they have a spot for me in their cabinet, if they happen to win. I even look good for a V.P. spot, depending on how the cards fall."

The men stare at each other for nearly a minute in silence. Patrick shakes his head ever so slightly. "All right," the governor waves his hand in disgust, "Speak!"

"I swear to you," Patrick confesses. "It was nothing more than a freak accident."

The governor processes the statement for a full minute trying to gauge whether Patrick is telling the truth. He finally gives a nod to Patrick, "I believe you."

The governor sighs, and Patrick mirrors him with his own deep breath as the tensions ease. "Ok," the governor begins to speak again after a swallow of water. "How are we on the schedule otherwise?"

Patrick perks up; he is in his realm; the construction discussion is his exact comfort zone, "Good, good," Patrick extols. "I had a nice conversation with the Feds the other day." Patrick is speaking a mile a minute, "Do you know Gary Hillmann? Anyway, I talked to him; he's with the Feds. I really think he might come around!"

The governor smiles and puts his arm around Patrick's shoulder. Patrick, a mountain of a man, leans down a bit to make it less awkward for the Governor, but it doesn't help. "Patrick," the governor says, "I like you. You're a good soldier, and I can always use good troops. I have plans for you in the future after I'm elected President or I'm the Secretary of Transportation...that's also been mentioned, among other appointments. Just finish this job...big plans ahead of us, Patrick!"

"Yes, sir!" Patrick calls out excitedly.

The Governor points to the door, "Randy will show you out. Thanks for coming by, Patrick."

Chapter 34

Green Onion

Quaint is the polite word people use when referring to Capitol City's Green Onion Tavern. Located across from the Kmart on St. Thomas Drive, the watering hole caters to a blue collar crowd. It isn't a tourist stop on the sightseeing trail. The non-descript building doesn't grab attention. The tavern sports one outside decoration; it is adorned with an historic satellite dish on the roof. The archaic dish now sports a hand painted shamrock, symbolizing…who knows what…the anonymous artist only knows why it's a shamrock and not an onion.

Even on the brightest of summer days the sunshine of four o'clock in the afternoon would not penetrate the windowless building. Blue collar customers, using a language of the less refined, have a word for the Green Onion…seedy. A bar where people keep to themselves and enjoy their liquor, make their bets with their bookie, and conduct their business out of the mainstream.

On this afternoon, Patrick Ruiz and Casey Baxter sit alone in the darkest back corner of the bar. The only light penetrating their shadowy nook is the neon Grain Belt Beer sign on the opposite wall. Patrick has dragged Casey for a post meeting drink. It was another meeting regarding T'rrain Trekker, updating the project management team on the fatal accident. Casey didn't put up much of a resistance to go for a drink; it was needed after the depressing details of the accident. They were the lone patrons of the bar, and they each nursed a long neck Bud Light. The conversation was sparse between the couple. The multiple televisions hanging on the walls flash sports highlights from ESPN, and Patrick and Casey divide their attention between their beers and the TVs.

Casey finally spoke. The emotions inside of her boiling and breaching the surface, "What the hell is happening, Patrick?"

"Stay calm. It was just an accident," Patrick replies and sips from his beer.

"A woman is dead!" Casey hisses, "She was just doing her job."

"It was an accident!" Patrick whispers through gritted teeth.

"I can't believe this," Casey sighs.

"Don't worry about it," Patrick consoles with a pat of his hand on Casey's shoulder. Casey flinches and pulls away as she sips her beer.

The door opens with a flash of light as a customer enters, letting the blazing sunlight flash through the bar for a second. The bartender barely looks up from restocking the cabinets with a load of clean shot glasses. The new customer stands near the door for a few moments, trying to let his eyes adjust to the darkness. He sees Patrick in the corner, walks directly to their table, and slides into a chair, joining them at the table. Casey leans back and looks at Patrick and then to the man that just sat down. The man slips a backpack from his shoulder. It is a pack a college student might use to carry books for class. Casey glares at the man, "Who the hell are you?"

Patrick holds up a hand, trying to calm Casey. "Casey, I don't know if you remember Dontrell Antonio, he is the governor's Chief of Security. You met him at Rio Ragma."

A look of recognition comes across Casey's face, and she nods to the man.

Dontrell speaks, "It's in the bag at your feet. The man will be here within the hour. Just give him the bag; that's all you have to do."

Security Chief Antonio slides his chair out and stands, "I'll get you two a couple more beers, and also pay for another round for when the man arrives. Have a drink, give him the bag, and that's it."

Patrick nods and Dontrell walks to the bar and speaks to the bartender. He points to Patrick and Casey in the corner, and the bartender's head bobs ever so slightly in acknowledgement. Dontrell drops two one hundred dollar bills on the bar, turns for the exit, and gives a slight nod to Patrick. Patrick touches his eyebrow with two fingers in a semi-salute back to Dontrell. The governor's Chief of Security departs. The light from outside washes over the gloomy bar again momentarily as the door opens and closes.

The bartender moves to their table, sets two more longnecks down, and clears the empty beer bottles, "Thanks," Patrick calls out as the bartender walks away.

"What is going on?" Casey questions. "What the hell is in the bag?"

"I assume it's money," Patrick replies sipping the fresh beer. "They say not to look in the bag, but you can if you want. Nobody'll know."

Patrick picks up the backpack and sets it in front of Casey; Casey grabs the new beer in fear of it being knocked over by the pack. She takes a sip of beer and shoots a puzzled glance from Patrick, to the bag, then to the bartender, and back to the bag.

Casey sets the beer down, unzips the main compartment of the backpack and looks inside. Her eyes widen upon seeing a cube of money wrapped in cellophane. She quickly zips the bag shut and shoves it into Patrick's gut. "What's going on, Patrick? How much money is in there?"

"Thirty grand...I think."

"For what?"

"How do I know," Patrick shrugs as he sips his beer, "I'm just delivering it."

"Jesus Christ, Patrick!"

Patrick scowls at Casey, "Keep your voice down."

Casey starts to hyperventilate, "I-I-I got to get out of here." Casey bolts from her chair, banging her hip on the corner of the table as she hustles out the door. Again the interior is briefly illuminated. Patrick watches the door shut tightly, sealing behind the outside sunlight. He sets the bag on the floor, sips his beer, and waits. He grabs Casey's beer, takes a sip, and sets it down next to his bottle. He rubs his face and smoothes his hair back, knowing what's coming next.

Chapter 35

Summer Scrimmage

"Thanks for getting me out of the house," Katrina whispers to Gary as they walk down the steps to the bleacher seats. Gary lets go of her hand as they move down the steep stairway, "You are very welcome."

The sun sets at University Stadium on the campus of the State University in Allentown. Tonight is a preview of the Mustang football team; it is the summer inter-squad scrimmage of offense versus defense; Maroon versus Black, the school colors at odds on this night. The Mustangs have not faired well in college football as of late, hovering around .500, but losing more than winning. But, hope springs eternal, and Mustang fans have made a decent showing this evening.

"I really miss her. Colleen was my rock…my confidant at the office," Katrina sighs.

Gary nods, "Well, let's not think about it tonight. You have been dwelling on it for awhile; it's time to block it out with some football, at least for an hour or two."

Katrina nods with a smile as the couple inches their way down the aisle, "Geez, I hate going down stairs like this in a crowd. I always get this horrible feeling I'm going to trip."

"Tell me about it," Gary opines. "Just add stairs to my list of fears. For me it's more going up stairs…I always envision myself tripping, falling, and being unable to break my fall. I have this vision of knocking my front teeth out." Gary shudders and runs his tongue over his teeth subconsciously.

"Teeth? Why teeth?" Katrina poses the question.

"I'm not exactly sure. I'm inclined to attribute my teeth fetish to my distaste for my orthodontist when I was a kid. It hurt so bad when they tightened the braces each month. For some reason I associate horrible pain with my teeth."

"Ok, weirdo," Katrina shakes her head as she points to the seats. "Here we are, safe and sound, teeth intact."

"Good crowd," Gary notes aloud as they sit down in row twenty overlooking the twenty-five yard line on the north end of the stadium. College students attending summer school have assembled a makeshift pep band and play *Roll Out the Barrel* as the Mustangs progress through pre-game warm up drills. The heat of the summer day slowly dissipates as the sun curves downward for a late 8:30 pm start time; the late start is a minor concession for combating the heat, at least for the players' sake. It is a start time rather than a kickoff. No special teams for the scrimmage; no kickoffs, no punts, no extra points; just back and forth between offense and defense. The 150 plus players are divided up, half on the Maroon sideline and the other half on the Black sideline. Most of these players will never see the field in a sanctioned NCAA football game, but tonight everyone will get at least a play or two on the field.

As the pep band plays a version of the Bill Haley & His Comets theme from the TV show *Happy Days*, Gary reviews the game program. Katrina surveys the crowd; she elbows Gary and points to a section over and down a few rows. Gary doesn't look up immediately and feels a sharper elbow to the ribs.

"Ow! What! At ease on the violence," Gary grimaces.

"I was just wanting to point somebody out to you," Katrina points, and Gary follows her finger. "Isn't that your computer guy with his daughter?"

"Where?"

"Are you looking where I'm pointing," Katrina whines.

"Yeah? I don't see 'em!"

Gary leans over into Katrina, craning his neck, "Oh yeah. Yup, it's them. It looks like Casey Baxter is sitting next to them. That must be Casey's daughter?"

"I guess their daughters must be friends," Gary shrugs, "Interesting that they would come to a football game."

"Just something to do, I guess," Katrina nods. "Are you going to go over and say, 'Hi'?"

"Hell no!" Gary's voice hits a falsetto.

Katrina laughs, "I was just kidding!"

"I should hope so," Gary shakes his head and smiles.

*   *   *   *   *

The scrimmage begins in earnest, and Maroon dominates Black up and down the field. The lopsided competition is exciting from the fans' perspective as long passes and long runs are common place. On the defensive side, interceptions and fumbles punctuate the off-season rust of the skill players.

Below Gary and Katrina, Casey and Chuck watch the game and share casual conversation. "What is going on with the train?" Chuck asks trying to make small talk.

"Did you hear anything in your office about the lady that got killed?" Casey replies with her own question.

"No, but, that's not what I was talking about. There was an inspector from the highway department over in our office the other day, I guess. I thought I overheard Gary talking to Diego about a whistle blower."

Casey's blood runs cold. She tries to remain calm, but she can't contain herself as she is gripped with concern. "What? Tell me everything you heard!"

Chuck continues, "I don't know what they said, something about inspection reports on a laptop. Bryan was going with this guy…Ricardo? I can't remember the guy's name. I don't know; I wasn't really listening. I was working on Gary's computer in the office next to Diego's. I thought maybe you'd know."

Casey's head spins. Her face turns ghostly pale.

"Are you all right?" Chuck inquires.

"Yeah…yeah." Casey nods.

The scrimmage grinds on, but Casey is a million miles away. Patrick is all she can think about. She knows she has to inform Patrick about what she has learned.

*   *   *   *   *

The banks of lights on the south end of the field suddenly flicker, dim, and go out, darkening half the stadium. To the mercy of the Black Team, the game is called and the rout ends favor of Maroon Team.

The public address announcer conveys the message that the game has been called due to the light system failure. He assures the crowd that everything will be in working order come September 2nd, the kickoff of the home season. "Drive safely!" the announcer's voice echoes through the darkness. "Good night."

*   *   *   *   *

The crowd begins to file out. Gary grabs Katrina's arm, "Let's hang back a moment," Gary announces. "I don't want to cross paths with Chuck and Casey."

Katrina nods, confirming the strategy. They see Chuck and Casey herd their daughters ahead and melt into the crowd of people. Gary gives the ok to begin to ascend the stairs a safe distance behind. After the couple climbs the twenty-five steps without a mishap, they merge with the stream of people moving its way toward the parking areas. Gary and Katrina shuffle along with the crowd, inching towards the stadium exit and parking lot. Gary suddenly arm-bars Katrina; she shoots Gary a dirty look. Gary grabs her arm and pulls her out of the stream of people. He points. A hundred feet ahead, a massive man, Patrick Ruiz, looks over the crowd of people from his position at the corner of the bleachers. "Let's just wait until he leaves. I don't want to have him see me and come up and start talking to me."

"Fine."

Gary and Katrina stand out of line, and people trudge by. Patrick is scanning the crowd intently as Gary and Katrina keep an eye on him. He finally moves out like a man with a purpose, pushing through the crowd toward the gate.

Gary turns to Katrina, "Ok, let's move."

Gary and Katrina move through the gate with a watchful eye. From the elevated position on the sloping ramp to the parking lot, they see Patrick Ruiz focused on something ahead of him as he walks slowly. The crowd passes him, and he stares at something. He is oblivious to anything else.

Katrina figures it out first, "Look, he's following Chuck and Casey. He's just staring at them. You remember that night at Juanita's? Patrick and Casey were there together; now it looks like Patrick is stalking Casey."

"Wow. That is weird. Come on, let's go home. Man, Casey sure gets around." Gary shakes his head. He grabs Katrina's hand, and they move down the ramp, keeping their distance from Patrick, Casey, and Chuck.

Chapter 36

Special Delivery

It's hard to fathom how many federal laws were being broken this afternoon in Gary's neighborhood. An actual postal vehicle, stolen from somewhere, or maybe as close of a facsimile to the real thing was mocked up by a creative individual for covert operations. The little postal truck meandered down the avenue, stopping in front of Gary Hillmann's street-side mailbox. It was a "special delivery" brought by a generic looking Hispanic man dressed in a postman's uniform; the man was not a postal worker; he was a hired killer; a hit man.

A casual observer would notice nothing but the mail being delivered; a serious neighborhood watcher might have found it odd that the mailman passed all the houses, delivered mail to one house, midblock, and took off not delivering any other mail. It was a very clever disguise. The bomb planted by the hit man was crude. A rudimentary explosive device, even by the hit man's own professional standard. The simple, black powder propellant, found at nearly any sporting goods and hunting stores in the area, was a purposeful effort. It was nearly untraceable in its commonality. The metal case enclosing the powder was some stock plumber's pipe, available in any hardware store. Added to the killing potency of the device was a handful of miscellaneous nails ranging in length, taped to the pipe by duct tape. All told, the approximate two pound package was sickeningly simple. The triggering mechanism was wired to the metal mailbox door; when opened, after about two-tenths of a second, the explosion would occur. The metal mailbox itself would provide additional shrapnel.

The setting of the bomb into the box took slightly longer than a normal mail delivery, but not enough to draw attention, even if somebody was watching. The packaged was delivered, and the impostor courier was down the street and disappearing into and out of the residential neighborhood, joining the city traffic with no one the wiser.

*　　*　　*　　*　　*

Gary and Katrina have finished up work and are returning to Gary's house after a long mid-week day. The evening was already planned: water the tomatoes and flowers in the yard, have a light supper and finally, after the evening has cooled down a bit, go for a walk... the usual big plans for a week night.

As Gary pulls his truck onto his street with Katrina in the passenger seat, he announces with a huge sigh of relief, "Anotha' day, anotha dolla', Dog!"

Gary's proclamation produces the usual result, a reaction of eye-rolling and contempt from Katrina, but in a playful sense. Katrina clicks her tongue and responds, "Why do you always say that?"

"Hmmm? Say what?"

"That stupid dog saying... Why do you always say that?"

"Huh, I was barely aware that I said it. That's funny. It's a long story and we're almost home," Gary waves to the driveway as he pulls the pickup truck past the drive and prepares to back up. He throws the truck into reverse, looks over his shoulder and backs into the driveway, finally parking the truck and killing the engine. "Anyhoo, it's a long story and we are home, so I don't want to get into it. I will tell you that it is sports related." Gary adds with his index finger extended straight into the air. "Let's talk about it later. Remind me when we go for a walk."

Gary begins to open his door, but the wind forces his door shut, "Gosh. It's really windy."

Katrina is in a feisty mood, and she jumps at a chance to attack, especially after being shut down on the dog story, "Really? 'Gosh?'" Katrina makes finger quotes. "Did you really just say 'Gosh'?"

"Yeah, it's an expression of surprise. The wind blowing kind of surprised me."

"What are you from the 1950's? Who says 'Gosh' anymore?"

Gary stares at Katrina as he holds onto the steering wheel. He is puzzled by her attack, shaking his head from side to side and flashing a crooked smile.

Katrina continues in a weird 1950's, overly enunciated TV accent, "Golly, gee Beave. Gosh, sure is windy!"

Gary lifts a hand as to partially shrug one shoulder while he continues to slightly shake his head in disbelief. He stares at her another moment and smiles wryly, "What?"

"That's how you sound!" Katrina retorts.

"Whatever."

Katrina exhales in a huff, "I'm just saying you sometimes sound ridiculous, and it bugs me." Katrina sighs again, "Just sometimes."

Gary lifts his eyebrows in wariness, "Okaaaay…I'm going to get the mail. Watch the door when you get out. The wind is gusty; I think we solidly established that fact."

Gary steps from the truck and walks in the street to avoid the wind-waving branches hanging over the tree-lined sidewalk. Katrina exits the vehicle, and her wide-brimmed sun hat is ripped from her hand by a gust of wind. The hat blows past Gary in a blink of an eye as it rolls down the street, driven by the breeze.

"Help! Gary! Get my hat!"

Gary reaches for the mailbox, but doesn't open it. Instead he takes off dodging back and forth across the street trying to corral the straw hat. A half block later he has captured the run away hat. He holds it up in victory as he walks against the blustery wind back to the house. Gary smiles and notes the postman turning onto his street. The mail man stops, delivers mail to the first house on the street, pulls to the next house, delivers, and finally passes Katrina with a wave before pulling up to Gary's mailbox. Gary walks down the middle of the street a couple hundred feet from the vehicle. Gary looks past the postal vehicle and sees Katrina opening his pickup's driver's side door, the opposite side of the truck facing the postal vehicle. Gary wonders for a moment what Katrina is grabbing from the truck, oblivious to the mailman opening Gary's mailbox and triggering the bomb. Gary is knocked to the ground from the concussion of the explosion even from 150 feet away. The postal vehicle is an unrecognizable, contorted, piece of metal; the frame is bent in a 90 degree angle. Letters and papers rain down in the air, swirling in the blustery breeze.

Gregory L. Heitmann

Chapter 37

Nailed It

The explosion picked Gary off his feet and flung him to the ground, bouncing him into the gutter a good twenty feet from where he had been standing. Gary pushes himself from the curb opposite from the middle of the street where he was just walking. Deafened and staggering, he holds his head and ears, pressure in his skull pounds his brain. Everything Gary sees has a tint of red; the shock wave of the blast squeezed his body in ways unimaginable; after a moment or two, the pain in every part of his body starts to subside.

Katrina's screams fall on Gary's deaf ears as he staggers toward the flames of the exploded vehicle. The fire produces a thick, greasy, black smoke. Gary curses and reaches for a pain in his lower leg but presses forward to see if Katrina is ok. Katrina peers out from the protection provided by Gary's truck and sees Gary stumbling his way down the street. She sprints from behind the truck and meets Gary near a chunk of the front end of the mangled postal vehicle. Katrina holds up a wobbly Gary.

Gary and Katrina peer down at the postman's twisted and bent body, pressed against the pavement by the vehicle's door and frame.

Gary shouts at Katrina, "Are you all right?" He is deafened by the blast and the ringing in his ears racks his brain.

Katrina is also suffering the effects of the concussion of the blast on her ear drums. She hollers back, "I think so!"

Gary holds on to Katrina as he tries to shake the cobwebs from his mind. The vehicle flickers in flames but has nearly burned itself and the letters in its cargo to nothing. Debris and papers scatter in the wind. A man emerges from a house three doors down with a phone pressed to his ear. One arm waving wildly, as if the 911 operator could see his beckoning motions.

Gary's eyes wander to the body of the dead postal worker, "Oh, my God!" he shouts.

"What?"

Gary points crazily at the body, "Look! Look at the man's name tag!"

"What about it?" Katrina squints as she leans toward the body but holding Gary tightly in restraint.

"His name tag, G. Zuss! G. Zuss! G. Zuss is dead! It's like, you know, Jesus."

Katrina screams at Gary, "What is wrong with you!"

Gary grips Katrina as tight as he can in his arms, "I'm just glad to be alive. I'm obviously in shock."

Katrina's tears flow freely as she holds Gary and leads him past the curb and eases him to the driveway. Katrina opens the tailgate of the truck and Gary sits. The first faint sound of a siren is heard over the roar of the breeze and the crackling of the fire. Several neighbors arrive on the scene and begin to offer assistance.

"I'm alright!" Gary insists as police arrive on scene, followed by fire and EMS.

Katrina grabs Gary and hugs him again. She pushes him back and grabs at his leg as she yells out, "Your leg! There's blood all over your pant leg! You're hurt!" She grabs at Gary's leg.

"Ow...ow...ow," Gary winces as Katrina rolls up his pant leg. "Dang it! These pants are ruined," Gary complains.

Katrina glares at Gary. Gary's khakis sport a small blood stain and as Katrina makes the final roll on his pants, the fabric snags and rips. "Owwww!" Gary cries.

Gary looks to Katrina. She is staring wide-eyed at Gary's shin. Gary looks down and sees a nail protruding from his leg. "Uh-oh," Gary mumbles, "This is not good."

Two neighbors observing Katrina's work, wince as they see the nail sticking from the leg. Emergency vehicles start to arrive from every direction. The quiet neighborhood street is turned into a disaster scene. Police burst from vehicles and corner the people gathering and begin a barrage of questions for anyone and everyone. But, no one has any answers. The fire has burned to nearly nothing, and firemen use extinguishers rather than hooking hoses to hydrants to squelch any remaining flames.

Katrina begins to hyperventilate as she continues to stare at the nail in Gary's leg. "Oh my God! Oh my God! Oh my God!" Katrina calls out in rapid succession as she gasps.

Gary grasps at Katrina, but can't reach her, "Take it easy."

"Paramedics! Help! We need medical assistance over here!" Katrina yells over her shoulder. She looks at the closest man standing nearby, a neighbor from across the street, "Go get a medic, please!" Katrina yells.

The man hesitates and nods. He turns and runs toward the emergency vehicles in the street.

"What the Hell happened?" Gary manages to ask Katrina.

Tears still stream from Katrina's eyes, "I don't know. After I lost my hat and saw that you got it, I moved to the other side of the truck to grab my phone. The phone had fallen from my purse onto the floor of the driver's side."

"Geez, you're lucky. The truck shielded you," Gary notes as Katrina wipes her eyes and leans into Gary, burying her head into his shoulder. "You're ok," Gary whispers as he pats her back.

Gary shakes his head in disbelief, "I didn't see anything. After I grabbed your hat, I looked up and saw you on the other side of the truck. I was wondering, 'what the heck is she doing now?' Next thing I know, I was laying in the gutter, against the curb."

Katrina looks up. She stares into Gary's eyes and kisses him. Gary wipes her tears. Katrina looks past Gary and says, "Hey, here comes a policeman, maybe he can tell us what happened."

The policeman is holding a notepad. He is dressed in his dark blue uniform and looks back and forth between Gary and Katrina, "What happened?" he inquires, pen in hand to take notes.

Gary and Katrina exchange puzzled looks. Katrina responds somewhat indignantly, "You tell us. We need a paramedic over here!"

The policeman looks over his shoulder and gestures with his pen, "They're coming. They're looking at the postman."

Gary scoffs, "That guy was definitely dead. His name is G. Zuss." Gary looks to Katrina, "Remember when I said that? They killed G. Zuss?" Gary turns his attention to the policeman, "I saw his name tag. It was G period then Z-u-s-s. If you say it fast, it sounds like Jesus."

The policeman writes it in his pad. A smile comes across his face as he says it out loud, "G-Zuss." He gives a small laugh, "It does!"

He looks to see Katrina scowling at him. The smile disappears from his face and is replaced by a solemn look.

"G-Zuss," Gary repeats one more time.

"Stop saying that!" Katrina shouts.

Gary smiles wryly, "I think I'm going into shock."

Katrina frowns, "Knock it off!"

Gary realizes he feels relatively fine, except for the nail in his leg, unscathed considering the circumstance. He sighs in relief, "I got a few scrapes, but if this nail is the worst I got...pretty lucky."

Katrina musters a bit of smile. The tears have subsided, streaks of grime and dust trace across the paths of the teardrops. She nods in agreement and hugs Gary.

The policeman interrupts, "First thoughts are that it was a bomb. There was the smell of cordite or gunpowder...pretty pungent when the firemen got the flames out."

Gary nods, "Yeah, I had that acrid taste in my mouth when I was in the gutter. I was downwind of the blast, I bet I have bomb residue all over me." Gary holds up his arms and looks at his dirty shirt and pants.

"Oh, God. I do not want to go to the hospital," Gary ponders out loud.

"You are going to the hospital! There is a nail in your leg!" Katrina insists.

The policeman grimaces, "Yeah, you are never supposed to pull out an imbedded object in your body by yourself. You might nick an artery or something. They taught us that at the academy."

"See?" Katrina raises a hand, deferring to the policeman.

As a paramedic approaches, Katrina continues, "Here's a medic; he'll tell you if you have to go to the hospital."

The paramedic looks at Katrina, "Are you hurt, ma'am?"

"No! It's my boyfriend," Katrina points at Gary's leg.

"Sir, are you injured?" the paramedic asks.

Gary looks at Katrina and back to the medic, "I think so. There is a nail sticking out of my leg."

"Mmm-hmm," the medic considers the wound as he looks at Gary's pupils and grabs his wrist for a pulse.

Gary looks back to Katrina, "You could say that I got nailed."

Katrina mockingly smiles, "Hilarious. Now, stop it! Sit still."

Gary looks to the paramedic and inquires, "Hey, do you have some really good drugs? Painkillers, per chance?"

Katrina interrupts, "Gary…"

The paramedic deflects the conversation, "I think you are going to be fine, sir."

"Good," Gary nods, "Now…about those drugs."

Katrina takes a swipe at Gary's head, "Knock it off," she growls through gritted teeth.

The paramedic looks at Katrina, "Ma'am, could you stand aside? Thanks." Katrina moves back, and the paramedic begins placing an I.V. in Gary's arm. The paramedic forces a smile, "We'll let a doctor decide on any pain meds. We are going to have to haul you in. A doctor's going to have to remove that nail."

The policeman pipes in, looking over the paramedics shoulder at Gary, "I told you." He gives Gary a thumbs up.

Gary rolls his eyes, "Great."

The paramedic stands and hands the I.V. bag to the policeman. "Here," the medic says, "make yourself useful." He looks down at Gary, "I'll get the gurney, and we'll get you loaded up."

Gregory L. Heitmann

Chapter 38

Bomber? I Hardly Know 'er!

Gary was adequately pain free. He was, by doctor's orders, administered a mild sedative and some morphine through his I.V. upon arrival. He was resting comfortably in the emergency room behind the drawn curtain. Miscellaneous other traumas were being tended to behind other partitions, but Gary's leg with a nail in it had fallen to a low priority. He was stable and feeling well thanks to the modern pharmaceuticals.

Gary smiled uncontrollably. The abrasions from skidding across the pavement on his arms and face resembled raspberries and looked menacing, but he smiled. Katrina sat by his side holding his hand. She was not smiling. She was exhausted. The adrenaline had long disappeared, and now the fatigue set in with a vengeance. Gary turns his head and looks at Katrina, "Why don't you go home? I'll call you if they discharge me. I'm fine…now. Go get cleaned up; get some sleep."

Katrina blinks back to reality from her daze. She runs her fingers through her tangled hair and rubs her eyes with the heels of her hands. Her eyes are dark and puffy from crying. "Uhg," Katrina grumbles, "I must look a fright."

Gary reaches and brushes her cheek with his finger, "You look as beautiful as can be for a victim of a bombing. I just don't like seeing the tear stains."

Katrina musters a smile momentarily. The smile disappears as the curtain around Gary's bed is flung open. "Hey!" Gary calls out, surprised by the flying screen.

A man with a trench coat and fedora, the uniform of every clichéd detective novel, appears before Gary. The man is large and Hispanic; he flashes a badge.

"Hi," the detective mumbles stashing his badge back in his coat pocket, "I'm Detective Navidad."

"Whoa…Detective Christmas," Gary points out quickly with a glance to Katrina.

"Yes, thanks for pointing that out," the man nods.

"Sorry," Gary drops his eyes in shame, but immediately returns his gaze to the detective. He points his finger at the man. "Wait a minute. I know you. Weren't you…"

Katrina finishes Gary's sentence, "…Betsy's date…at the party with her sister, Sarah?"

The detective puts his hands up in defense, "Guilty." He digs in his coat pocket and pulls out a notepad and pen. "What happened today?"

"I got a nail in my leg," Gary announces loudly.

"I can see that," the detective replies sharply. "What caused that to happen? Who did you piss off? Who would want to blow you up?"

"What?" Gary asks.

"Oh, my God!" Katrina cries, "Someone tried to kill him?"

"What?" Gary inquires again, straining to understand.

The detective closes the notebook and unclicks his pen. "Well, the preliminary look shows that the bomb was in your mailbox. At first we thought it might have been in the truck with the way it was damaged, but they are pretty sure it was in the box. They screwed it up. They missed the obvious trigger of the actual postman setting it off."

"Oh, my God!" Katrina shouts again. "You were just about to get the mail. If my hat hadn't blown off." Katrina's lip quivers and her eyes well again with tears.

"Why would somebody want to blow me up?" Gary poses the question with a puzzled look.

The detective opens his notebook again, "Do you have a disgruntled neighbor? Did you cut somebody off in traffic recently? What about work?"

Katrina gasps and loses all color, "T'rrain Trekker," she whispers, her voice husky and trembling.

"What? Are you kidding me?" Gary shakes his head, "Who would want to kill me?" Gary looks to Katrina and back to the detective. "No way. Nobody wants to kill me. It was probably mistaken identity if anything."

"You and your office are pissing off all kinds of people!" Katrina insists. "That stupid train, especially."

"What?" Gary grunts the word incredulously, "Me? I'm a low-level bureaucrat. Nobody cares what I do!"

"Stop saying 'what,'" Katrina orders. "You guys…Diego, Bryan, and you…y'all touched a nerve. That train is the governor's baby."

"Yeah, right," Gary waves away her accusation. "The train is practically built; nobody in my office has stood in its way. What are you talking about?"

Katrina throws her head back in disgust and stares at the ceiling, "This is making me sick. I can't believe this is happening."

Gary is mystified, "What? Nothing is happening."

"The stations, Gary," Katrina snaps. "The commuter rail stations."

All three fall silent. The detective finishes his notes. A commotion behind an adjacent curtain occurs as another trauma is brought in.

Detective Navidad breaks the silence with a staccato-monotone delivery of facts, "It was a bomb. You are very lucky to be alive. Your mailbox was packed with explosives and shrapnel intended to kill. That nail in your leg...exhibit A. I'm also here to collect that as evidence."

"What?" Gary cries, "Seriously? I don't even get to keep it as a souvenir?"

"Seriously," the detective replies, "that's evidence."

"Jesus," Gary says in disgust. He pauses and repeats the homophone, "G. Zuss."

The detective flips through his pad, "Yes...Mr. G. Zuss. Guillermo Zuss. Three years on the job as a postal carrier. Dead. He was the lone fatality. Killed by the bomb meant for you."

Detective Navidad exhales deeply, "Well," the detective removes a business card from his notepad, "here's another card," the detective hands the card over with a wink. "I assume you lost the one I gave you at the party. If you think of anything, give me a call." He smiles and points a finger at Gary and then to the nail protruding from Gary's leg, "Don't forget that nail is mine. Don't even think of asking the doctor to give it to you."

The detective departs, flinging the flimsy, curtain divider closed.

Chapter 39

If I Had A Hammer

When the doctor finally pulled open the curtain two hours later, Katrina and Gary were numb. Gary numb from painkilling drugs, and Katrina just plain rung out from the drama. They did wake up to see a doctor staring at a clipboard reading Gary's chart. They both turn to each other and exchange puzzled looks of people having a prank pulled on them. The doctor spoke without looking up, "Hello, my name is Doctor Cohen."

When the doctor finished reading the chart, he looked up to see two blank-looking faces staring holes through him. Gary points at the doctor, "You know…you look like…"

The doctor cuts Gary off. "Ah," he laughs, "I see you were fans of ER."

Doctor Cohen removes his circular, wire-rimmed glasses and steps closer. "As you can see," he continues, "I kind of look like character Dr. Mark Greene, played by Anthony Edwards. Yes, yes, I realize this. No need to point it out." The doctor puts his glasses back in place.

Katrina chimes in, "It's got to be distracting to resemble a famous TV doctor."

Dr. Cohen sighs, "Yes, the funny thing is, I'm almost a foot shorter than Anthony Edwards." The doctor laughs again, "I often think about who has it worse, Anthony Edwards, who people think is a doctor, or me…who people think I'm an actor, possibly playing a doctor."

Katrina speaks up apologetically, "I'm sorry; it just seemed like it had to be pointed out. It was the elephant in the room. You look so much like Anthony Edwards."

"Talk to me, Goose," Gary offers smiling.

Katrina tries to stifle a laugh and snorts, "Good one."

Dr. Cohen shakes his head, "I hear that less and less, but I still hear it."

"Come on," Gary interjects, *"Top Gun* was a classic…Tom Cruise…Kelly McGillis….awesome movie."

Dr. Cohen bends down to look at the nail sticking out of Gary's leg. He puts his face within an inch or two of the nail, observing the injury. "Hmmmm," Doctor Cohen emits a sound befitting the puzzling injury. He grabs onto the nail with his hand, presses down on Gary's leg with the other, and pulls on the nail.

Gary howls, more in surprise than in pain, but still in some pain. The nail doesn't budge. "Yup," the doctor nods, "Pretty standard 16 penny nail, galvanized."

Doctor Cohen lets go of the nail and backs away. He grabs his chin and rubs it, thinking. "I guess," Doctor Cohen says, "it's in the bone pretty good. The galvanized surface helps hold it in there."

"So?" Gary wonders aloud, "What's next?"

Doctor Cohen shrugs, "What else can we do? We need the proper tools. Guess I'd better find a hammer." The doctor smiles and gives a knowing nod, "I'll be back with a hammer, a piece of wood, and a couple nurses to hold you down…Don't worry, you're going to be fine."

Gary laughs, dismissing the doctor's proposed procedure as a bit of medical humor. Gary's eyes nearly popped from his head when the curtain opened again, and the doctor, accompanied by two hefty nurses, entered. The nurses grabbed Gary's leg, one at the knee, the other at the ankle. The doctor moved in quickly, "I checked your x-ray again; no problems."

Doctor Cohen places the short two by four chunk of scrap next to the nail and announces, "I had this hammer and pieces of wood in my truck. Pretty lucky."

The doctor attaches the claw over the nail and pries the nail out with steady pressure. As the nail eases free, a trickle of blood oozes from the hole. Gary, virtually paralyzed at the quick action of the doctor, does not say a word or cry. He is too surprised at everything that just happened; his only reaction is eyes as big as saucers. A nurse puts pressure on the wound, holding gauze over the blood.

The doctor admires the nail in his gloved hand. He holds the nail between his index finger and thumb. "Hmm, didn't even bend it," he remarks offering it to Gary.

Gary takes the nail in his hand. The doctor gives a smile, "You can't keep it. The detective already told me he needs it as evidence. Who knows, maybe someday you'll get it back."

Gary hands the nail back to the doctor, "Thanks, Doc. That barely hurt."

The doctor hands the nail to a nurse, and she places it in an evidence bag left by the detective.

"No problem," Doctor Cohen replies. "We aim to please. Listen, you are going to have to take it easy for month or so. That nail probably weakened your tibia, so, no exertion like sports or running. Get out and walk...drink some extra milk."

"Ok," Gary nods.

"The nurses will get you bandaged up; I'll get you a script for an antibiotic...wait a minute," the doctor grabs the chart and flips through. "Ah," he resumes the instructions, "the nurse will give you a tetanus shot too, just in case. That should do it...we'll get you outta here within the hour."

"Thanks again, Doc," Gary acknowledges.

"Thank you, *Dr. Greene*," Katrina says with a smile.

Dr. Cohen returns the smile and moves to the next curtain.

When the final nursing chores were completed, the last remaining nurse announced, "There you go. Give us forty minutes to get the papers filled out, and we'll send you home."

Gary nods to the nurse. If Katrina was tired before, she was exhausted now. She climbs into the bed and settles next to Gary. Gary pulls her close, "You want me to wake you when we're home?"

Katrina closes her eyes and nods, "I need to rest so I can keep you safe."

Gary runs his fingers through Katrina's hair as she settles in closer, "What do mean?" Gary whispers.

Katrina whispers back, "You know what I mean. I'm from Capitol City; I know how the politics work." Katrina opens her eyes and looks at Gary for a moment, then closes her eyes. "Don't worry; I won't let the bad men get you."

Gary smiles and laughs silently, shaking the bed, "You have a vivid, conspiratorial imagination." Gary continues to stroke Katrina's hair, gently untangling strands as he carefully passes his fingers through her locks. "I only wish I had the power and influence you and others seem to think I have."

Katrina smiles and wriggles closer trying to get comfortable, "I told you; don't worry, you are safe with me."

Gary shakes his head. He kisses Katrina's cheek. Gary whispers, "You should be more concerned about how we are going to get home, than about these boogey men out there. We'll have to get a taxi."

Gary closes his eyes and waits for his discharge papers.

Gregory L. Heitmann

Chapter 40

To Be Brief

When all was said and done for the week, Gary missed a couple of days of work and was healing at home. Meanwhile, Bryan's leg was mending on the job. He was already rid of his crutches and in a walking boot surrounding the fiberglass cast. He insisted that even with some pain, he would rather be putting weight on his leg, rather than letting the muscle atrophy away to nothing inside a cast.

The first thing on Tuesday morning was an impromptu staff meeting to discuss the recent happenings. Diego had asked Bryan to round up everyone in the office in order to provide an update. At 9:30 a.m., everyone was situated in the conference room. The room is longer than wide with a large table that comfortably sits twelve people. The most dominating feature in the room was the large television monitor, a 45-inch flat screen for video-conferencing. Opposite the monitor was a white board stretching from the floor to ceiling. Diego was the last to take his seat amongst all the full chairs surrounding the table. Diego cleared his throat, "I will be brief. I just wanted to talk to everyone about the rash of incidents that have occurred in and out of our office. As you are well aware, there was a fatality on the T'rrain Trekker project last week. A good friend of this office, Colleen Davison, was killed. I know some of you will be attending her funeral services. We have a card circulating for her family. Please sign it."

Diego pauses to smooth the fabric of his black suit jacket's lapel. He is dressed in his black suit and red tie with white shirt for his weekly meeting later that afternoon with the highway department executive management. He taps a finger on his lips and continues, "Our very own, wounded warrior, Bryan, can update you on his status and Gary's condition, Bryan."

"Thanks, Diego," Bryan acknowledges. "Well, everyone, I'm feeling a lot better. I got the ok from my doctor to ditch the crutches. I'm still not back on my bike yet, but in a couple weeks, I'll be as good as new." Bryan gives himself a thumbs up.

Bryan looks at his notes in front of him before continuing. "I'm not sure if everyone knows, but Gary was injured in an explosion outside his house, right on the street."

Sylvia interrupts, "What caused the explosion?"

Bryan shakes his head, "All that was reported on the news and in the paper was that it was either a defective postal vehicle or letter bomb being transported by the vehicle."

Sylvia follows up with another question, "Is Gary going to be ok?"

"That's some of the good news I have to report," Bryan sighs with relief. "I did speak to Gary and he's fine, resting comfortably in the care of Katrina for a couple days."

"Did he say what happened?" Sylvia inquires.

"He took a piece of shrapnel in his leg, right in the shin. Doctors had to yank it out, but he said doctors assured him he will have a full recovery. He'll be out for a couple more days."

"Thank God," Sylvia exhales and looks to heaven.

"Thanks, Bryan," Diego nods, "Why don't you go over the safety briefing."

"Sure," Bryan continues, "in the wake of all these accidents: my bike crash with a dog, Gary's random explosion, and Colleen's worksite death, we thought it would be a good idea to review some of the safety policies of the office."

Bryan hands out some papers. "First of all, accidents happen. We will never be able to avoid every accident, but we can minimize risk. I've handed out a list of simple policies for construction inspections, i.e., vests and hard hats. Plus," Bryan looks at Chuck, "I've also included a handout about safety in the office. Chuck, please note the information about fire safety including extension cords and overloading outlets."

Tension is lifted in the meeting slightly as everyone gets a small laugh at Chuck's expense as they recall the recent fire in the server room. Diego gives an approving nod and takes control of the meeting. "Finally, I wanted to say a few words about the commuter rail project. You have probably heard lots of rumors about the train. Let me assure you, we are working with the highway department through the processes to get it built. There have been a lot of negative things said in the paper and on the TV news about the slow development and apparent lack of cooperation from our office."

Diego pauses to wipe his glasses. He replaces his spectacles and continues, "I don't want you to get caught up in all the politics of this train; that is my job as the director of this office." Diego looks around the room, meeting the eyes of the employees.

"There will continue to be additional scrutiny on the T'rrain Trekker, especially since the fatality at the construction site," Diego continues coolly. "Just continue to do your jobs. Review the safety precautions outlined in the handouts Bryan provided. The commuter rail is drawing national attention with the governor's Presidential bid. Make sure we follow all our processes including the safety processes. Cross all the 't's,' dot all the 'i's. If there are questions about the train, feel free to direct them to me."

Diego pauses and surveys the room, "Are there any questions?"

Everyone looks around at each other, but there are no questions. "Ok," Diego notes with all seriousness, "I want to thank everyone. Keep up the good work. All I can ask is that you continue to do the right things, right."

Diego pauses a moment, leaning forward in his chair. He sweeps his finger around the room, "The discomfort you sense coming from the highway department…that is a sign that we are all doing our jobs. I commend everyone on a job well done."

Diego nods, satisfied and proud of his team, "Thanks again. We'll get through this tough time. I know there are a lot of personal feelings and emotions involved with all that is going on; I ask that you do your best to manage them and be professional with our partners. I know you will. Is there anything else, Bryan?"

Bryan raises his hand and announces, "Yeah, one more thing. I will be out tomorrow; I have to go to Mora for a preconstruction meeting. I might be late getting back, so I probably won't be in until the afternoon, the day after tomorrow."

"Safety first, out there. No shortcuts. Thanks, everyone," Diego calls out as an adjournment to the meeting.

Gregory L. Heitmann

Chapter 41

Mora

The morning started earlier than usual for Bryan. He was at the office before 7:00 a.m., waiting for Rico Suarez to pick him up to travel to the town of Mora. A pre-construction meeting with a contractor was set to take place at 9:00 a.m., and if they drove steadily from Capitol, they would make it in time to maybe grab a cup of coffee and a donut before the meeting. The unincorporated village of Mora lies on the eastern edge of the Sangre de Sustantivo Mountains. Considered a gateway into the wilderness areas of the mountains, Mora is the largest of several communities along State Highway 51 as it winds along the Mora River; Schulman, Chico, Farnsworth, and Lloyd all lie along the Mora River Valley.

As the crow flies from Mora to Capitol City, it is a little more than forty miles; by highway, it is more than double that distance. The road trip from the capital to Mora skirts the southern end of the Sangre de Sustantivo Mountains on Interstate 11, traveling through Baptiste Pass along Baptiste Mesa to reach the largest community found in the northeast part of the state, Eli. The trip from Capitol City to Eli on Interstate winds through some rugged country, actually taking you south a few miles before straightening and delivering a northerly reckoning, according to Interstate signage. Thirty miles north of Eli on Sate Highway 51 is where the highway department patrol yard is located; a maintenance depot for the care of state designated highways in the region by government forces.

The winter is a very busy time for this patrol yard, plowing snow and maintaining access to Shoshone Ski Resort, but on this summer day, the thought of snow was far from anyone's mind. Today's pre-construction meeting was for routine highway construction activities consisting of what is known as a "mill and fill." Old asphalt pavement is removed via a grinding or milling machine, the mill portion. Next is the fill portion, a

191

new layer of asphalt is placed, providing an improved surface, hopefully maintenance free for the next five years.

It is not clear where the Village of Mora got its name. The arguments range from the Spanish term "lo de mora," or stopping place, possibly a surname Mora from Spanish settlers after the Pueblo revolt, or even another Spanish term moras, or mulberries found sporadically along the river. Where the name derives from is a mystery that will probably never be solved, but one thing that is not a mystery is the tough reputation of the area. As rugged as the mountains themselves, the settlers and their descendents still maintain a lifestyle reminiscent of the Wild West, a last vestige in which to be proud.

Rico Suarez, a long time construction inspector, was familiar with the "character," as he politely referred to it, of the Village of Mora. Rico was not from Mora, but he grew up close enough to hear the tales and outlandish goings-on of the region. The Capitol City Journal has file cabinets of odd stories from the locale, enough to write multiple volumes of the area's escapades. As Rico drove his highway department truck toward Mora, he related several of his favorite legends that he had heard, true or not.

As Rico converses with Bryan, he reveals that he is still not comfortable visiting the area and probably never would feel at ease. "They just don't like outsiders," Rico sums up the area's dislike for strangers. "It's a beautiful area, seemingly attractive to tourists, but they just don't want 'em. They don't want intruders, period. And, they pretty much have kept them out with their cool reception of outsiders."

"I'll keep that in mind," Bryan notes as he rubbed his leg still in its cast.

"How is your leg?" Rico notices Bryan massaging his leg and inquires as they drive onward.

"Eh," Bryan frowns, "it's healing good, it just itches like crazy."

Rico laughs, but turns his emotion to seriousness quickly. "I have the laptop stowed in the backseat. It's got all the original inspection reports, before they were modified."

Bryan nods, "Ok, just give it to me when we get to the patrol yard. I'll put it in my backpack." Bryan pats his backpack/bookbag, a holdover from his college days, in lieu of an actual briefcase. He is quick to defend his backpack with the argument that he rides his bike so much that he needs to strap it on his back, and a briefcase would never allow for that.

After driving in silence a minute or two, Bryan reflects contemplatively, "You know, I'm a little surprised at today's pre-construction meeting and that the project is even going forward. With all the money the state has spent on the stupid train, how can there be any money left over for actual highway work?"

"You got that right," Rico nods affirmatively.

"I guess that is a question," Bryan whines, "I should be asking the governor, and my state legislators for that matter. They voted to approve the money-sucking train."

The men pass through the city of Eli, now off the Interstate, and pass through the home of Cortez University. Rico shares some history of Eli that coincides with the Mora area. Eli has a "colorful" past, but has modernized, in part, due to the success of Cortez University and the blending backgrounds and education. If the historic buildings surrounding the plaza could talk, they would relate words of classic Western confrontations and disagreements that ended with gunfire.

Eli lies on the open range, at the foot of the Sangre de Sustantivo Mountains, but after passing through the community, the road immediately begins climbing higher and higher into pines. The first pine trees are the piñon pine intermixed with juniper; after another few hundred feet of elevation, the ponderosa pine make their appearance. Soon the altitude brings you to a mix of spruce and ponderosa pines. A smattering of aspens emerge in between the evergreens for good measure. State Highway 51 winds its way parallel to the Mora River. The topography limits the widths of lanes to bare minimums. Vertical and horizontal curves are also built to a standard falling below highway engineering practice; government approved design exceptions for the curves are on file at the highway department for State Highway 51. The speed limit for the road reflects the character of the route. The typical speed limit sign for Highway 51 indicates 35 miles per hour with its black letters and numbers on a white background. The road side is littered with cautionary speed limit signs. These signs, black lettering on the yellow background, show a variety of sweeping arrows indicating curves ahead and a suggested speed in order to navigate the turn. The signs often suggest slowing to speeds less than 25 miles per hour.

The narrow roadway with segments constructed between thirty and fifty years ago does not afford room for guardrail in many areas. Nothing but careful driving separates a vehicle from exiting the highway and disappearing 500 feet below into the ponderosa pines, next to the Mora River.

Rico concentrates on driving the winding road, and Bryan takes in the breathtaking scenery as a few miles go by in silence. Rico looks in his rearview mirror and catches a glimpse of a rapidly closing vehicle behind him. Rico's eyes bounce from the mirror to the road in front of him and back, "What the heck is this clown doing behind us?" Rico calls out in fear.

As Bryan cranes his neck to see what Rico is looking at, he has but a moment. Instinctually, Bryan calls to question what he sees, "What's going on? Is that a highway department vehicle?"

Those are the last words exchanged between Bryan and Rico as the truck behind them smashes into their vehicle driving it from the road down the steep embankment. Their highway department truck tumbles violently down the steep grade, end-over-end, bouncing off boulders and continuing to barrel roll down the talus slope until it plows through sapling ponderosa pines before snagging into the larger pines.

Chapter 42

Invisible

The crashed vehicle is invisible from the highway lanes above. The wrecked truck is shrouded in the evergreen boughs. Rico and Bryan, oblivious to any threat, now lie hidden in the trees trapped in a crumpled vehicle. The only trace of their departure is a scant skid mark from Rico's slamming of the brake pedal. The anti-lock brakes reacted, but the tires chattered against the force of the crash in a futile attempt to grip the asphalt.

The other truck involved in the crash is long gone, disappearing into the wilderness along this lonely stretch of highway leaving Rico and Bryan stuck at the bottom of a ravine.

*   *   *   *   *

The shadows of the steep walls provide an early darkness to the bottom of the canyon. An unearthly glow is the first thing that Bryan notices as he regains consciousness. The vehicle is right-side up, but he has no immediate cognitive recall of any of the "who, what, where, when, and why" of his situation. All Bryan notices is the gloomy shadows to his side window and the glow of the lights through the windshield. The sun is setting and the sky is ablaze in reds and oranges of refracted sunlight in the clouds.

Bryan winces at every movement he makes. His legs are pinned under the dashboard. He is unable to move. Slowly he gathers his senses. "Rico," Bryan grunts.

There is no answer. "Rico!" Bryan shouts mustering some strength; still no answer.

Bryan reaches next to him where Rico sits behind the wheel; a shadowy, blurry figure is all Bryan can see. His hand touches Rico's face.

Rico is slumped over the steering wheel and, immediately, Bryan recoils, drawing his hand back away from the man. The feel of the cold skin to Bryan's touch immediately registers in his mind. Rico is dead. Bryan's mind spins through what happened. He remembers the pickup, the crash. He remembers nothing else, but notes the darkness and how cold Rico felt. Bryan figures Rico was killed instantly, and his body had cooled considerably in the shade. Bryan winces again as he tries to free himself and realizes he is pinned in the vehicle next to a dead man.

Bryan's urge to panic is dulled by the slow gathering of his wits. By his estimate he was either unconscious or drifting in and out of consciousness for ten hours. Ten hours. That would explain why Rico was so cool to the touch; he'd likely been dead for ten hours and that thought rattles through Bryan's mind. The panic kicked up a notch as Bryan realized those ten hours had gone by and there was nobody helping him. It wasn't like the movies and TV; there were no emergency vehicles here in the wilderness. Nobody would probably even miss him for another twenty-four hours. What had he said at the office? He was going to be late…maybe Rico would be missed sooner, but the fear moved to another level at the unknown time frame of even being noted as "missing" by anyone.

Hope blossomed for a moment as Bryan felt in the dark for his backpack. He had his cell phone in the bag. He found the pack below his legs, unzipped the pocket, and removed the phone, relieved…momentarily.

What was he thinking? He looked at the service indicator on the phone. A large "x" was displayed where the service bars would be. Phone service was spotty in the mountains as is, even on the peaks. Bryan sank down in his seat, angry for allowing himself this fleeting hope.

For the first time he looked up the canyon wall and noted how steep the ravine was. He shook his head. Even if he could pry himself from the vehicle he would have no chance at climbing to the road; he would have to follow a path suitable for his damaged body; he vowed he would do it, even if he had to crawl.

He felt again around his pinned legs. The edges of the fiberglass cast were jagged. The cast had crushed. This was the first bit of good news to register in Bryan's mind. The cast had provided a modicum of protection for both his legs from the crushed front end of the truck. A smile crept across his face realizing something positive. The smile compounded when he realized he had a bottle of water and a granola bar in his bag. Food and water…both. Something to quiet his mind as well as feed his hunger and thirst. For the first time in the hour since he had regained consciousness, he thought he was going to survive. "I can do this," he says aloud, as he unwraps the granola bar from his pack. "I can make it. I'll eat and drink.

That will give me some strength, and I can push the dashboard off my legs!"

Chapter 43

Back in Black & Blue

"Welcome back," Diego called out in exaggerated excitement. "How is the leg?" Gary stood before the copy machine in the business center of the office. He smiled and bounced on his injured leg, hopping ever so slightly to try to indicate he was indeed fine. "Doctor told me no demanding physical activity for a couple months."

"Oh, yeah?" Diego raises an eyebrow. "It was that serious?"

Gary rolls up his black nylon sweat pants revealing his bandaged shin. Outside of the bandage, from his knee to his toes, his leg and foot entertain a bruise displaying different shades of black and blue, even some hints of a hideous greenish tint.

Diego grimaces at the grotesquely colored leg, "Yikes. I had no idea. It is serious; at least it looks serious."

"I guess," Gary shrugged. "They are worried that the nail might have weakened the bone enough to break if stressed. I'm supposed to drink extra milk, so the calcium will fill the hole in the bone." Gary rolls his sweats pant leg down, "You'll have to excuse my casual dress for a week or so. "I'm sure your suit and tie will more than offset my sweat suits and tennis shoes."

Diego brushes the sleeve on his dark grey, herring bone patterned suit jacket. He looks at his suit pants and smooths the crease, "Yup, don't worry; I got us both covered. Wow, I sure am sorry about your leg." Diego shrugs, "If you need more time, just take it. Between you and Bryan, maybe you guys can get a working pair of legs."

"I think I'm doing fine; I didn't even need a cast," Gary laughs. "Funny, they advised me to avoid golf. The torque from a full swing could snap my leg."

"That's what happens when you get old," Diego slaps Gary on the back. "What are you workin' on?"

"Oh, nothing. This is just some of the annual reporting of the crash numbers that the highway department provided. I'm just getting them in the right format so you can forward them to your boss."

"That's what I like to hear," Diego nods satisfactorily. "Keep up the good work." Diego turns to leave but stops, "Hey, when I saw you here at the copy machine, I thought Bryan had gotten the information on the train. Have you heard from him?"

"Nope," Gary shakes his head as he sorts through some of the papers on the copy machine.

Diego twists his mouth as he thinks, "Tell him I want to see him as soon as he gets in. We all should sit down and talk when he has the laptop." Diego signals back and forth with his finger pointing to himself and Gary. "Give Bryan a call when you get a chance."

"Sure thing."

*   *   *   *   *

After sorting through his papers from the copy machine, Gary returns to his office. Stashing the papers, he picks up the phone and dials Bryan's cell phone. The phone rings a few times and goes to voicemail. Gary leaves a message for Bryan to call him.

*   *   *   *   *

A little while after lunch, Gary heads to Diego's office. Diego sits at his desk, and Gary leans against the door frame. Diego looks up from his computer, "What's up?"

"I tried Bryan's cell phone. No answer. I just left a voicemail," Gary reports.

"Hmmm," Diego shrugs.

"Something probably came up," Gary folds his arms. "It's getting late in the afternoon; we can catch him tomorrow."

Diego rubs his chin and purses his lips as he thinks. He stares through Gary as he contemplates. "Block some time on our calendars to go over the information. I have calls into headquarters, our legal counsel, and the OIG. I'd like to be able to report something to them tomorrow."

"Will do," Gary affirms with a nod. He gives his head another nod to the door, "I have to leave early for another x-ray on my leg. I'm going to take off in a few minutes, but I'll see you tomorrow. Later."

Diego gives a wave, "All right. Later."

Chapter 44

An O.K. Samaritan

It's hard to understand why things happen the way they do. God's plan? Maybe. It's as good as an explanation as anything else. Nearly two days since Bryan had gone missing, an anonymous driver rounded the curve on his way home from his job as a custodian at the Eli Regional Hospital; the rays of the sun were at just such an angle. It was a perfect angle that revealed the skid marks on the road. Those skid marks were virtually oblivious to the naked eye, but when viewed through a tinted windshield, while wearing polarized sunglasses, with the perfect angle of the sun…well, they were plain as the nose on a person's face. The choppy, intermittent, black tire residue from braking quickly hinted that a vehicle had left the road. The observant driver pulled to the shoulder when there was room along the narrow highway, about a quarter mile past the spot where he had noticed the tracks. He walked back to the spot of the tread marks on the faded, gray asphalt. The first indication of a crash was a small sliver of red plastic taillight. He found another piece, then another. Something had happened.

It was a good five minutes of looking, kneeling, turning his head at an angle first with his left eye then with his right eye close to the pavement before he was again able to spot the skid.

He looked over the edge of the road, down into the canyon and could see a blemish in the scree of the talus slope. The weathered rock along the slope had been disturbed; the muted reddish brown boulders covering the slope had slashes of darker streaks in a field of red stone. The dislocated rocks looked as if they were damp, but it was only the rock faces that had not been exposed to the harsh sun for years on end. The freshly turned cobbles glinted in the sunset.

The man could see nothing in the trees, but noted an almost imperceptible gap in the smallest of the pine saplings ringing the outer edge of where the forest picked up again and hid the Mora River below. There was no possible way the fifty plus-year-old man could descend the slope from this point on the highway. He decided he would have to report this to the authorities. He returned to his car and drove to his home, a small cabin on the outskirts of Mora. After a brief discussion with his wife, he dialed 911 and reported his observations.

*   *   *   *   *

Katrina was in full caregiver mode. She had insisted that Gary stay with her at her house while he recovered. She worried about him taking his antibiotics. She worried about his over doing the pain pills. She wanted to make sure the bandage and dressing were properly changed. Gary was not one to deny her demands; besides, he was enjoying the pampering.

After a nice dinner of hamburgers and hot dogs from the grill, Katrina and Gary took a walk to stretch their legs. The walk was cut short due to the summer monsoons. The rainy season had picked up, and a few rain drops fell from the evening cloud cover. The couple high-tailed it back to Katrina's house and settled on the couch to watch a movie on DVD.

Katrina donned her proverbial nursing hat and dispensed Gary's medication after the movie. Katrina tuned into *Dave Letterman* on the television, and Gary settled into a recliner in the living room. He was sleeping with his leg elevated at night to thwart some of the swelling. As the pain killer worked its magic over Gary's eyelids, he dozed.

At around 11:30 p.m. Katrina called it a night as she secured the house and powered down the TV. Gary's cell phone buzzed on the counter. She retrieved the phone and saw that it was Bryan calling. She hesitated for a moment before waking Gary, opening the phone. "Gary," Katrina called out as she shook his shoulder. "It's Bryan calling. Didn't you say you needed to get a hold of him?"

As Gary groggily understood he grunted, "Hmmm? Yeah, give me the phone."

Katrina handed the phone to Gary. He looked at the caller ID and put the phone to his ear. Without even saying "Hello," he began talking. "Dude? What's going on? It's like 11:30 at night. You were supposed to bring the information, weren't you? Diego was asking about it."

There was silence on the other end of the phone for a moment before a woman's voice asked in a serious tone, "Is this Gary Hillmann,"

Gary's face twisted in a perplexed expression as his eyes widened and he turned to face Katrina, "Uh, yes, this is Gary Hillmann."

"Sir, I'm calling on Bryan Baker's phone at his request. You were listed as his ICE, In Case of Emergency, contact in his phone. I confirmed with him, and he asked that I call you."

"Emergency?" Gary calls out.

"Bryan is in surgery," the voice over the phone matter-of-factly states.

Gary shrugs as he looks at Katrina, still trying to grasp the situation, "What is going on? Who is this?"

"Sir, my name is Cindy Gallegos. I'm the emergency room administrative nurse here in the Eli Regional Hospital."

Gary tenses, "What happened? How bad is it?"

"I do not have the details of his condition other than he was taken in for surgery following a car crash near Mora."

"You said, 'Eli Hospital'?" Gary repeats.

"Yes, sir."

"Ok, thank you. I'll be right there, bye," Gary closes the phone.

Katrina puts her hands on her hips, "What's going on? What do you mean, 'You'll be right there?' You are not going anywhere."

"Bryan was in a car crash; he's in surgery. I'm his emergency contact, I guess."

"I'll take you in the morning," Katrina declares, taking the phone from Gary and tucking the blanket around him. "You are in no shape to go anywhere."

Gary fights to sit up, but Katrina pushes him down. Gary grabs his head, "Maybe you are right. Those pain pills are good. My head does feel like it's full of cobwebs right now. We'll go tomorrow."

"Yes, we will," Katrina affirms. "Lie back down and go to sleep," she orders.

Gary sighs and closes his eyes, "Ok, remind me to call Diego first thing in the morning."

"I will," Katrina whispers, kissing Gary goodnight.

Chapter 45

Eli's Coming

Gary and Katrina have driven up to visit Bryan in the Eli Regional Hospital. Much to Bryan's chagrin, they have brought Ashley, Bryan's recent ex-girlfriend. The visitors find Bryan propped up in bed in the late afternoon. He is awake and alert, checking out ESPN sports updates on the television. Bryan welcomes the visitors and mutes the TV, excited to see some familiar faces. Bryan's smile is reduced to a neutral expression as the surprise visitor, Ashley, enters the room last, hesitating and a little shyly.

"Nice room," Gary observes taking in the surroundings, "1957 chic decorations. I knew that Eli was a historic community, but I didn't know to what extent they played things out. Do they even have an x-ray machine here at the hospital, or are they still treating all ailments with leeches and such?"

Gary gets a backhand to the belly from Katrina, "Stop mocking!" she scolds. "How are you, Bryan?"

Bryan shrugs, "Better than yesterday."

Gary stares at Bryan's legs. Bryan has both legs elevated. His injuries were limited to his legs, but now he has two broken legs. The more recently broken leg has steel rods protruding from his skin. The steel criss crosses and looks to be the beginning of a toy Erector Set building in place to support Bryan's lower leg. Bryan notes Gary's fascination with the steel framework surrounding his leg, "Pretty fancy, huh?"

"Dude," Gary replies. "This is quite the monstrosity of a system in place to keep your leg immobile."

Bryan smiles, "A feat of engineering even I can enjoy. You should see some of the counter-weights they've been hanging off the sides of my ankles. They can't seem to decide how they want to torque everything to get the healing started."

Gary closes his eyes and rubs his temples, "Wait a minute...yes...I see it. I see more surgeries in your future."

Bryan manages a laugh as Katrina backhands Gary in the belly, causing him to drop his hands from his temple in self defense.

Katrina speaks up again, "So, what happened?"

Ashley slowly moves closer to Bryan but is still afraid to speak. Bryan watches Ashley inching forward and begins to explain. "I was riding up to a pre-construction meeting with Rico Suarez. He's an inspector for construction projects. I asked him to drive 'cause of my leg in a cast. Anyhoo, we basically got run off the road by some maniac."

Katrina covers her mouth in shock, "Somebody ran you off the road."

Ashley covers her mouth, and her eyes begin to well with tears.

"Yeah," Bryan continues, "Rico's dead. I woke up probably ten hours after the crash. Rico was ice cold by then...I was pinned in the truck, by the dashboard. It crushed my leg. Funny thing is, if I hadn't had a cast on my other leg, you'd be looking at a double amputee. The doctors told me it was a one in a million chance that both legs were spared. The cast had just enough strength to prevent the circulation from being cut off in my legs, just below my shin."

"Wow," Katrina remarks, stunned.

"Of course," Bryan continues, "I'm not out of the woods yet. Cross your fingers that this steel fortress around my leg will work."

Gary, Katrina, and Ashley heave a collective sigh, having been unconsciously holding their breaths listening to Bryan's story. They soak in the tale a few moments more in silence. Bryan interrupts the quiet, "Can I speak to Gary in private a few moments...guy stuff."

Gary looks at Katrina and Ashley, "You heard 'im. Everybody out!"

Gary herds the women out into the hall. As Ashley moves to the door she yells out, "I still love you, Bryan!"

Gary shuts the door to the private room, before he closes it completely; he winks to Katrina and motions with his thumb to Bryan, "Guy stuff."

Katrina glares at Gary as the door shuts.

Gary returns to Bryan's bedside and pulls out a chair and sits, "What's up buddy?"

Bryan shakes his head, "Thanks for coming, but...seriously? Ashley? What on earth? Why in the world would you bring her?"

"I'm sorry, man. Katrina. She made me do it. But...I think it's going to work out for you. Just think...she'll take care of you. Hey," Gary bounces his eyebrows, "sponge baths? Hmmmm...huh?"

Bryan rolls his eyes.

"Forget Ashley for a minute," Gary waves his hand deflecting the eye roll. "Tell me what happened."

"You, of course, know why I was with Rico," Bryan exhales deliberately. "I swear it was a highway department truck that rear ended us. It had a light bar on the roof. The guy just pushed us over the edge like nothing." Bryan gestures with his hands flailing.

"Wait; was it a guy that was driving?" Gary questions.

"I don't know, guy...person...just other driver in general. Rico saw the driver coming up fast behind us as we went around the curve. He yelled out. 'What is this clown doing?' I turned and looked over my shoulder and thought I saw a highway department vehicle."

Bryan settles back into the hospital bed and folds his arms in disgust.

"Take it easy. You want me to call the nurse for a sedative?"

Bryan looks to the ceiling, "No, I'm fine."

"Not for you, I was thinking I might need one."

Bryan's shoulders shake as he holds back a laugh.

"I told the police all this," Bryan continues, "I don't think they even believe me! But...somebody ran us off the road! Rico...is dead!"

"I know," Gary acknowledges.

There is a long silence as Bryan looks out the window. Gary speaks up, "Count your blessings. Do you know how lucky you are? Some random, anonymous citizen, just passing by saw some nearly invisible skid marks and a piece of broken taillight on the road. He stopped and checked it; called it in when he got home."

"Psssh! Lucky!" Bryan reacts incredulously, "Have you looked at my leg?"

"You know what I mean. It was a miracle the guy stopped and then reported it. You might still be suffering at the bottom of that canyon if not for him."

"Yeah," Bryan reluctantly admits.

"The thing is, in my mind anyway," Gary continues, "how is this a hit-and-run out in the middle of nowhere? I'm a bit of conspiracy theory guy, but this one is too much for me."

"Who knows?" Bryan throws his hands in the air. "It was probably some drunk...I sure don't remember anything other than it was a truck that hit us."

"Drunk at nine o'clock in the morning?" Gary scoffs. "Did you tell the cops that?"

Gary exhales and straightens in his chair, "Do you think it's a coincidence that you and a whistle blower are run off the road...the same week somebody blows up my mailbox?"

Bryan practically leaps out of his bed, "What?!?!" I thought it was a defective vehicle?"

"Hell no!" Gary retorts and shakes his head in disgust. "The police are keeping information under wraps during the investigation. The newspapers are reporting random speculation."

"So, you think running us off the road was intentional? This is all connected?"

Gary raises his eyebrows, "If I was a betting man..."

Bryan leans back in his pillow and stares at the ceiling, "Jesus."

They sit in silence for a moment. There is a tap at the door, "Can we come in?" Katrina inquires through the slightest opening in the door.

Gary turns in his chair and faces the door, "Give us another minute or two."

"Ok," Katrina accepts the answer and shuts the door.

Bryan finally turns his eyes back to Gary, "They blew up your mailbox, eh?"

"I constantly have visions of leaning down and peering into the mailbox as I look to see if anything is inside as the bomb goes off and takes my head with it." Gary mimes opening a pretend mailbox and craning his head down as if peering in the box.

"These guys aren't messing around," Bryan states as he resumes his inspection of the ceiling tiles.

"Did you get the laptop from Rico," Gary asks.

"Nah, he was going to hand it over to me when we got to Mora. It was just sitting in the backseat of the pickup."

Gary breathes a sigh of defeat.

"Who in the heck found out about this stuff?" Bryan says aloud as he searches for an answer to who might have leaked information. "Do you think Rico accidentally told somebody?"

Gary shakes his head, "Nah, I think he was frightened enough just in telling us."

Bryan shakes his head and whispers in a husky tone, his voice rising, "That evidence is long gone! If somebody knew enough to come after us, they know about the laptop."

"God," Gary nods, "You're probably right. I got to talk to Diego."

Gary stands and moves to the door to let the women back in the room, "Hey," Bryan calls out. "Find out where they hauled the wrecked truck. Couldn't hurt to check and see if the laptop is still there."

Gary grabs the door handle. He thinks about Bryan's suggestion, "I will. I'll make a phone call and find out."

Bryan adds, "For all we know, they piled all the debris into the back of the truck and hauled it to the Mora Patrol Yard. It could be sitting in the wide open."

"I don't know. Trying to salvage that truck from the ravine is going to be an operation in itself." Gary smiles a crooked smile, "I can't believe how lucky you are to be alive having this conversation with me."

Bryan grins, "You're the lucky one...you get to talk to me."

Gary nods, opens the door, and the Katrina and Ashley return to Bryan's bedside.

Ashley's eyes are swollen from crying and as she nears Bryan, the sobs well up inside her again. The conversation is stilted as Ashley cannot maintain her composure. A nurse mercifully arrives and shoos everyone out the door to let Bryan rest and give him his medications.

Chapter 46

Cheers...

After the emotional visit to Eli Regional Hospital to see Bryan, a nice relaxing supper is the perfect remedy to recover from the draining day trip. Tired of the traditional take out options, the evening meal was agreed upon: salad and ham with scalloped potatoes. Gary, as usual, is less than enthralled with the selection of salad, but holds his nose and drowns the lettuce with Italian Dressing.

Katrina and Gary eat with minimum conversation, mentally tired from dealing with all their own recent hospital drama and now compounding the excitement with Bryan's episode. The television displays the local six o'clock p.m. news. The sound is muted, but the couple casually eats and watches the news. The top story for the night remains the threat of cutbacks to the Air Force base in Allentown. Several important politicians are interviewed, and they all proclaim they are fighting for the Air Force base against Department of Defense bureaucrats. Governor Reid-Salazar finishes as the last interviewee of the story, and Channel 13 news anchor, Dick Forsine, segues seamlessly to the next story also involving the governor.

"Un-mute, un-mute it!" Gary cries out. "I have to hear what they're saying...it looks like something about T'rrain Trekker."

Katrina reacts instinctively, jumping to grab the remote control and restoring the sound. Gary points to the TV, "Check out who's on stage with the governor at the press conference."

Katrina remains standing, looking and listening to the news story, "I see them. They are like celebrities."

Katrina shakes her head as she watches Governor Stuart Reid-Salazar extol the greatness of transit, flanked by Patrick Ruiz and Casey Baxter. A thirty second sound bite from the governor covers the great accomplishment of continued construction and the on-time delivery of multiple stations along the route. "Thanks, everyone," the governor beams, "I will turn it over to the technical team leaders, Ms. Baxter and Mr. Ruiz. They can answer your more specific questions."

The governor steps back from the podium. With a hand on the back of each person, Casey and Patrick step to the microphones and begin to answer questions shouted at them.

Gary howls as if he is in pain, "Seriously, I'm going to puke if you don't change the channel immediately! I've had all I can stand!"

"Quit being such a drama queen. They're your peers, the media darlings."

Katrina turns the TV off.

"My peers! That's not even remotely funny. Hey since you are up, can you grab me a beer?"

"I'm not your servant."

Gary points to his leg, "What about my leg?"

Katrina rolls her eyes and reluctantly gets a beer from the fridge. "There."

"Thank you. You should probably get one for yourself. I have to talk to you about something."

Katrina cocks her head suspiciously, but follows orders, grabs a beer, and sits. They sit and sip on their beers for a few moments in silence. Gary eats, while Katrina watches and waits. She can't stand it any longer and yells, "Tell me! What did you want to talk about?"

Gary stops eating and drinks from his beer, "Promise me you won't hit me."

Katrina makes a questioning, scrunched face, "Ok? I promise."

"I know you're not going to be happy," Gary continues as he stares at Katrina and drinks from his beer, "but, promise me you won't hit."

"I promise! Just tell me already!"

"You also have to swear to keep this secret."

"I swear," Katrina whines. "Just say it!"

Gary sets down his beer. He folds his hands on the table and leans closer to Katrina sitting across from him. "Bryan was with Rico Suarez because Rico is…was blowing the whistle on the T'rrain Trekker."

"Shut up," Katrina whispers as her eyes widen.

"Bryan said that they were run off the road by somebody…somebody tried to kill them both."

"Oh, my God!" Katrina shouts.

"Somehow the word got out that Rico was blowing the whistle. Rico met with me and Bryan, but someone ratted him out…" Gary exhales. "I think you were right…somebody tried to kill me with the bomb in the mailbox."

Katrina turns pale as the room spins. She grabs the table trying to remain calm. "I knew it," she whispers breathlessly. "I knew it. I knew it. I knew it!" she repeats in rapid fire. What are we going to do?"

"We are trying to get evidence to turn over to the OIG. Bryan was supposed to get a laptop with evidence on it. It had some original testing reports that showed the concrete was failing. Patrick Ruiz had forged some other ones on the system, but these originals were unmodified, stuck in the laptop's memory cache when it died…it's complicated."

Katrina nods, "I'm familiar with the electronic construction diaries."

Gary nods, "Let's just say Patrick Ruiz is a *bad* man."

Katrina continues to nod. "You know what I'd like to do?"

Gary shrugs, silently questioning.

"I'd like to just take all this information you shared and give it to my friend at the Capitol City Journal. She could always use the scoop."

"Don't you dare," Gary wags a finger of warning.

She stands and quickly moves close to Gary and punches him in the shoulder. "Owww!" You promised not to hit," Gary howls.

"I promised that before I found out you weren't telling me the whole truth! What are we going to do? We're not safe!"

"Well, we are going to be careful. I'm going to find that laptop and get the evidence off of it. It was in the truck when they crashed. I'm going to find out where they hauled the salvaged vehicle."

"That doesn't tell me how we are going to stay safe," Katrina pleads.

"With Rico dead, my guess is that things are going to settle down. They probably think they are in the clear…whoever they are. Either way, maybe you should go stay with your parents a few days down in Allentown."

"Lord, Jesus," Katrina prays, eyes skyward. She falls into her chair at the table and tips the beer bottle steeply up in the air and chugs her beverage.

Gary hoists his beer, "Cheers…we'll get this figured out."

Katrina moves her drink to complete the toast with a touch of the bottles, instead she taps down on Gary's longneck bottle. Foam rises up and overflows onto Gary's hand. "Hey!" Gary cries, maneuvering to contain the river of foam streaming across his hands.

Katrina smiles mischievously, "That's what you get."

Gregory L. Heitmann

Chapter 47

Asylum

Gary sits in his office at the United States Transportation Department. He is on the phone trying to track down the wrecked highway department pickup Rico was driving. Katrina raps on the open door and enters.

Gary covers the phone, "I'm on the phone with Risk Management. Have a seat."

Gary points to a chair and Katrina sits; he turns his attention back to the phone and speaks, "So, you're telling me the salvaged vehicle *is* sitting in the Mora Patrol Yard?"

Gary listens for a minute. He smiles at Katrina and points to the phone. "Ok," he says, "I can go get Bryan's computer from it, no problem?"

Gary waits and nods happily, "Good. Thank you very much."

Gary hangs up the phone, stands hastily, and hops on his good leg in celebration. The phone cord is snagged on his finger as tries to raise his hands in victory. The phone drags across his desk, falling to the floor, taking a stack of papers and most of everything from his desktop to the carpet.

Gary looks at his mess and his hops get smaller and smaller. "Oops," Gary quietly quips. Katrina tries not to laugh, but can't hold back. She literally slaps her knee and bursts out laughing. She wipes tears from her eyes and slowly recovers.

"Too dramatic?" Gary asks.

Katrina holds her thumb and index finger together, "A bit."

"Well, I'm actually going to get my hands on that evidence. I can't help it. It's the first good news I've had in awhile."

Katrina shakes her head, "Why did you lie about the computer belonging to Bryan?"

Gary picks up a stack of papers from the floor, "I don't want word to get out anymore than it is. The way I figure it, anyone could be a snitch; anyone and everyone at the highway department."

"Even me?" Katrina points to herself and bats her eyelashes, innocently.

Gary concedes the point with a shrug, "Present company excepted."

Katrina sits smugly in her chair, arms folded, "Didn't I say right away when they blew up your mailbox that this was related to the T'rrain Trekker? I knew it!"

"Yeah, yeah," Gary acknowledges.

"I am still half inclined to call my friend at the newspaper and give her this info. Imagine the headline: 'Reckless Governor Crashes Train'."

"Don't even think about it!" Gary glares at Katrina.

"I won't. I just like to make sure you know that I have some say in this matter," Katrina points a finger back and forth between them. "These are our lives we're talking about." Katrina shivers with disgust, "Uhg! This whole debacle frustrates me."

Gary finishes putting things back in place on his desk. "I know," Gary nods, moving around to the front of his desk. "I'm glad you're going to spend some time with your folks. Just get away a few days; if anything happens, you'll only be tucked away in Allentown. You'll be safe, and we'll have all this figured out in no time."

Katrina stands and wraps her arms around Gary and kisses him. She sighs, "I know; it will be done soon."

Gary squeezes Katrina tightly and loosens his grip. Katrina slips from his arms, "Get back to work!" she orders. "I just wanted to stop and say 'bye' on my way out of town, so bye." Katrina kisses Gary, they walk to the front door and they part, neither confident in the situation, but neither wanting to show any fear.

Chapter 48

Salvage Mission

Bright and early in the morning, Gary checks out a government car and heads north, destination Mora. He leisurely makes his way north on Interstate 11, passing through Eli. Gary notes to himself that he will have to stop at the hospital on his way back and check on Bryan. On State Highway 51, Gary drives carefully. He searches for the curve where Bryan and Rico were forced off the road. It is not the way he envisioned; when Gary rounds a bend on the snaking mountain highway, he comes across a small wooden cross surrounded and draped with flowers. Rico's friends and family have constructed a makeshift memorial along the narrow highway, a *descanso*, Spanish for resting place. Bouquets of flowers are spilling into the driving lane. Gary slows to a near stop, but decides that he will wait until the trip back to look over the side of the road and into the ravine to see where the truck came to rest.

Speeding onward, as fast as the G-car sedan will handle the curves, Gary travels the last ten miles in about a half hour. He pulls into the Mora Patrol Yard and sees only a few orange highway department maintenance trucks parked in a row. The snow plows for the trucks stand in a neat alignment opposite the trucks. Machines that sit in the bed of the trucks to spread sand, hang by chains from high metal stanchions, waiting to be reinserted into the truck beds and put into use as soon as the cold weather returns. Gary notices the elevation of the mountains surrounding the benched area on which the community sits, nestled cozily in the mountains. He imagines that winter comes earlier and stays later up here.

Gary steers his car on past the patrol yard's office, as he spots the crumpled pickup truck he was hoping to see. He pulls up next to the wrinkled and twisted metal that loosely resembles a Chevy extended-cab truck. Gary exits the vehicle and looks around the yard for anyone else. He sees no one, shuts his car door, and pushes his sunglasses to the top of his head. Both front doors from the pickup are gone and upon closer inspection, Gary sees the doors in the box of the truck, realizing the doors were removed to extract Rico and Bryan.

The doubt creeps in as Gary moves closer to the truck, "No way," Gary says quietly to himself, "the laptop is long gone."

Gary reaches the driver's side and catches his breath. He sees the blood stained floor mat under Rico's driver's side seat. Gary decides to move to the other side of the truck and look inside from the passenger's compartment. He runs his hand over the undulating metal, being careful of the sharp creases on the hood and front quarter panels.

Upon inspection of the passenger's side front seat, Gary finds Bryan's backpack; he extricates the straps from snags on the crumpled crash cage of the vehicle. He sets the pack on the ground and pauses. He takes a deep breath, looking at the wreck, contemplates searching the backseat of the truck. Gary takes another deep breath, squeezes into the passenger side, ducks his head, and climbs into the caved-in passenger side of the vehicle. He wriggles his way into the compartment, kneeling and facing backwards in the passenger seat. Gary looks in the backseat; the "*Holy Grail*" rests in plain view on the floor of the back seat area, the laptop computer. Gary releases an audible gasp, surprising himself. He smiles at his own reaction and leans forward. The laptop edges away from Gary's restricted reach. The crushed-in cab of the truck makes it difficult to extend his body. With great effort, Gary finally hooks a fingernail into an air vent on the back of the computer and slides it close enough to pick up with his thumb and index finger. "Got it," Gary says in quiet satisfaction as he lifts it over the seat and into the front cab.

He wriggles out the door in a smooth motion while lifting the computer. Out of the truck he bends and slips the laptop into Bryan's bookbag. While kneeling he hears a voice thirty or forty feet away, "Whatcha doin' there?"

Gary's head snaps around to see a man approaching.

Chapter 49

Got It

Gary stands, calmly hoisting the book bag onto his shoulder, and faces the man approaching him from across the patrol yard. He holds the book bag over his left shoulder hooking it in place with the thumb of his left hand. The man looks to be about 45-years old. He is dressed in faded blue jeans, a well worn flannel shirt over a plain red t-shirt, lace up work boots, and a brand new Colorado Rockies baseball cap. "Hey, how's it going," Gary calls as the man presses to within twenty feet, but doesn't reply.

"Hi, my name is Gary Hillmann," Gary says, "I'm with the United States Transportation Department," extending his hand.

The man looks at Gary suspiciously, edges forward, and shakes Gary's hand. "My name is Adrien Martinez. What are you doing here?"

Gary points to the bookbag, "I called around to find out about the salvaged vehicle from the wreck the other day. One of my engineers, Bryan Baker, was the guy that was injured."

Gary pauses then continues as Adrien nods, "Bryan is in the Eli Hospital and he asked me to get his backpack from the wreck."

Gary slightly lifts the backpack from his shoulder and shifts his eyes to it for a split second. It clicks for Adrien and he nods, a little more fervently as he offers, "I think I talked to you on the phone." Adrien points at Gary, "Yeah, was it yesterday? Yeah, you asked about the salvaged vehicle. What a shame about Rico."

"Horrible," Gary acknowledges. "He was a good guy. He was doing a lot of work for us."

"A real tragedy," Adrien adds with a sigh. "How is your guy? Is he going to be ok?"

"Still iffy with his leg, but doctors are more confident every day. Hopefully he can keep his leg." Gary replies with due concern. "He is going to live."

Adrien manages a weak smile, "I won't bother you; go ahead and do what you need to do."

Gary hikes up the book bag on his shoulder and points to it again, "Actually, I got what I came for. I'm taking this bag to Bryan on my way back through Eli. I'll visit him in the hospital and make sure he's doing ok."

"Good," Adrien nods and extends his hand. "Nice to meet you."

Gary shakes Adrien's hand, "Likewise."

Each man turns his separate way, Adrien headed back to the patrol yard shop and Gary to his G-car. Gary sighs in relief as he opens the back door of the car and tosses the bookbag inside. He climbs behind the wheel and drives out of the patrol yard heading down the winding mountain road towards Eli on Highway 51. Twenty minutes later, he is back at the location on the road where the truck departed its lane and jumped over the edge to the bottom of the canyon. Gary drives past the flowers and wooden cross and creeps forward slowly looking for a place to pull safely off the highway. He finally finds a wide enough shoulder and parks. He hikes the quarter mile back to the memorial and looks over the edge of the road. He lets loose with a low whistle as he observes the drop off of the road to the canyon below. The talus slope shows a fair number of scars now since the emergency rescue operation and the salvage operation of the truck. "Yikes," Gary comments out loud.

He removes a small camera from his pocket and snaps a few pictures of the canyon down below. He photographs the uphill view of the highway running away from him and turns and does the same for the downhill view. Gary looks around and absorbs the mountain views and takes a few more scenic pictures of the emerald peaks surrounded by clouds. Gary has seen enough and returns to the G-car. He opens the back door and grabs the back pack and extracts the laptop from the bag. He throws the bag in the back and shuts the door. He powers on the laptop and climbs into the front seat as the machine comes to life. "Hmmm," Gary grunts, surprised to see the machine appearing to work and that the wreck did not damage the computer.

Gary clicks on the recently viewed files symbol and several choices labeled by date appear. He clicks on the file labeled June 27; a formatted Portland Cement Concrete Testing Record fills the screen. Gary removes a portable memory drive from his pocket and spends the next fifteen minutes using his camera as best as he can to photograph the screen as well as copy the twenty plus files to his memory drive.

The laptop beeps and flashes a warning of low battery, and Gary, satisfied that he has enough information backed up, powers the computer down. Pleased with his work, he places the computer on the passenger seat, stows his camera and jump drive, and heads to Eli to see Bryan.

*   *   *   *   *

When Gary arrived at the third floor room and knocked at the partially closed door, he heard a monotone answer, "Come in." The television was off, and Bryan rested a paperback novel bent over his suspended leg. His eyes were closed but sprung open like the window shades in a cartoon when he heard Gary's voice, "Hey, Bry."

Bryan smiled and pushed himself more upright in bed. "Thank God," Bryan sighed, "I'm going stir crazy, stuck with my leg in the air."

"What's the prognosis?" Gary asks as he pulls a chair along side the bed and sits.

Bryan rolls his head back and forth in agony on the pillow, "I had an x-ray this morning…just a few minutes ago the doctor comes by and tells me one more week like this."

Gary smiles and stands, "Maybe this will cheer you up." Gary slides the straps of Bryan's backpack from his shoulder and sits down again as he hands the bag to Bryan.

"My backpack!" Bryan hollers. "Thank the Lord! I got my Playstation game in here at least. Hey, what's in here?" Bryan questions as he unzips the bag.

He pulls the laptop from the pack. "No!" Bryan hisses as his eyes widen. "Is this what I think it is?"

"Yup," Gary responds. "We got 'im! I looked at some of the reports…plain as day…the ones filed were modified."

Bryan beams as he soaks in the news. "At least it's not going to be for nothin'…my leg…Rico. I had visions of nothing happening." Bryan hands the laptop back to Gary.

"I'll get this back to Diego. He already has the FBI, OIG, and our legal counsel on notice, just waiting to get this thing." Gary smiles satisfactorily.

Bryan heaves a sigh of relief that is echoed by Gary.

"Changing the subject a bit, how's Ashley?" Gary asks.

"Good, good," Bryan nods. "She drives up from Capitol City every night after work to see me. We're gettin' along good."

"See…" Gary smiles smugly.

"It's nice to have her around. She's going to take care of me when I get out of here, hopefully in no more than a week."

Gary points to the book bent over Bryan's leg, "What're ya reading?"

"I don't know. Some Swedish book about a lady with a tattoo that stepped on a bee hive or something. It's some mystery that's supposed to be great, but its ehhh," Bryan wobbles his hand.

The men talk for an hour or so as Gary updates Bryan on the latest news, including sending Katrina to Allentown. The nurse shows up for her rounds, and Gary heads back to Capitol City.

Chapter 50

Give It Away

Gary arrived back at the office with the evidentiary lap top computer in tow, satisfied, but exhausted by the adrenaline of the day's find. The building is empty except for Diego in the office next door to Gary's. Gary enters his office and sets his briefcase down. He calls out to Diego, "You're the last man standing, huh?"

Gary moves out of his office into Diego's. He holds the laptop out to show Diego as Diego reads from his computer screen and answers Gary's question; only half paying attention, "Yeah, everybody's done for the day. I was just trying to…"

Diego stops midsentence as he turns and sees Gary holding out the computer. He smiles, "You got it!"

Gary smiles and shakes his head, "Mission Accomplished! Where's my banner?"

"All right!" Diego shouts. He takes the laptop from Gary. "I'll give legal and the others a heads-up. They're going to flip out when I call them. I think all of them had some pretty serious doubts about our story."

"We'll see who gets the last laugh now," Gary continues to smile. "I'm out of here. I'll be in tomorrow."

"Sounds good," Diego says giving a wave as Gary departs. "Bye."

*   *   *   *   *

Fifteen minutes after Gary departed the office, Diego powers on the laptop handed to him by Gary. The machine lies lifeless on Diego's desk. As it turned out, Chuck was returning to the office as Diego was leaving for the evening.

Chuck has spent the afternoon lounging at home as he had left the diagnostics to cycle in the server room and had returned to analyze the report and provide any tweaks necessary to make sure the office network was running as smoothly as possible.

Diego started to leave his office and the laptop on his desk, but when he noticed the server room door open and could hear Chuck click-clacking away on a computer keyboard, Diego went back to grab the laptop.

Diego held the laptop in one hand as he stepped behind Chuck in the server room. The fans cooling the machinery prevented Chuck from detecting Diego's approach, and as Diego called out his name, Chuck flinches, frightened. Diego laughs, "It's just me, Chuck. No need to be scared."

"Holy cow! You scared me," Chuck gasps as he holds his hand over his heart.

Diego nods, "Good to see you're back on track keeping things in order."

"Yes, sir," Chuck replies. "Just running the network diagnostics to make sure everything is runnin' smooth."

"Here," Diego says as he extends his arms and shoves the laptop toward Chuck. "Take this and see if you can have it running for me tomorrow."

"Yes, sir. What's wrong with it?

"I don't know. It won't power up. I don't have a cord, so…"

Chuck nods, "I'll charge it and check it out. I'm sure I got a power cord lying around here someplace."

"Okey-doke," Diego gives a jerk of his head to the door. "Lock it up when you leave. See you tomorrow."

"See ya," Chuck replies and lifts his hand in a partial wave.

The front door closes and Chuck examines the laptop a little more closely. His heart skips a beat when he sees the State Highway Department property tag on the bottom. He and Casey just had a conversation about a laptop from the department that was missing. What was it again? Chuck attempts to recall his conversation. Something about a whistleblower stealing a laptop and information on the train. Could this be the computer? Rico! That was the whistleblower's name! Chuck remembers. He starts to shake as he reaches for his cell phone case on his belt. He presses the button to dial Casey's number, his hand's barely able to hold the phone he is so nervous.

"Hello," Casey answers.

"You are not going to believe this," Chuck whispers huskily into the phone, "I think I was just handed the computer you were looking for."

* * * * *

An hour later at Chuck's house, Casey and Chuck are looking at the computer screen and information regarding the concrete testing reports. "What is all this stuff?" Chuck asks.

"I'm not exactly sure," Casey replies. "Listen, I need to take this computer with me."

"I don't know…Diego said I needed to give it back to him tomorrow morning."

"Don't worry about it," Casey assures Chuck, "I'll get it right back to you."

"But my job is on the line, Case! I can't afford to lose it. I have child support to pay. I'm already on thin ice since I just about burned the building down."

Casey giggles and gets a smile from Chuck. "Listen," she soothes, "I'll be back in an hour. You'll have the computer back in your hands in no more than one hour."

"Ok," Chuck concedes.

Casey kisses Chuck and smiles, "I'll be right back."

The computer is powered down and closed. Casey leaves him with a smile.

*   *   *   *   *

In less than an hour, true to her word, Casey returns with a computer. She has met with Patrick Ruiz and exchanged an almost exact replica highway department laptop for Rico's laptop. No one is the wiser, and Chuck breathes a sigh of relief when he sees the laptop back on his kitchen counter in his house, delivered by Casey.

Casey is not in the mood she left with when she returns to Chuck's. "Do you want to stay for a late supper?" Chuck offers.

"No thanks," Casey waves the offer away.

"Something wrong?" Chuck asks.

"I just don't feel good."

"Is it Patrick? Every time you go see him, you get angry!"

The knock down, drag out argument between Casey and Patrick over the cover up never came to blows. It was the closest to a physical confrontation that Casey and Patrick had come to during their ongoing dispute about the T'rrain Trekker. It wouldn't have been much of a fight; Patrick is almost double the size of Casey. The mental toll of the continued argument had worn on Casey, and it showed.

"I'm just going to go home and go to bed," Casey announced with a dreary monotone.

"Fine," Chuck leans over and kisses Casey on the forehead. "You want to talk, just call me."

"Sure," Casey smiles weakly. "Bye."

Chapter 51

Casey's Flight

Today - August 27th

On the day that Casey "Took Flight," as some people referred to the suicide leap of Casey Baxter, the world didn't end anywhere else, the world stopped only for her and her alone. Casey had told her husband that she had an early morning meeting in Capitol City and would be departing early, really early. She lied. Don't think she was being impulsive, as rash as her suicide might have seemed; she had purposely planned this date for a long time. It was her kids' first day of the new school year. Ken was a stay at home dad and would be handling things this year, but beyond the idea of timing her own demise for her benefit, she had reasoned that this was the best time for the children. They would be distracted by the excitement of the start of a new school year. Besides, she convinced herself out loud on the drive north, "They'll barely miss me since I'm never at home anymore."

Casey had made sure in the previous weeks that her affairs were in order. There were no loose ends to stop the execution of her plan. The calm she realized was strange as she made the two-plus hours drive from Rio Loma to the Rio Caballo Gorge Bridge. It was a weight off of her shoulders, and she had no regrets.

She had been careful to not let on to anyone of her state of mind the past month and a half; maybe Patrick had picked up on her emotion, but it was too late. That was all in the past. The only slight hesitation Casey felt in her mind was a twinge of doubt over her choice of the method of suicide. The Gorge Bridge had seen a rash of jumpers over the past ten years, but they were in cycles, and there had been none recently. Casey had checked, and there had been no suicide by bridge in the last ten months. That was her one fear on the drive up north to the bridge. Would there be people around that might try to stop her?

She had debated the method for several days before deciding on the gorge. She didn't have a gun; carbon monoxide in the garage would be too close to home and maybe traumatic for the kids. Pills seemed too iffy. No, the Gorge Bridge was the way to go. Nobody survived the landing; it would do the trick.

*   *   *   *   *

Everything worked as planned and timed. She said goodbye to Patrick at sunrise and made her leap into the abyss of the Gorge. She was free at last, no guilt, no doubts, free at last.

Chapter 52

Do You Know Who I Am?

After a long day on the T'rrain Trekker construction site, an exhausted Patrick heads back to his Capitol City home. He merges onto the busy Interstate 11 Highway. His mind is a million miles away, still trying to understand the morning's events. How could Casey have jumped from the bridge? It did not seem real in his mind. Patrick had avoided the radio and TV all day, hoping to avoid hearing and seeing the reports. He did not want to be somehow dragged into Casey's suicide. Patrick's mind turned the drama from the Gorge Bridge over and over in his head. The graphic visual of Casey falling churned away in his thoughts.

He had fled the scene, and a man, that vendor, had watched him leave the bridge. The man…he had even said something to Patrick. Patrick racked his brain, trying to figure out how to reconcile the situation. He is engrossed in his own thoughts so deeply that he doesn't even see the car not yielding at the Exit 64 Interchange. A car trying to merge onto the mainline Interstate traffic is going to sideswipe Patrick. He brakes, but it is too late. The car hits the passenger side of his Laramie Engineering Truck. Patrick curses wildly and pulls to the shoulder. Patrick flips the switch of the flashing light bar atop his truck to warn passing traffic. The un-yielding car does yield now, pulling in behind Patrick.

Patrick exits the vehicle and a woman emerges from her late model Chevy Malibu. The woman is apologizing profusely, "I'm sorry, so sorry. I was on the phone."

Patrick manages a weak smile. He heaves a sigh wondering how things could be worse. "It's all right," Patrick mumbles. "We can exchange information and contact our insurance."

The middle-aged, Hispanic woman's face brightens, "I am in insurance. I'm Betsy Lucero with Freedom Insurance." She extends her hand, and Patrick shakes it.

"Patrick Ruiz," Patrick states with a far off, melancholy tone.

A passing State Patrol Officer with his own lights flashing pulls behind the vehicles on the shoulder. The officer takes over the situation and writes an accident report. A half hour later, he hands carbon copies to Patrick and Betsy.

"There you are, ma'am. You can take off. Be careful merging back into traffic," the officer says with a smile.

"I will, Officer," Betsy says with a smile and a wave.

She heads to her car and Patrick turns to go to his truck but is hailed by the officer. "Mr. Ruiz, can I talk to you a minute."

Patrick turns back to the young patrolman, "Sure, what is it, officer?"

"Sir, you have some other damage on your truck. I'm pretty sure it didn't contribute to the cause of this crash, but you need to get it fixed. It looks like your front left signal light and headlight might be out."

An exhausted Patrick is pushed too far by the lecturing officer, "Do you know who I am?" Patrick raises his voice. "My uncle is the Secretary of Public Safety. One call and I can have you sent to serve the next two years patrolling the Black Rock Desert in the teeming metropolis of Gerlach."

Patrick is sweating and his breathing is coming in gasps. "Is that what you want?" Patrick continues to question the young officer. "Don't sit here and lecture me about safety."

"Please sir," the officer says calmly. "Don't get excited. I just want you to get it fixed." He smiles soothingly, "I'm just doing my job to make sure vehicles are in good-working order."

Patrick is huffing and puffing. He grabs his chest.

The officer steps forward, all smiles aside now as he sees Patrick's distress. He grabs Patrick's shoulder, "Sir, just go ahead and sit down alongside the shoulder. I think you might be having a heart attack."

The officer eases Patrick to the edge of the pavement as Patrick nods silently, gasping for breath. The patrolman moves to his vehicle and grabs his radio calling for assistance as he tries to comfort Patrick.

The officer turns to Patrick, "Sir, I'm going to get you in my vehicle and take you to the emergency room. It will be faster than waiting for an ambulance. Don't try to speak. Save your breath. Nod if you understand."

Patrick nods and the officer assists Patrick into his patrol car. In a moment the officer is flying down the Interstate with lights flashing and siren blaring.

*   *   *   *   *

It wasn't until later, after doctors had diagnosed Patrick with an acute anxiety attack, that Patrick had the near coronary that he thought had gripped him earlier. Jeremy Montoya, Secretary of Public Safety, and close friend of the governor paid his nephew a visit in the hospital emergency room. "Patrick," Jeremy called out in polite concern as he approached the bed where Patrick rested, "I'm so glad to hear that you are ok."

Jeremy swung the curtain divider closed, separating the men from the rest of the room. He reached to shake Patrick's hand as Patrick smiled, "Uncle Jeremy…" he raised his hand and began to respond, but was immediately cut off as Jeremy squeezed Patrick's beefy hand tightly and pulled himself to Patrick's scared, twisted face.

"Listen, Patrick," Jeremy growled through gritted teeth. "Don't you ever! Don't you ever cast my name around in trying to influence anyone! Do you understand me?"

Patrick was frozen in fear.

Jeremy growled again and squeezed Patrick's hand tighter, "Do you understand me?"

Patrick managed a slight nod.

"Say you understand," Jeremy rasped.

"I-I-I understand," Patrick stammered.

Jeremy loosened his grip and brushed his dark suit of any wrinkles and straightened his tie. "I am glad you are ok, son," Jeremy continued in hushed tones, "I really am. About this other stuff with the T'rrain Trekker. Get it fixed, and get it fixed now. You talk to that Hillmann fellow and get those train stations finished up. No more delays."

Jeremy stared at his terrified nephew. Jeremy slowly forced a smile of pity on his nephew, "Come on now…buck up Patrick. I know you can do this. We're all countin' on you at the Governor's Office."

Jeremy reached toward Patrick, and Patrick flinched. Jeremy paused before he finished reaching to tousle Patrick's hair. "You're ok. You'll be home in an hour or two. The nurses will discharge you, and I'll drive you home myself. I already called and had your truck taken to your house. I'll get you home safely to your wife and kids, no sense in frightening them needlessly with this hospital business."

Chapter 53

Phone It In

Gary stands in the doorway to Diego's office. He leans on the door frame, "Did you see the paper this morning? Casey Baxter? Taking a leap off the Gorge Bridge by Verde. Holy cow, that is crazy!"

Diego sits at his desk and pulls his hands from his keyboard and interlocks his fingers behind his head. "God rest her soul," Diego replies, his mouth twisted in concern.

Gary enters Diego's office and falls into a chair in front of Diego's desk, "I just can't believe it. Her poor family…what the hell could have been going on in her life to do that?"

Diego sighs, "The best laid plans of mice and men often go awry."

Gary forces a smile, "Thank you, Robert Burns."

Diego drops his hands from behind his head and shrugs, "At least I didn't try an Irish accent." Diego pauses a moment and repeats the Burns' poem with a lilting accent:

"The best laid schemes o' mice an' men / Gang aft a-gley"

Gary laughs uncomfortably, "Wow, that seems wildly inappropriate. By the way, I'm pretty sure Burns was Scottish, not Irish."

Diego waves away the correction, "Scottish, Irish, same thing."

Gary laughs and tries his own attempt at a Scottish accent, "Aye, laddie, 'tis sad, still."

Diego's eyes widen, "Wow, you are right. That is inappropriate." Diego shifts in his chair and continues with a serious tone. "We should send a card to her family from our office. We worked with her quite a bit on the train."

"That's a good idea," Gary agrees, "At least I'll feel a little better. I had given her quite a bit of grief lately at the T'rrain Trekker meetings." Gary sighs deeply, "My God, was she even forty years old?"

"I think the paper said forty-two…two kids in elementary school," Diego offers.

Gary leans forward and rubs his knees with his hands in an unconscious nervous habit, "This freaks me out. This is just crazy."

The men sit in silence a moment or two, each lost in their own thoughts. Gary massages away at his knees as he looks out the window past Diego. He finally breaks the silence, "Speaking of crazy, have you seen Chuck?"

"No. Why?"

"The guy is AWOL," Gary continues.

Diego thinks back, "I haven't seen Chuck since I gave him Rico's computer. It wouldn't power on, and I wanted him to get it going. I guess the battery was dead. He charged it." Diego looks at Gary, "You and I haven't had a chance to talk, but there was nothing on his computer that I could find. I talked to legal and the OIG. I told them to stand fast until we figure this out."

"What?" Gary responds incredulously. "I took photos of the screen with my camera and, I backed up all the files I could find on a jump drive." I got the portable memory drive right here in my pocket," Gary taps his pants pocket.

"Well, there was nothing on the computer when I looked," Diego shakes his head.

"I showed the stuff to Bryan. What the hell is going on?" Gary asks. "Never mind," Gary sighs as he stands, "I'll handle it."

Gary stands in front of Diego's desk for a moment. His mind turns over the information Diego shared about the computer. He shakes his head, not able to understand, "Anyhoo, I'll give some money to Sylvia and ask her to pick up a card and send some flowers to Casey's family. I'll talk to you later."

Diego nods, "Later."

*   *   *   *   *

Gary moves through the hallway at his office building and heads to the front desk to see Sylvia. "Hi, Sylvia," Gary calls out as he reaches into his pocket.

"Hi, Gary. How are you?" Sylvia replies without looking up from her typing.

"I'm fine," Gary chirps as he pulls some money from his pocket. "Would you do me a favor?"

Sylvia looks up, "Sure, what is it?"

Gary hands Sylvia sixty dollars, "We need to get a card for the office to sign and send to Casey Baxter's family."

"Oh," Sylvia grimaces in pain. "What a shame about that poor woman."

"Yeah," Gary concurs. "We'd like to send some flowers too."

"That would be nice," Sylvia nods. "I will do that right away."

"Thanks, Sylvia," Gary says as he starts to turn away, but stops. "One other thing…have you seen Chuck? Did he call or email you"

Sylvia shakes her head from side to side emphatically, "No, I'm a little worried. No one has heard from him."

Gary's frustration shows, "Ugh, I'm sick of him. I wish Diego had fired him when he almost burned the office down."

Sylvia tries to soothe Gary, "It will be fine, Gary. We always seem to work our way through these things."

Gary manages to smile at the positive support from Sylvia, "The worst part, Sylvia, is that I asked him to look at my personal laptop on his off hours. I think it had a virus and I was hoping he could fix it. I told him I'd pay him, and I gave him the computer to work on at his house. Now, I'm afraid that computer might be out the window for me; I have some personal financial stuff on there and a bunch of my tax info."

"It's not the end of the world, Gary," Sylvia offers reassuringly. "Try calling him again."

"I've already left him about ten messages. I'll try again, I guess." Gary reaches for the cell phone in his pocket. "I'll see later, Sylvia. Thanks again."

Gary turns and walks toward his office as he pushes the button on his phone to call Chuck's number. Chuck's voicemail picks up again. The beep sounds, and Gary leaves a message, "Hey, Chuck. Gary again. I was wondering about my laptop. I do have some financial stuff on there and some tax stuff I'm going to need soon. I think I'll swing by your house to see if you are around. Give me a call if you get this message before this evening."

Gary leaves the message while he walks through the office, and he reaches his desk as he closes his phone. He stands by his desk frozen, thinking for a moment. He turns around and heads back out of the office, passing by Sylvia's desk.

"Sylvia," Gary says as he passes her desk, "if anybody needs me, they can reach me on my cell phone. I'll be back in a half hour or so."

"Ok, Gary," Sylvia responds. "Bye."

Gregory L. Heitmann

Chapter 54

Blood Red

As Gary drove his truck through the mid-afternoon traffic along Corral Road, he fumed. He cursed under his breath and out loud at Chuck's absence. Traffic was slow as he maneuvered along with the other cars. Why? Why had he given Chuck his computer? To save a buck? Gary questioned his decision-making ability. On top of this, now Rico's computer was void of the information he had verified. What had happened to it when Diego had handed the laptop to Chuck to get it up and running? Did the laptop get mixed up with some other machine? What in the world could have happened to the files on that machine? Gary finally convinces himself that Chuck accidentally swapped out a similar computer with Rico's machine. A visit to Chuck's house would now be clearing up two mysteries involving computers.

The ten minute drive from the office to Chuck's neighborhood flies by in flash as Gary's thoughts are consumed by the computer situation. Gary pulls his truck into a residential neighborhood off Congress Avenue. The homes are part of the affordable housing development of Tierra Rojo. The Pueblo-style houses are squeezed closely together with little or no yards to speak of. The neighborhood is new and the concrete shows the sharp edges of the forms in which they were poured along with the pale tint of the curing compounds. When Gary rounds the corner and begins to look for the house number corresponding to Chuck's address, a passing vehicle's driver waves. Gary unconsciously lifts his index finger from the steering wheel to return the greeting, but momentarily delays a look to the rearview mirror. When he does look, Gary notes the resemblance of the vehicle to a highway department pickup truck. "I wonder who that was?" Gary questions out loud before returning this attention to the task at hand, locating Chuck's house. Gary cranes his neck to see the house numbers. "Eleven thirty-five War Eagle," Gary repeats out loud. "There it is."

Gary eases to a stop in front of the house. The simulated adobe, stucco structure is light pink with a dark brown double garage door. Gary notes to himself there is no vehicle in the driveway as he observes the house from the curb while deciding whether to go knock on the front door. "This is stupid," Gary says out loud. "What am I waiting for? I can just go knock. It's no big deal. I'll just ask him for my computer and then ask him if he is ok and maybe if he is going to come to work. No problem."

Gary has psyched himself up enough to exit the vehicle. He makes a mental note to himself and laughs. This is the first time in his career that he can remember somebody from work going to an employee's house to check on them. He walks up the driveway and swings around the curved sidewalk to the porch. Gary shakes his head knowing that this can't be the first time an employer has had to make a house call. He rings the door bell and waits. After a minute he rings the doorbell again and knocks loudly on the door. Gary can hear the doorbell ring inside from his position on the porch, so he knows it is working. The picture window overlooking the street is shielded by curtains tightly shut. Gary tries to see around the edge of the drapes, but they overlap with the wall enough to seal the view. Gary rings the doorbell once more and listens intently for any movement inside. Nothing.

Gary twists his lips in an undulating frown as he calculates his next move. After a brief argument with himself, he ventures to the side of the house and finds a gate to the fenced backyard. The gate opens with a shrill squeak, drawing the ire of the neighboring dog that begins a fit of barking. Gary jumps back from the gate, unsure of the capability of the wooden fence to contain a whirlwind of howls from what sounds like a rather large dog.

The fence proves durable, and Gary swings the gate open and enters the back yard, a twenty foot by thirty foot area, mostly covered by paving stones forming a patio. The rest of the area is neatly kept river rock. "Hello?" Gary calls out to no answer.

The back entrance is a sliding glass door between the patio and the house. A blind is partially opened and Gary moves close to take a look inside. He shields his eyes with his hand over his head to block the reflection of the bright sun outside and presses his cheek to the glass.

The neighboring dog provides an intermittent, half-hearted woof, sensing the activity of Gary next door. It takes a moment for Gary's eyes to adjust to the shadows inside, but in a half minute he is able to see as much as his sharp viewing angles through the opening in the blinds allow. Gary observes the kitchen and dining area as his gaze bounces around the rooms. When his eyes fall to the wood floor as part of his inspection, his body instinctively steps back from the window. The floor is a light colored laminate wood flooring; a large crimson pool is visible oozing from behind the kitchen counter, blocking Gary's full view of the kitchen floor.

Gary's flinch and step away from the window backs him into the gas grill on the patio with a crash, the commotion once again drawing the full onslaught of the neighboring dog's barking. Gary stumbles away, bouncing from the grill to a patio chair as he trips again. He finally gathers his balance and stares into the house another moment before retreating quickly through the gate to howls of the neighbor's dog. Gary makes a beeline for his truck.

*　　*　　*　　*　　*

Safely in his truck with the vision of a pool of blood burned into his mind, Gary quickly races to a conclusion that Chuck's dead body rests behind the counter blocking his view. Gary reaches for his soft sided briefcase and digs wildly inside for his day planner. He surprises himself as he flips through his organizer and quickly finds what he is looking for: A business card.

Gary rifles through his briefcase again and produces his cell phone. Trying to remain calm, he dials the number from the card, he presses the send button and midway through the second ring, Gary hears a voice on the line, "Detective Navidad."

"Hey, Detective," Gary replies into the phone, "This is Gary Hillmann."

"Hi," the detective offers and pauses until the name clicks into place, "Yeah, Gary, how are you? Your leg ok?"

"Sure, sure," Gary deflects the small talk, trying to get to his point, "I got a bit of a situation."

"What's going on?"

"My office computer guy has been AWOL for, oh…the last couple days. I'm at his house to check on my laptop and another computer he was going to take a look at…Anyhoo, there was no answer at the front door, so I swung around to the back to take a look…I looked in the back, through the patio door, and thought I saw a big pool of blood."

"Uh-oh," the detective grunts, "Give me the address. I'll be right there."

Gary provides the address, and the detective declares he will be there in less than ten minutes. "Sounds good, Detective," Gary sighs somewhat relieved, "Do you want me to wait?"

"No, go ahead and leave," Detective Navidad counsels at first, but quickly amends his statement. "Wait, did you go in the house?"

"No," Gary adamantly responds, "I'm sitting in my pickup. I retreated so quickly I never even checked to see if the doors were locked."

"Just get out of there then," the detective orders.

"Yes, sir!" Gary responds.

"I'll let you know what I find out."

"Sure thing, Detective," Gary ends the call, turns the key to the ignition of his truck, and puts it in gear, taking a last look at the house before driving away.

Chapter 55

Crimson Pool

Gary could sense the movement outside his office door. Somebody was moving quietly down the hallway toward his office. He watched as the shadow darkened his door for a moment followed by the appearance of Detective Navidad. Gary smiled when he recognized the detective in his doorway. He seemed bigger than Gary remembered. Not fatter, just bigger in general, taller, maybe even broader in the shoulders. The detective was wearing a summer time, tan, seersucker suit jacket and tie along with khakis.

The detective's blank look of observing his surroundings melded into a smile as he recognized Gary sitting at his desk. He stepped into the office and spoke, "How ya doin'? Your secretary up front just sent me back this way."

"Howdy, Detective," Gary offered as he stood to shake hands with the man.

"I hope it was ok for me to just come barging back here."

Gary laughed, "No problem. Have a seat." Gary gestures to the chair, and the detective sits as he returns to his own chair.

"You got a minute to talk?" Navidad asks.

"Sure, what's the good word on Chuck? I assume you didn't find a body since you probably would have been stuck there a few hours and not visiting me if there'd been a corpse in the kitchen."

"Yup, looks like a false alarm. The front door was locked, but I went to the back like you had done. I looked in the window and saw what appeared to be blood on the floor. I thought it looked like probable cause, so I tried the patio door, and it was open."

Gary nods as the detective pulls a notebook from his jacket pocket and continues. "I found a package of rib-eye steaks on the counter, probably left to thaw. They were hanging over the edge of the plate and blood had escaped the package and run onto the floor. You couldn't see that from the patio door."

Gary sighs, "Well, that's good. I had the worst-case scenario envisioned."

"You and me both. When I saw the blood pool, I thought I was in for a long night," the Detective admits. He refers to his notebook and flips through to the page he wants. "Nobody in the house. A car was in the garage. No sign of any suspicious activity. The house was quite neat and tidy, except for his computer workshop. We found a note to Shelly. All it said was that 'he would be right back.' It was sitting on the counter near the steaks. I threw down a bunch of paper towels on the blood."

"Hmmph," Gary grunts, "I'm pretty sure Shelly is Michelle, his daughter. I think Chuck is divorced and splits custody with his ex-wife. That's about all I know about that."

The detective nods, "What about his car?"

Gary shrugs, "The only car I've seen him drive is an older BMW. It's a rusted 1970's square looking thing."

The detective continues to nod, "That was the car in the garage."

"Maybe he has another car," Gary observes.

The detective shakes his head, "No, I checked the vehicle registrations. Nothing else showed up."

"Hmm," Gary grunts. Hey, you didn't happen to see and confiscate my laptop did you? It had A Minnesota Vikings sticker on it." Gary smiles at the impossible request he makes.

Detective Navidad snorts a laugh, "Sorry, no such luck. I did see that there was a whole room dedicated to computers. There had to be sixty to seventy laptops and desktop computers in different stages of repair or disrepair for that matter. That room was a mess, but, like I said, the rest of the house was clean as a whistle."

Gary shakes his head in disgust, "It turns out both the IRS and the State Tax and Revenue want me to provide some additional info for the previous taxes I filed. I have the data on that stupid laptop."

The detective shakes his head, "Man, I'm really sorry. I checked the police reports; there is no missing persons notice on file. No suspicious calls from neighbors."

Gary shrugs and throws his hands in the air, "Oh well, I'll keep trying his cell phone. He's been doing work in the movies being filmed around Allentown as an extra…just standing in the background. Who knows? Maybe he got a bigger role in a remote location."

The detective closes his notebook, "I'm sorry I couldn't be of more help."

Gary timidly stands, "No, I'm sorry to waste your time and get you involved on some meat-thawing incident. This is embarrassing."

Detective Navidad stands and laughs. He extends his hand to Gary. "Don't worry about it. It was pretty exciting there for a moment or two. It was a good to see you. I'll show myself out."

The men shake hands. "Nice to see you too," Gary adds. "See you around."

Gregory L. Heitmann

Chapter 56

Puppy Love

The effort to visit Bryan was simplified when the doctors at Eli Regional Hospital cleared him for transfer to a branch of the Capitol City Medical Center. The Cedar Wing of the medical center campus is an assisted living center for patients that fall outside of the full care of the hospital but are still in need of specialty care.

An evening visit to Bryan found him in good spirits; Ashley provided him some company, as she was settled in at his bedside. Gary and Katrina had brought along Sarah with her bubbly personality to cheer up Bryan. "Oh my God!" Bryan calls out when he sees the trio of visitors barge in the room. "Sarah, really? You had to bring Sarah along?" Bryan's voice drips with sarcasm.

Sarah lets out a cackle of laughter, "Come on! I'm standing right here, and you talk that way?"

Gary throws his hands in the air, "She wanted to see you!"

Bryan turns his fake frown to a smile, "You know I'm just teasing, Sarah? Don't you?"

"Yes," Sarah rasps huskily as she leans down to hug Bryan propped up in his bed, both legs still elevated. Bryan's left leg is still in traction provided by a robotic system of pulleys.

Gary points to Bryan's leg, "So, how's it hanging?" Gary doubles over in laughter at his own joke. He slaps his knee and stands straight again, met by unwelcome stares from everyone. "Come on, it was kinda funny."

"No," Katrina opines succinctly.

Sarah moves to hug Ashley and Katrina follows with a hug and greeting for Ashley.

Sarah turns a concerned eye to Bryan, "So, how are you doing? Are you feeling better?"

"Sure," Bryan nods, "They are very liberal with the pain meds."

Sarah laughs loudly again, causing everyone to join her laughter.

"And," Sarah continues her line of questioning, "when are they going to let you out?"

"Oh, yeah," Bryan smiles, "that's the best news yet. They told me that I can go home in two days. I got lots of rehab," Bryan turns and grabs Ashley's hand, "but with Ashley helping me at home, they said they would release me."

"Wow," Katrina offers, "that is good news."

The group falls silent absorbing the update from Bryan. Sarah breaks the silence, "I brought you a special visitor."

Bryan sits up and looks to the door. "What? Who?"

Sarah reaches into her monster-sized purse and produces a tiny puppy. "Shhh. I snuck him in. This is the puppy I want to give to Katrina and Gary. They haven't actually adopted him yet, but I can tell they are weakening." Sarah gives a look and smile in Gary's and Katrina's direction.

"We didn't adopt him yet," Gary chimes in, "but we named him. His name is Soos, as in Heh-soos, a.k.a. Jesus."

Bryan frowns, "You named your dog, Jesus?"

"Technically," Gary responds with a finger raised to make a point. "He's not my dog yet."

Sarah rolls her eyes and shakes her head, "Blasphemy," she calls out towards Gary.

"I don't think Blasphemy is a very good name for a dog," Gary shrugs. "It's too long. You need a short name, like Rex or Soos."

Sarah clucks her tongue and heaves a sigh of disgust for Gary's benefit.

Katrina takes the puppy in her hands, and in the voice of a child squeaks, "He's just so cute!"

Gary waves the comment away, "I know I am."

Katrina holds the puppy in one hand and puts her other hand on her hip to posture her anger, "Shush! You know I meant the dog!"

Gary defends himself, "Yes, heaven forbid you call me cute."

Sarah laughs at the mock argument but settles her attention quickly to Bryan. "Do you want a puppy, Bryan? He's got a brother if you do. You and Ashley could share him."

Bryan shrugs, "I guess I can think about it."

"Great!" Sarah bubbles.

Bryan turns to Gary, "What's going on at the office?"

"You heard about Casey jumping of the Gorge Bridge?" Gary questions.

Bryan shakes his head in disbelief, "Yeah, that's one of the weirdest things I've ever tried to comprehend since I've been in this state. I just never suspected her secret desperation. All the meetings we were in with her…I never knew anything about her."

Gary sighs, "Katrina and I saw her with Patrick and with Chuck on separate occasions. It looked like they were romantic meetings. Maybe her sneaking around finally caught up with her. It just goes to show that you never really know people. You might think you know somebody, but you don't."

A silence falls across the group before Katrina speaks up, "Did you guys hear that Patrick Ruiz had a heart attack?"

"No kidding?" Gary blanches, "You never mentioned that before."

"I just remembered," Katrina shrugs. "It's just gossip."

"Well," Bryan remarks, "Patrick is the poster child for a heart attack. He is so overweight."

"Fat, you can call him fat," Gary grins. "We're in polite company here.

A chuckle goes around the room.

"I guess he's going to be ok, in case you were wondering," Katrina adds.

"Good," Gary nods.

"What else, besides the T'rrain Trekker stuff?" Bryan begs for more gossip.

"Let me think…Chuck's AWOL." Gary declares.

"Chuck? The movie star?" Bryan frowns, "What a dud,"

"You're missing all the fun!" Gary exclaims with feigned excitement.

"No…I don't miss it," Bryan smiles wryly, "but, it would be better than lying in a hospital bed all day."

Gary tells the story of his adventure to Chuck's house, the pool of blood, and his subsequent meeting with Detective Navidad.

Another period of silence covers the room as people contemplate what Gary has shared. "Why don't you ask Shelly, Chuck's daughter?" Bryan offers. "Just call her and see if she has seen her dad lately."

A light bulb goes on for Gary, "Yeah! That's a great idea! Heck, maybe she would take me to her house to see if I can get my laptop back and see if Rico's laptop is there!"

Bryan is puzzled, "Rico's laptop?" he asks.

Gary tries to cover his tracks in front of everyone, "I mean my personal laptop that I gave to Chuck to fix." Gary gives Bryan a look that says "help me cover."

Bryan picks up on the look, "Oh, yeah, your tax stuff, right?"

Katrina nods, understanding the cover up in front of Sarah and Ashley. They both let the comment pass. "Well, thanks, Bryan," Gary offers, "I'm glad I came to visit you. First thing tomorrow, I'm going to get a hold of Shelly and her mom."

Chapter 57

Keyed Up

Through the proper channels of Chuck's contract employer, IT-Dynamo, Gary was able to gather the information he needed in two simple phone calls. It would have and should have been one phone call, but his first call was a voice mail referring him to a second phone number, because as the message dictated, "Larry Torrez was out of his office for the week."

It was surprising to Gary how easy it was to get such personal information. He guessed if you sounded like you knew what you were talking about, people were generally lazy enough not to want to question your motives. Thus it was that Gary found the contact information for Chuck's ex-wife, Traci, and daughter Shelly.

Gary waited until just before lunch to try to call Traci. On the third ring, just when Gary was thinking of the message he would leave on an answering machine, Traci picks up with a simple greeting, "Hello?"

"Uh, hi," Gary replies, "Uh, um, I'm sorry, I thought I was going to get an answering machine. My name is Gary Hillmann, with the United States Department of Transportation…"

Traci interrupts, "Oh, Chuck works for you!"

"Yeah, that's what I'm calling about. Have you seen or heard from Chuck lately?"

"I knew it," Traci's voice goes flat. "I knew something was wrong. He would never go this long without talking to his daughter. What happened?"

"I don't know. I'm trying to figure it out. Chuck's been AWOL for a week, and he was working on a couple laptop computers that we need."

"Oh, God," Traci moans, "I wonder if he fell off the wagon."

"Oh, I didn't know…"

Traci cuts Gary off, "He's been sober for nearly ten years, but you never know."

"I know this is asking a lot, but would it be possible for you to let me in his house?" Gary asks, his voice losing steam as he makes a request he knows sounds ridiculous.

"I don't have a key," Traci abruptly responds.

"I understand..." Gary offers, but is cut off by Traci.

"...but Shelly has one. She could let you in."

"Really?" Gary is excited, "She would do that? That would be super. Do you want to meet over there?"

Traci balks, "Why don't you just pick us up and bring us back. I'll just wait in the car. I just as soon avoid Chuck as much as I can."

"I understand," Gary grins as he nods. "Why don't I just come over after lunch and get you two, say one o'clock."

Traci agrees to the time, and Gary gets the address from her. He hangs up the phone raising his arms in victory, celebrating the best news he's had in awhile. Gary whistles with a bounce in his step as heads out for lunch passing Sylvia's desk on the way out the door. Sylvia notices Gary's good mood, "Why are you so chipper, Gary?"

"I'm just going to lunch, but afterwards, I'm going to hopefully finish some business Diego and I have been working on for a couple weeks."

"Good for you," Sylvia offers with a smile. "I will see you later then."

"Bye," Gary replies with a wave and resumes his whistling as he heads out the door and across the parking lot. He grabs his cell phone and calls Katrina. She answers her cell phone from her parents' home in Allentown. "Hi, what are you doing?" she asks immediately.

"Nothing, just about to solve all our problems and put the T'rrain Trekker mess to bed," Gary replies matter-of-factly.

"What are you talking about?" Katrina replies with skepticism.

Gary tells her the plan to go to pick up Chuck's daughter, who has a key to Chuck's house, and hopefully find the missing laptops. Katrina does not respond for a moment or two. "Hello? You still there?" Gary yells into the phone.

"I'm here. I just don't think much of your plan. Are you sure this is a good idea?"

"What else would you suggest," Gary counters.

"I don't know? Maybe call the police."

"That didn't work. Detective Navidad went to the house on that welfare check and found nothing," Gary argues.

"I don't like your plan," Katrina counters. "Using that little girl that way. What if something is really wrong?"

"Her dad is missing. Her mother said she knows something's wrong. Chuck never goes that long without calling or seeing his daughter."

"My point exactly!" Katrina yells.

"I'll tell you what; we'll know a lot more after I go look."

"You just want to find those stupid computers!" Katrina yells again.

"I don't deny that. Hopefully, we'll find out where Chuck is also. His ex-wife said he is almost ten years sober. He could be on a bender or in jail for all we know."

Katrina is at her wit's end, "Fine, just call me later."

"Okey-doke," Gary signs off and continues to whistle a random tune as he approaches his truck.

Chapter 58

Shelly

After a quick sandwich at home, Gary made his way to the west side of town. Off Cold Water Street near a small park, he found Traci's address. He knocks on the door of the tiny, one thousand square foot, old, adobe house, just a couple minutes after one o'clock, and Traci opens the door with Shelly by her side, as if they had been waiting right in the entry way.

"We'll be back in an hour or so," Gary says as they move down the sidewalk to his truck parked on the street. Gary goes around to the driver's side and gets in the truck as Traci places Shelly in the back seat. She buckles her seat belt on the passenger side. Gary gets the truck back on Cold Water Street and heads toward the south side of the city. He smiles and attempts to strike up a conversation with Shelly, looking in his rearview mirror. "Do you work on computers like your Dad?"

"Yes," Shelly responds.

"You ready for school to start?" Gary tries again.

"Mmm-hhmm," Shelly affirms with a hum.

"What grade are you in?" Gary asks.

"Fourth grade," Shelly says crisply.

Gary raises his eyebrows and tries to think of something to carry the conversation past the barrage of one word answers, as they make their way across town. "You like computers, huh?"

"Yeah," Shelly nods.

"Do you ever help your dad fix the computers?"

"Sometimes."

Shelly looks at Gary after a minute or two of silence, "My dad works for you?"

"Yeah," Gary nods.

"You yelled at him before, didn't you?" Shelly accuses.

Traci scolds her daughter, "Shelly!"

Gary shakes his head, "No, it's ok. I did yell. He accidentally started a fire, and everyone was scared and I did raise my voice."

"He told me about that," Shelly continues. "He said he understood why you were mad."

The trip takes them across Airport Boulevard and into the Tierra Rojo neighborhood and finally down War Eagle. Gary parks the truck and Shelly bursts from the vehicle and runs to the front door key in hand. Gary hustles as he trails her. He gives a wave to Traci, who stays behind, waiting in the truck.

Shelly unlocks the front door and yells as she crosses the threshold, "Dad! Are you home?"

Shelly stands in the entrance hall and waits for an answer. There is no response, and she heads for the kitchen. Gary closes the door and follows her, looking down the hallways and sizing up the layout of the floor plan. Gary notes the neutral colors and modest, but tastefully decorated living room. A large mule deer head and shoulder mount has the place of honor on the living room wall. "Did your dad shoot that buck?" Gary inquires with awe. "It's nice!"

"Yeah," Shelly yells back from the kitchen. "My dad is a hunter. We have a freezer full of deer meat in the garage!"

Shelly grabs the note from the kitchen counter next to a plate of packaged meat. Blood is at the rim of the plate. Blood-stained paper towels line the floor. "Gross," Shelly mumbles as she sees the bloody towels and meat. She reads the note. She looks back to Gary, who is now moving into the kitchen area. Gary observes Shelly holding the note the detective had mentioned. Shelly explains the note, "It says that my dad will be right back."

She gestures to the meat then the towels on the floor, "Look at this mess." She giggles, "My dad is messy."

She reaches down and wipes at the blood with the towels. She drops the soiled paper towels in the trash.

"Hmm," Gary grunts, "Shelly, can you show me where your dad kept the computers he was working on?"

"Sure," Shelly nods. "They are in the back office. Follow me."

She passes Gary and heads down the hallway with Gary in tow. The framed pictures along the hallway document Shelly's ten years of life. Gary sees the master bedroom and Shelly's bedroom. The third bedroom is the office. Shelly waits for Gary in the middle of a cramped ten foot by ten foot room crowed with shelves cluttered with computer parts and disassembled computers. Cords of every color, shape, and size are strewn throughout the room. A small card table sits in the corner; it appears to be on the verge of collapse, weighted down with an assortment of laptops and desktop computers.

The main workbench is a homemade table of two by four construction solidly sitting against the far wall of the room. The bench is littered with wires, chips, disks, and every possible computer part needed to assemble a working machine. A soldering iron sits unplugged on its heat resistant rest. A laptop computer punctuates the middle of the workspace with its cover off, frozen in mid-repair. Stacks of laptops litter the floor.

Gary emits a whistle as he takes in the mess. "Wow," Gary rasps, "how did your dad work in here?"

Shelly stands still in the middle of the room. Her gaze sweeps across the computers. She shrugs a shrug of a disinterested ten year old.

"Did you ever see a laptop with a purple sticker on the cover? The sticker said 'VIKINGS'," Gary asks as he forms a square shape with his hands attempting to indicate a computer.

Shelly shakes her head, "I don't remember."

"Did your Dad say where he was going when you talked to him last?"

Shelly shakes her head again, "Uh-uh, he didn't tell me anything. I'm supposed to be with him this week. My mom is mad because it's his week, and he never called or anything."

Gary bends down and looks at a stack of about ten computers. He shuffles through them one at time trying to find his computer or Rico's.

Shelly turns to the door, "I'm going to go get some juice."

"Ok," Gary replies without looking up from the second stack of computers.

A thump emanates from the kitchen and catches Gary's attention. Gary stands and moves to the office door, "What was that noise?" he calls down the hall. Gary hears another puzzling thump, but no answer from Shelly as he moves down the hallway toward the kitchen. He hears and sees the source of the thumping from beneath the refrigerator door, as he watches a white package bounce off the floor. He moves into the kitchen and looks in the fridge stuffed full of butcher paper wrapped packages. The packages are marked with handwritten notes of deer, a date, and what kind of cut. Gary reaches for a package on the floor marked "Steak."

Shelly is incredulous, "What are all these packages in the fridge for? I can't reach the juice."

Shelly's attention is drawn to something behind Gary, and she leans to get a better look behind him. Gary is puzzled by a smile across her face and her distracted look. He is not ready for what he hears next as Shelly squeals with delight, "Hi, Uncle Patrick!"

Gregory L. Heitmann

Chapter 59

Gotta Go

Gary turns around slack jawed as he sees the monster of a man now standing behind him holding a rifle. Shelly runs past Gary, brushing his arm as he tries to reconcile the situation. Shelly hugs Patrick, now kneeling with one leg on the floor. "Your mom," Patrick smiles as he looks at Shelly, "told me you were here. I just came over to borrow your dad's deer rifle. It's getting' close to huntin' season again."

Patrick stands to his full height and works the mechanism of the bolt action .30-06. Gary sees that a round of ammunition is chambered and his eyes widen. Patrick grins wildly as he sees the fear in Gary's eyes. "Shelly," Patrick says softly, "Would you go wait with your mom. I just need to talk to Gary a minute."

"Ok," Shelly replies cheerfully. She moves past Gary, out of the kitchen to the living room, and out the front door. Gary and Patrick stare at each other as Patrick waits to hear the door open and close. The door opens and Shelly calls from the living room, "Uncle Patrick…"

Patrick cuts her off and yells loudly, "Just wait with your mom. I'll be there in a minute, sweetie."

Shelly is scooped up at the door by a policeman and hustled to her mother next to a police cruiser at the curb.

Patrick hears the door latch and turns his attention back to Gary. A knowing, creepy smile curls across Patrick's lips.

"You're her uncle?" Gary quizzically offers and quickly follows with a second question, "Wait, didn't you have a heart attack?"

Patrick rolls his eyes and shakes his head, "Chuck and I were best friends." Patrick's smile disappears and is replaced by a frown as he re-grips the rifle pointed in Gary's general direction. "We aren't related, but we were like brothers; a term of endearment. And, no…I did not have a heart attack. Apparently it was just anxiety. Now, I ask you to come to the garage with me."

The standoff between the men continues in silence.

"How did you know I was here?" Gary whispers.

"I wasn't sure, but I asked Traci to call me if you ever contacted her for anything. Chuck was a good friend of mine. Traci and my wife are still best friends."

Gary tries to break from the shock of the situation with a quick shake of his head. "I gotta go, Patrick," Gary gestures a thumb to the door.

Patrick shrieks, "You will move to the garage!" Patrick is a man possessed; he raises the rifle to his shoulder and sights down the barrel at Gary. His mouth foams from his scream, and his breathing is rapid and shallow.

"I was just looking for Chuck or for my laptop. I didn't see either. Now I'm going to leave," Gary states matter-of-factly.

"Get on your knees!" Patrick yells. Sweat begins to stream down his face.

"You haven't seen Chuck, have you?" Gary asks.

"Get on your knees!" Patrick spits the words, appearing to be a man having a psychotic break. "Chuck's not around anymore!"

Patrick attempts to wipe sweat from his brow with the sleeve of his shirt, "You killed Casey! Now, I kill you!"

"No, wait," Gary shrugs as he holds his hands up in plain sight, "I don't understand. I didn't kill anybody."

"You killed Casey," Patrick's voice huskily pronounces. "The pressure of completing the train…You… you and Chuck killed her. Chuck stole Casey from me…you and Chuck caused her to jump! I was there. I saw her jump. One last cruel act. She called me to the gorge. I tried to stop her, but she made me watch her jump. I can't get that image out of my head."

"I'm sorry…"

"Shut up!" Patrick screams in a near ear-shattering volume. "I loved her, and you killed her!"

The neighbor's dog begins a barking fit, drawing Patrick's attention to the patio door. A uniformed policeman casually moves outside trying to see inside the glass door, fighting the glare and reflection of the window. "What the hell?" Patrick calls out.

He turns his rifle toward the window and man outside. He fires the rifle, shattering the glass of the patio door.

Gary breaks for the front door. He moves past the wall between the living room and kitchen when he is knocked to the floor by Detective Navidad. Navidad maintains his balance and steps around the corner of the kitchen with his weapon drawn, shouting orders at Patrick, "Drop your weapon!"

Patrick freezes for a moment and hears a repeat of the order from the detective. Patrick works the action of the rifle and slowly turns the rifle toward Navidad. Navidad does not hesitate, but fires four times in rapid succession striking Patrick square in the chest. The mountain of a man is knocked backward, separated from his rifle. He falls in a heap and doesn't move.

Gary shakes his head and gathers his senses from his position on the living room carpet. He props himself up and stands. He eases to the wall and peeks around the corner. Detective Navidad holds Patrick's rifle and checks Patrick's neck for a pulse. Two more uniformed policemen have joined the detective, having entered through the shattered patio door. Their police radios chatter, and one officer talks calmly into the microphone affixed to his shoulder.

Gary eases around the corner, "What the hell are you doing here?"

The detective flashes a smile, "You're welcome."

Gary looks around at the police and the bloody body of Patrick, still stunned. "What just happened?" Gary inquires as he stands with arms extended from his sides.

"Again," Detective Navidad states, "You're welcome. You should also thank both Katrina and Sylvia for calling and asking me to check on you."

"How long were you guys here?" Gary asks.

"We got here just as the little girl came out the front door. We scooped her up before she could yell back a warning."

"What took you so long to step in? He could've killed me!" Gary whines.

Detective Navidad shrugs, "I was listening to his story. It was interesting."

Gary repeats himself shrilly, "He coulda killed me!"

"He didn't though," Navidad smiles, "did he? Again, you are welcome."

Gary exhales and looks to his hands still shaking. He's still breathing as if he just finished a mile sprint. "Good Lord," Gary mumbles, "now what happens?"

Sirens wail and emergency vehicles fill the entire neighborhood. Detective Navidad hands the rifle over to a uniformed officer and steps close to Gary. He puts his hand on Gary's shoulder, "Let's get the paramedics to look you over and make sure you aren't traumatized." Navidad leads Gary out the front door.

"Wait!" Gary stops and shouts, "Check the freezer. I'm pretty sure you'll find Chuck in there. The fridge was jammed with packages of meat. Patrick must have made room in the freezer for something."

The detective steers Gary toward the front door, "We'll check it out. Let's get you looked at."

Gary and the detective move outside and pass Shelly standing with her mother and a uniformed officer. Gary sighs, "Oh, my God. Shelly. Her dad...Chuck." Gary whispers and looks at Navidad, who acknowledges the realization with a frown. Shelly has lost her father.

"She's ok. She's with her mom," Navidad answers back quietly.

Navidad directs Gary to an EMS vehicle where he sits down and an EMT begins to work checking his pulse, pupils, and other signs of shock. Gary looks up at the detective, "Do you think Casey had some assistance from Patrick in her leap off the Gorge Bridge?"

The detective exhales deeply, "That is a good question. I dumped the phone records for Patrick, Casey, and Chuck. These people were like the three musketeers in exchanging phone calls. I still have a guy sorting out the web of phone calls between the three of them."

"This is some sort of love triangle?" Gary speculates out loud, his face scrunched with a look of bewilderment. The EMT continues to work on Gary, checking his blood pressure.

Detective Navidad shrugs and shakes his head, "You heard him, Patrick said he loved Casey. You and Chuck had caused Casey to jump." The detective throws his hands in the air, "I hate to say it, but ultimately this seems to be love gone bad. Nine out of ten times that's what it is."

"Unbelievable," Gary mumbles. Gary looks away from the detective a moment. After a few seconds he turns back to the detective, "But, the laptops and the T'rrain Trekker. Patrick must have gotten help from Chuck and Casey in his cover up."

"What?" the detective asks.

Gary rubs his face with his hands, "Patrick was forging inspection reports on the T'rrain Trekker construction. It's a long story."

Gary slumps down in the EMS vehicle, "I just can't believe all this."

The detective leans down and offers his hand. Gary looks up and grabs his hand. "Thanks," the detective says. "Let the medic check you over. I gotta get back in there." The detective nods toward the house.

"No," Gary replies. "Thank you, Detective. You saved my life," Gary pumps the detective's hand and let's go.

The detective gives a nod to Gary, "We'll talk more and sort this out." As he turns away from Gary, he gives a nod to the medic and departs.

Chapter 60

Hard Mann 2 Love

After Gary was released by the paramedics, he went straight home. In his driveway sat Katrina in her car waiting for him. As Gary exits his truck, he is met with an angry barrage of questions, "What? You don't answer your cell phone anymore?" Katrina shouts.

"I'm sorry," Gary replies extending his arms and pulling Katrina to his chest.

Katrina speaks, her voice muffled against Gary's shirt, "It's all over the news. Are you ok?"

"Barely," Gary states with great effort. "Let's go inside. I'll tell you the story before the news reports it anymore incorrectly than possible."

"I think I need a margarita," Gary declares as they move through the garage and into the house.

After an hour, and one and a half margaritas later, Gary has completed the story. Recounting the story, including pacing back and forth and acting out some of the drama, Katrina sat wide-eyed and dazzled by the tale. She had scarcely interrupted the story, only a few times for clarification. Now they both sat on the couch relaxing. There was a short debate, but they decided to turn the six o'clock news on and see what was being reported.

"I shudder to think how this story is going to be reported," Gary declares. "Let me say upfront, I'm guessing that they'll get it wrong."

"Shhh," Katrina hushes Gary. "Just watch."

The KLTW news anchor opens the news cast, "Breaking news from Capitol City," Dick Forsine announces seriously. "Governor Reid-Salazar is demanding a full, independent, investigation into the police shooting of the project manager of the T'rrain Trekker construction."

The news footage cuts to the governor standing before reporters, wagging his finger, and demanding answers.

"Oh, my God!" Gary howls. "I told you they'd report this wrong. The governor running for President, of course, is the lead story!"

"Lord help us," Katrina chimes in.

Gary angrily grabs the TV remote and turns the television off. "Let's go for a walk," he orders, standing from the couch.

Katrina smiles wryly, "Yeah, let's walk along the rail trail."

Gary can't help but laugh. Katrina stands and puts her arm around Gary and they move to the door. The garage door shuts behind them, and they walk casually hand in hand down the sidewalk for a block in silence. Finally Gary speaks, "Do you think Kevin Fowler will be back in town soon?"

Gary struggles to whistle the tune *Hard Man to Love* as Katrina shakes her head stifling the urge to laugh.

The End.

Greg Heitmann has worked for the Federal Government for nearly 20 years, which pays the bills while pursuing a writing career. His life experiences have been an inspiration for much of his writing. Look for a future book in the vein of one of Greg's writing heroes, Tony Hillerman. Tony Hillerman was a renowned author from the Greg's adopted home state of New Mexico. Hillerman penned nearly twenty novels focusing on two Navajo Tribal Policemen. Greg is borrowing this Native American theme, but relocating the geographical setting nearly 1500 miles north and east, to the land of his upbringing, northeast South Dakota and the Sisseton-Wahpeton Indian Reservation. Look for Greg's first novel in this series:

Long Hollow – A Charlie LeBeau Mystery

The novel is expected to be available in January 2014.

www.ingramcontent.com/pod-product-compliance
Lightning Source LLC
Chambersburg PA
CBHW061605170626
46811CB00001B/320